JOEL BEN IZZY

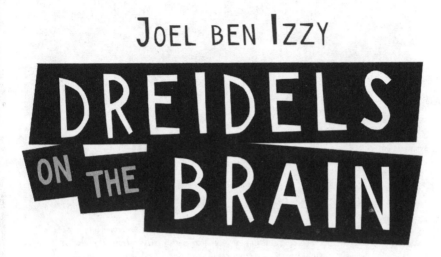

DREIDELS ON THE BRAIN

Dial Books for Young Readers

Dial Books for Young Readers
Penguin Young Readers Group
An imprint of Penguin Random House LLC
375 Hudson Street
New York, NY 10014

Library of Congress Cataloging-in-Publication Data
Name: ben Izzy, Joel, author.
Title: Dreidels on the brain / Joel ben Izzy.
Description: New York, NY: Dial Books for Young Readers, [2016]
ISBN 9780803740976 (hardback)
Summary, Subjects, and Classification available from the Library of Congress

Printed in the United States of America
10 9 8 7 6 5 4 3 2 1

Design by Nancy R. Leo-Kelly
Text set in Garamond Premier Pro

This is a work of fiction . . . and of friction—the kind that filled the author's childhood. Although much is based upon actual people, places, and events from his life, he has taken great liberties in all these realms—as well as spelling—to recount a story set over the course of the eight days of Hanukkah, 1971. While some characters represent real people, they have been fictionalized, and other characters, incidents, and places are entirely the product of the author's imagination.

For my parents, Robert and Gladys,
who lit candles in the darkness.

For my children, Elijah and Izzy,
who carry light into the future.

And, always, for Taly.

Contents

THE FIRST CANDLE: Chopped Liver

I could have stopped at three and called it a miracle.

After all, three in a row is good. Not just good—great. You know the odds of that happening by itself? Miniscule. A dreidel has four sides, so the chance of getting a single *Gimel*—which is the letter you want—is one in four. The chances of getting two in a row is one in sixteen. And three in a row—which I had just spun—is one in *sixty-four*.

And the number three makes a lot of sense. There are all kinds of things that come in threes: tic, tac, toe, three in a row; Snap, Crackle, Pop; third time's a charm; three strikes, you're out. And stories—which I love—are filled with threes. It's always the third son who sets off to seek his fortune and actually *finds* it—which works for me, because I'm the third son. There's Goldilocks and the Three Bears. The Three Little Pigs.

But those things aren't Jewish. Especially the pigs. They

are, as my dad would say, *goyish*, which is the Jewish word for non-Jewish things. For Christians, three is a magic number, like the Holy Trinity. And maybe if I wasn't Jewish, spinning three Gimels in a row would have been enough. Then again, if I wasn't Jewish, I wouldn't have been spinning a dreidel in the first place, trying to figure out whether I should believe in magic, or God, or miracles, or anything at all.

For Jews, things come in fours, like the four sides of a dreidel. Just look at Passover: You drink *four* cups of wine, ask *four* questions, tell about the *four* types of children. Besides, four was the deal I'd made with God before the first spin.

"Hey, God," I'd said, "happy Hanukkah."

I never know how to talk to God, and always end up feeling foolish. "I'm looking for a sign. Nothing big. Nothing fancy. No lightning or thunder bolts. Just a little sign. Between you and me." I held up the dreidel. "So I'm going to spin this dreidel four times. And if you're there, I'd like you to give me four Gimels in a row."

That didn't seem like too much to ask—just one lousy miracle.

And why, you might ask, did I think this Hanukkah should be different when everything else in the first twelve years of my life has been so amazingly, astoundingly, unbelievably *un*miraculous?

Well, for one thing, I could feel it in the air. Outside, it was really cold, even misty, that kind of feeling you get just before it snows, when the world gets all quiet and the light becomes soft. At least that's how I think it feels. I've never actually seen snow, on the ground or falling from the sky, though I've read a lot about it in books.

But it had been raining all day, a cold rain, and I had just checked the barometer on the front porch for the tenth time, and I could see it was between 29 and 30, pushing toward SNOW. The windows were so foggy, I couldn't see outside, so I could pretend I was somewhere else, anywhere else but here in Temple City, California.

It was also the perfect time for a miracle. The house was quiet and I was alone. I had looked through the garage and found the cardboard box of Hanukkah decorations. Sifting through the dreidels, which were mostly crooked or broken, I found a perfect one, made of wood, painted orange, with gold letters. I don't know where we got it, but it was nicely balanced. Just to be sure, I spun it a half-dozen times. Just a regular old normal dreidel—excellent.

Then I cleared all the junk off the table—a bunch of papers, my dad's electronics stuff, and some glow-in-the-dark phone dials—and piled it on the washing machine. I wasn't going to let anything interfere with these four spins, so I took the sponge from the sink and cleaned off the table-top so thoroughly that I could see the little gold sparkles among the black and gray swirls of the Formica.

"All right, God," I whispered, "this is your chance. Four Gimels in a row. One little Hanukkah miracle. Right here, right now."

I spun. A good, solid spin. And when the first Gimel came up, I was impressed.

"All right," I said. "That's one."

But when the second Gimel came up, everything changed.

"Excellent," I said, trying to play it cool. "That's two."

I tried to act casual, like miracles happen to me all the time, as opposed to *never*. I wound up the dreidel and spun again, hard as I could.

Gimel!!! This time, I went wild.

"Yes!" I shouted. "YES! That's it! Woo-hoo!" I completely lost it, jumping around screaming "Man-O-Manischewitz!"

"Be quiet!" said Howard, who had come out of his room. "You're making too much noise. I'm trying to concentrate."

When I said I was alone, I wasn't counting Howard. He's my oldest brother, and he spends all his time in his room with the door closed, studying math. That's all he ever does. He's fifteen and he's in high school, and is supposed to be some super-brilliant genius. At least that's what he tells us. The only time he stops studying is to come out and eat or when Kenny and I are making noise. Kenny's my other brother, who is two years older than me, and actually *likes* to have fun. His real name is Kenneth, but everyone calls him Kenny. But no one calls Howard "Howie"—he won't let them. When Kenny and I make noise, Howard stomps out and yells at us, then goes back into his room and shuts the door. That's one reason Kenny and I hardly ever have friends over.

But at the moment, I couldn't have cared less about Howard. This was between me and God.

"All right," I whispered, suddenly feeling nervous about the next spin. "Three in a row is pretty good," I said. "Really good. But it's not a miracle. Not yet. It might just be luck—after all, it's just a one in sixty-four chance." I stopped myself, because weird as it feels to talk to God, it's even weirder to lecture God about math. I brushed off any microscopic dust that might have settled on the table. "Just one more Gimel," I said, so quietly, only God could hear me. "That's all I'm asking."

I wound the dreidel between my thumb and middle finger—and spun.

I realize none of this will make any sense to you if you're not Jewish and don't know what a dreidel is. Even if you *are* Jewish and know all about dreidels, it still won't make much sense, because the whole game of dreidel doesn't make sense. Nobody can agree on the rules, which is how you know it's a Jewish game.

A dreidel is a spinning top with four sides. Maybe you've heard that stupid, inane, insipid song, the one that always gets stuck in my head this time of year: "I have a little dreidel, I made it out of clay! And when it's dry and ready, oh dreidel I shall play!"

Shoot. Now it's stuck in my head. I'm sorry if it's stuck in yours too. From now on, I'll just refer to it as "The Horrible Song." Anyway, "The Horrible Song" by itself wouldn't be so bad, but when the choir sings it at school along with the Christmas carols, and everybody acts as if they've done us Jews a big favor, it makes me want to barf.

Back to dreidels, which, by the way, can be made of wood, plastic, metal, even Styrofoam—anything *but* clay. They date back to the time of Antiochus, this mean Seleucid ruler who wouldn't let the Jews study Torah, which is the one thing Jews love to do most, like Howard studies math. So the Jews came up with this trick of keeping dreidels handy while they studied. That way, when the soldiers came by, they'd hide their books and whip out their dreidels, and the soldiers—who weren't too bright—figured they were just gambling, not studying. As soon as the soldiers left, out came the Torah. That's another totally Jewish thing. Other people might have toys they play with in secret to *avoid* studying. But Jews have toys we *pretend* to play with, so we can study in secret. Go figure.

Anyhow, there are four Hebrew letters on a dreidel—*Gimel, Hey, Nun,* and *Shin.* Gimel is the best—everyone agrees on that—and when it's your turn to spin and it lands on Gimel, you win whatever is in the pot, which is usually pennies or stale chocolate coins. That's easy to remember because *Gimel* sounds like "gimme-all!" When you get Hey, you get half of what's in the pot. After that it gets confusing. *Nun* means "nothing," but some people play that when you get Nun you *do* nothing, while others say it means you're supposed to *have* nothing, so you lose everything you've got. The last letter is Shin, which is always bad, because you lose something, or maybe everything. The only good thing about Shin is that when you get it, you can shout, "Oh Shin!" It's pretty vague between Nun and Shin, and that's where the whole thing falls apart. I have never played a game of dreidel that hasn't either fizzled out or ended in an argument.

If you still don't understand the rules, don't worry, because no one does, but here's my point: If you spin a dreidel again and again, sooner or later it has to land on Gimel. You don't need some kind of giant computer brain to figure that out. I'm not saying it should happen every time, or even very often, just once in a while.

If, however, you keep spinning and it only ever lands on Shin or Nun, then something is seriously wrong. Maybe the dreidel is loaded, like the dice they have at Berg's Studio of Magic—my favorite place in the world, by the way. It's on Hollywood Boulevard in Los Angeles, and Mr. Berg knew all the great magicians and tells stories about them. There's a display shelf of illusions and, right in the center, there's a straitjacket that Harry Houdini actually escaped from! There's even a picture of him wearing it, hanging upside down from a crane over a street in Chicago, and the rope is on fire!

I asked Mr. Berg if I could touch the straitjacket, but he just laughed, then gave me a pair of dice to play with. Every time I rolled them, they landed on five and two. Sometimes one would land on another number, then flip over, like Mexican jumping beans. He said the dice were loaded, and would always win in a game called "craps," which I've never played, but is a fun word to say.

Back to dreidel. If it's not a loaded dreidel, and all you ever get is Shin, you have to wonder. It's like the farmer who wakes up on a beautiful spring day, walks out of his front door, and steps on a rake. It flips up and hits him in the face—wham! Dazed and confused, he staggers and reaches his hand out to lean on a wall. Only it's not a wall, it's his bull—who doesn't like it one bit! The bull chases the farmer all over until he dives onto his tractor for protection, but his hand accidentally hits the lever and the thing starts up. Only he's not in the driver's seat, he's hanging off the side, from one suspender of his overalls, getting dragged through the mud all over his fields, until the tractor finally runs out of gas. And as he's lying there in the mud, all beat up, the bull comes back, sniffs him, then poops right in his face. And the farmer looks up and says, "Why, God? Why are you doing this to me?"

Then the sky parts and this booming voice says, "There's just something about you that really bugs me."

I heard that joke from Brian, my best friend, and it's pretty good. But I would like to believe it's *just* a joke. I would like to believe that God is not up there snuffing out lives like cigarette butts. In particular I would like to believe, all evidence to the contrary, that my father—who never gets a break, no matter how hard he tries—is not one of those being snuffed out, and our home is *not* the ashtray. That even though we've lost again and again until now, we're not actually *losers*. We just haven't won *yet*. Because it seems to me that if life is a game of dreidel and you keep spinning enough times—and there's a God who doesn't hate you—it will eventually land on Gimel.

And by eventually, I mean *now*. Hanukkah, 1971.

It was a perfect spin, and went on so long that the dreidel moved slowly toward the edge of the table. That got me thinking about a whole moral question—if it dropped to the floor, could I still count the fourth Gimel?—when it began to wobble, and finally fell—right on the edge of the table, half on, half off.

Oh Shin.

This is the first night of Hanukkah. Or, if you prefer, Chanukah. Or Hanaka. I've even seen it spelled Khanukkah. That's how you know it's a Jewish holiday—we can't even agree how to spell it. Mr. Culpepper—my seventh-grade English teacher, who is really tall, with a beard, and so cool that he's practically a hippie—told us that the word *catsup* can be spelled more ways than any other word in the English language: ketchup, catchup, katsup, katsip, catsoup—there are about twenty different spellings. Really, you can combine those letters almost any way you want and it works. So that's what I'll do with Chonikah—keep trying different spellings until I find the best one. But however you spell it, catshup is about what you put on hamburgers and French fries. And Hanuukkka is all about miracles. At least it's *supposed* to be.

Growing up Jewish, you hear plenty about miracles: Moses crossing the Red Sea, manna in the wilderness, Daniel in the lion's den. There's a whole song about miracles in *Fiddler on the Roof,* which we've seen more times than I can count. So I know all about how miracles are *supposed* to work. But they don't. Not for me. And not for my family. What we get is the exact opposite.

Mr. Culpepper says you need to define your terms or no one knows what you're talking about. According to Rabbi Goldberg, who took over at our temple after Rabbi Buxelbaum died, a miracle is when the *exact* right thing happens at the *exact* right time, just when you need it the most. It comes as a surprise. You can't believe it, but there it is! Clear as day! And you say, "Wow! It's a miracle!"

But Mr. Culpepper also said you can define a term by its opposite, which is called its antonym. So what's the word for the exact opposite of a miracle? Like when you really, *really* need something to happen, even though it's a long shot. So you hope and you hope and then when you can't hope any more, you start to pray and ask God to please, please let this one thing happen, and if it does I'll believe in you for the rest of my life. And then, finally, when it seems like time has run out and there's no hope, at the last minute . . . *it doesn't happen.*

I've been looking for a word for *that* for a long time. Then, a couple of weeks ago, I found one. Actually, two. My mom was talking to her friend Esther—she actually has three friends named Esther, but they're easy to tell apart. This is the one who used to smoke, and keeps on quitting. I'm glad, because smoking stinks and is disgusting. Not only that, it kills you. Now that Esther has quit smoking again, she has a new hobby: complaining about her husband, Harold, who doesn't pay enough attention to her.

"So there we were at the Finkelsteins' daughter's wedding reception, I'm wearing my new chiffon burgundy dress for the very first time, but does Harold even notice? No, he's too busy staring at Mrs. Fenig—God knows why, she's skinny as a stick—and he says to her, 'That's a lovely dress. And those are beautiful earrings, Mrs. Fenig.'"

Then Esther says to my mom, "So what am I? Chopped liver?"

I'd heard the phrase before, but never really thought about it.

"Mom?" I asked later. "Why did Esther say she was chopped liver?"

"What?" she asked, confused.

"Chopped liver!" I said again, louder. My mom doesn't hear very well. I have to look right at her when I speak. "Esther asked if she was chopped liver. Why?"

"Well," she said, "'chopped liver' is an expression that means 'nothing special.'"

"Like 'This weekend I have no plans, so I'm chopping liver'?"

"Not exactly," my mom said. "You only say it to complain, when you feel like nothing special: 'What am I? Chopped liver?'"

It was funny to hear her say that, because she never complains about anything, even when she should. Everyone's heard about the Jewish mother who makes you feel guilty. She gives you two shirts for Chchchcanukkah, and when you try one on, she says, "What's the matter? You don't like the other one?"

That's not my mom. She wants to believe everything is wonderful, even when it's not, which is pretty much all the time. And I'm the type of kid who tries to make everything wonderful for her, because I can't stand it when she's miserable. Sometimes I manage to do it. But, when I can't, I end up feeling worse than the kid with two shirts.

Even though the words *chopped liver* are English, it's a Yiddish expression. Yiddish is a Jewish language, like Hebrew, except Hebrew is for praying and Yiddish is for complaining. And for making jokes—it's really good for that. There are a bunch of Yiddish words that are just plain funny, like *"Gesundheit!"* That's what you say when someone sneezes, but it works as a punch line all by itself. If you don't believe me, try shouting it out sometime, you'll see.

As for chopped liver, I think "nothing special" understates the case. It isn't just unspecial—it's *revolting*. That's one of those funny words that can mean different things. The Maccabees in the Kchanukah story were revolting in a *good* way, the hippies are revolting in a *confusing* way, and chopped liver is revolting in a *disgusting* way. As a phrase, though, chopped liver is great—and the perfect name for when the exact right thing *doesn't* happen. You pray for a miracle, and what do you get? Chopped liver.

The weird thing is, old people seem to like the stuff. Last year we were at a bar mitzvah party for the son of another one of the Esthers. This one wears a wig that spins around on her head when she sneezes, which she does fairly often, because she has allergies. And if that isn't enough to remember her by, her whole name is Esther Nestor. And her husband—get this—is actually named Lester, so they're Lester and Esther Nestor. I like the name, though I don't know how she felt about it when she married Lester. He must have *impressed* her. But maybe it *stressed* her. Or *depressed* her. Kenny and I joke about it, but never to her face, lest we *pester* Esther Nestor.

Anyhow, it was her son's bar mitzvah, though his name is something of a mystery. He's called—don't ask me why—Steve. They could have named him Chester or even Fester, like the uncle on *The Addams Family* on TV. He could learn to juggle and become a *jester*. Or a banker—Chester Nestor, Investor. The party was at this fancy hotel in downtown Los Angeles, with a huge buffet of Jewish foods like bagels and lox, and right there in the center of the table, like some kind of wedding cake, was the head of President Nixon—sculpted entirely from chopped liver!

We all gathered around staring at it until Marty Finkelstein said that if they were going to go to all the trouble to make a president's head out of chopped liver, they should have chosen a good president, like John F. Kennedy. We all agreed—everyone knows Nixon is a crook—until Sidney Applebaum pointed out that it might not be right to have everyone scooping out chunks of Kennedy's head, given how he had died.

Everyone laughed. Then, suddenly, we stopped. There was a long, awkward pause as we all stared at our shoes. I don't know what everyone else was thinking, but I was remembering that morning in 1963 when I was in line with my mother picking up the turkey at the Midway grocery store. When we finally got to Mr. Chen, the cashier, he was crying. I was four, and had never seen a man cry in a grocery store.

"Mr. Chen?" my mother asked. "Are you all right?" He just stood there, shaking his head, and we all stood there, not buying groceries.

That year for Thanksgiving the whole country ate chopped liver. And three years ago, when President Kennedy's brother Robert was killed, we had leftover chopped liver. And now Nixon is president.

But Hanukkyah is not supposed to be a chopped liver holiday—it's a *latke* holiday. And so, after the almost-but-not-quite-miracle with the dreidel, I got out the Veg-O-Matic and potatoes and went to work. With three Gimels in a row, I figured, God was at least *watching*.

"All right," I said. "Maybe dreidel isn't your thing. I agree. It's kind of a dumb game. But how about this: Supposing I make this the most perfect Kquanukkah ever, starting with the latkes. And if you want to do me a little miracle, you can make it snow. Is it a deal?"

Latkes, in case you don't know, are potato pancakes. It's also a Yiddish word, and sounds a lot like another Yiddish word—*gatkes*—but that's completely different. *Latkes* means "potato pancakes" while *gatkes* means "underwear." Some people make latkes with grated potatoes, while others use mashed. Of course, no one can agree, which is what makes them a Jewish food. But everyone *does* agree they should be crispy, not soggy, and fried in plenty of oil, because Khanakah is supposed to be all about the miracle of the oil.

Last year, though, my father tried to make latkes without oil, so they would be healthier. He's always trying to make healthy food, like his sugarless cheesecake made with cottage cheese and sweetened with grapefruit juice. Yuck. But his latkes kept sticking to the pan, so he added a bunch of oil, which pretty much undid any health benefits, and we ended up with clumps of greasy potato mush. When latkes come out right, they're delicious and you eat them with sour cream and applesauce. I like them with jam, because that's how they eat them in Chelm, the Jewish village of fools. But you don't eat latkes with katsayp. Or kitshoup. Or catsip. None of those.

I couldn't find a recipe book, but then I remembered we have this little red 78 RPM record called "Let's Make Latkes!" I found it and put it on the record player, and it actually sang the recipe for latkes—including onions, which burn your eyes when you grate them, but it's worth it.

I followed the recipe exactly and made a sample one to test. It came out crisp and golden brown. Tasted like a dream! Perfect latkes for the perfect Kchahanukkah.

I covered the batter so it wouldn't get gray and disgusting, then went to decorate the house. I had time—Kenny was with my mom, at McVey's hobby shop. He's fourteen, and had his bar mitzvah last June. He also has a paper route and has been saving up money to buy a model airplane kit, which is the latest thing he's into. He makes them from balsa wood and coats the wings with tissue paper, then hangs them from the ceiling in his room.

As for my dad, he said he'd be home a couple of hours ago, and we were going to cook latkes together, but he's always late.

It usually bugs me, but in this case it may be good, because he was meeting with this guy named Forentos who has some serious investors lined up for "Omni-Glow." That's my dad's new business, which is all about glow-in-the-dark plastics. If you haven't heard about them, you will soon. My dad says they're the next big thing, and the world is waiting.

That's what makes Omni-Glow a sure bet, unlike the Garage-O-Matic, which was what last Chanakayah was all about. It actually began a couple months before, after Halloween, when we were driving home in the Dodge Dart. The rain was coming down in buckets, and my brothers and I got into an argument about who had to get out and open the garage door. Guess who lost? Me, that's who. The youngest. That was really unfair, because I had already lost the argument before that one, and had to sit in the middle of the backseat, where there is a big, uncomfortable bump. Usually the middle seat isn't so bad, because of the hole in the floor that lets you watch the street zip by below. But with the rain it's a whole different story, and I was getting soaked. Having to get out to open the garage door—well, that added insult to injury.

I didn't think much more about it, but my father stayed up late that night, and every night for weeks, fiddling with wires and switches and other little electronic gizmos. Finally, one day, he took us out to the garage to show us what he'd built. Hanging from a pulley was a contraption with a rope and all the weights from Kenny's weight lifting set—which explained where *that* went.

But we didn't care about the weights, because our dad was so excited. We stood outside the garage, he flicked the switch, there was a loud grinding and banging noise, and suddenly—voila!—the garage door began to lift all by itself! We couldn't believe it.

You know how many garage doors there are in the world? A lot. And how many people there are who don't want to open them? Even more. So my dad called his brother, my uncle Morrie, who is a total *schmoozer,* which means "he knows everybody." Uncle Morrie flew out all the way from Cleveland and lined up some big business people, ready to pay real money for my dad's invention—five thousand dollars! Three of them actually came to our house, driving a Cadillac, just to see our garage! We even cleaned it up just for the occasion. Everyone watched as my father pressed the button. There was the grinding and, a moment later, it opened up! You should have seen their faces. They were as impressed with the Garage-O-Matic as we were. They did it again and again, opening the door, then closing it. This was it.

There was a loud pop, and I turned to see my uncle Morrie, who had opened a bottle of real champagne for the occasion, which bubbled all over the driveway.

"Here's to the Garage-O-Matic!" he said.

They were just about to shake hands on the deal when my dad started to tell them the whole story of how he invented it. While he was talking, one of the investors— Mr. Rosenberg—went over to examine the mechanism. Just then an airplane flew overhead and must have triggered the garage door to close. By the time Mr. Rosenberg noticed, it was too late. We didn't see his face, but his legs were sticking out from under the door, like the Wicked Witch of the East, and he was screaming about a law suit.

The deal was dead, nothing left but a puddle of champagne.

Like I said, Chanaykayah isn't supposed to be a chopped liver holiday. Of course, in Hebrew school, Cantor Grubnitz reminded us that it isn't even a *major* holiday, and we shouldn't get too excited about it. A major holiday is Yom Kippur, in the fall, which is the end of the beginning of the Jewish New Year. Let me tell you, Yom Kippur is not fun. You dress in uncomfortable clothes, go to temple, and sit there forever, not eating, standing, then sitting, not eating some more, then standing again, listening to Rabbi Goldberg go on and on, and to Cantor Grubnitz, who lives to hear himself sing. The two of them dress up in black robes and pointy hats and tell you to say you're sorry for everything you've ever done and a whole bunch of things you've never even thought of doing. Then, when you get back to school, everyone says, "Wow, you got the day off? Lucky!"

This year was even worse than usual. My dad was in the hospital—again—recovering from another operation. So we were in temple with my mom, praying for him. And Cantor Grubnitz decided to sing extra operatically with notes that lasted for hours and nearly shattered the stained glass windows. *That's* a major holiday. Some fun.

Major holiday or not, I was going to make this a perfect Kchanakkah. I hung all our decorations. We had two letter chains—HAPPY HANUKKAH and HAPPY CHANUKKAH!—so I put both up, one in the kitchen and the other in the living room over the fireplace. Then I cleaned up our menorah, which I don't think had ever been cleaned. It's gold with blue-and-white enamel, and has eight soldiers, who I guess are supposed to be the Maccabees, each standing on one leg and holding up a torch, which is where the candle goes. There's a ninth soldier in front, a little taller than the rest, who I suppose is Judah, the leader of the Maccabees. My parents brought it back from their trip to Israel when I was in the third grade, and I thought it was the coolest thing ever. Now it seems a lot less cool, and the soldiers look more like the USC marching band than the Maccabees. Even so, once it was clean and shiny, it looked pretty good.

That done, I picked out candles for the menorah. That's always my job, partly because no one else cares and partly because it lets me choose the *shammes*. I've always had a thing about the shammes, which is the helper candle, the one that lights all the others. It's not really part of the holiday, just a little bet I have going with myself each night, to see whether the shammes is the last candle to burn out. Because you light it first and it burns the whole time you're singing the blessings and lighting all the other candles, you'd think it would be the first to burn out. But I've noticed that a lot of times it actually stays lit longer than the rest, like it's being rewarded for sharing its light with the other candles. The first time I noticed, it seemed like a mini-miracle. Now I look for it to happen. Actually, I do more than look; if one candle is a little longer, I'll choose it for the shammes. Maybe that's cheating, trying to force a miracle, but I'll take what I can get. Tonight I chose a longish blue one for the shammes and a yellow one for the first night.

Only then did I allow myself to think about my Chahah-nukkah present. I had noticed that my parents had been running mysterious "errands" in the past week, to Los Angeles, and I figured they had gone to Berg's Studio of Magic to buy me the one thing I've wanted for the past five years: a real silk top hat.

I do magic shows—that's my thing. While Kenny goes from one thing to another—baseball, then coin collecting, then rock collecting, then weight lifting, and now model airplanes—magic has been my one and only thing. It started when Kenny got "Sneaky Pete's Professional Magic Show" from Steve Klein, who lives next door, then lost interest in it, and gave it to me. Now I do magic shows around town, at birthday parties and libraries. Lots of my tricks involve a hat, but all I have is a crummy felt one. What I've always wanted is a real spring-loaded top hat, like the one Mister Mystery has—he's my magic teacher. They're from the old days, for going to the opera, made so you could take your hat off and press it down flat so you didn't block the view of the people sitting behind you. Then, when the opera was over, you'd whack the brim against the back of your wrist and—pop!—it was a full-sized hat again!

You should see the audiences when Mister Mystery opens his. It's not even a trick, but they're amazed. And they have one for sale at Berg's Studio of Magic. It costs $50, but once when I was there with my dad, Mr. Berg said he'd sell it to me for $38, which is still *a lot* of money—my felt one only cost three dollars. I've never asked for a gift for my birthday or anything else—what's the point?—but I know my dad saw my face when I tried it on.

🔨 🔨 🔨 🔨

If it seems like I know a lot about Chaynukkayyah, I do. I'm kind of an expert. It began in December of first grade, when my teacher brought out song sheets and started leading the class in Christmas songs—first "Frosty," then "Rudolph," then on to "Silent Night."

"Mrs. Grumbacher?" I said, raising my hand.

"Yes, Joel?"

"These are Christmas songs. But my family doesn't believe in Christmas. We have our own holiday, which is even better."

I had been giving this a lot of thought. My brothers and I were the only Jews in Bixby Elementary School, which goes from first to eighth grade. When Howard started fourth grade, he came home and told us how the kids in his class had figured out he was Jewish and threw pennies on the ground to see if he would pick them up. He did, and they laughed and said, "Jews love pennies!" The next time he didn't pick them up, and they laughed again and said, "Why don't you pick them up? Jews *love* pennies!"

Howard, in response, said, "You're all stupid jerks." In retrospect, this was not the cleverest comeback line. He may be an Einstein genius in math, but he has never been too smart at dealing with people, and quickly became the least popular kid in his class. Unlike Howard, Kenny gets along with pretty much everyone, so he didn't think the Jewish thing would be a problem. But when some kids in his class discovered he was Jewish, they started asking him questions, like if he was rich, and whether Jews had horns and could they see his. He came home crying.

Being the only Jew in my class had never affected me personally. In kindergarten I hadn't said anything about it, and no one had asked. We sang all the Christmas songs, and when we got to the ones that mentioned "Jesus" or "Christ," I mouthed the words, like Jews are supposed to do. In fact, the only time the Jewish thing ever seemed like it might be a problem for me was at the start of first grade when I was at Jimmy Bowen's house and met his parents for the first time. His dad looked at me and said, "So, this is the little Jew-boy?"

Then Jimmy's mother, who is really nice and always gives us sweet iced tea, said, "Oh, Donald, don't say that!"

Then his dad said, "No, it's fine! We like Jews, right? The chosen people!" Then he shook my hand so hard, my fingers hurt. That started me thinking about the Jewish thing, and I decided it would be better to strike first, like the Maccabees, which is why I had raised my hand.

"Oh, yes," said Mrs. Grumbacher. "I've heard of your holiday, the Jewish Christmas. It's called 'Cha-nu-kah,' isn't it?" She said the *Ch* like in *chocolate*. "There's even a song on our song sheet. . . . Ah, here it is!"

"Actually, Mrs. Grumbacher, it's pronounced Chhhhanukah," I said, clearing my throat to stop her from singing "The Horrible Song." "And it's eight times as good as Christmas, because it lasts for eight days and nights. It's a time when miracles happen!" This was a little hard to say because saying the *Chhhh* in *Chhhhanukkah* had generated a big loogie in my mouth, which I couldn't spit out but didn't want to swallow.

My comments caused a ruckus. Every kid in that class lived for Christmas—the best day of the year by far—and the notion that some holiday they'd never heard of might be even better was inconceivable. Finally Arnold Pomeroy shouted above the rest.

"Oh yeah? Well, Christmas lasts for twelve days, so there!"

"Yeah, but do you get presents on *all twelve* days?"

That's when Mrs. Grumbacher stepped in.

"Children, both holidays can be wonderful, and this is a good chance for all of us to learn about another religion. We don't have time now, Joel, but perhaps tomorrow you would like to tell the class all about"—there was a pause as she prepared to clear her throat—"Chhhhhanukah?"

Now *she* was stuck with a big loogie, and I had just what I wanted: a chance to show off to the class. If I got it right, I would not be a bully magnet. I would be a star, and every first grader in Bixby School would be wishing they were Jewish.

The next day I arrived early with a paper bag full of supplies: a large Styrofoam menorah, a bunch of dreidels, and chocolate Choinykah gelt, along with the string of letters that said HAPPY HANUKKAH! I got Mrs. Grumbacher to stand on a chair and pin it above the blackboard, over the letters of the alphabet.

"Class," said Mrs. Grumbacher as they took their seats, "today we will have a special presentation from Joel, who is one of the Jewish people and will tell us all about his holiday. The one he mentioned yesterday, which comes at this time of year. That isn't Christmas." She had given up on saying the actual word.

I stood in front of the class. "Once, in ancient Israel, there was this big, mean, hairy guy named Antiochus who thought he knew *everything about everything*. He told everyone how to dress and what to eat and who to worship: the Greek gods. He put up giant statues and made everyone bow down to them. The Jews didn't like it one bit, but what could they do? If they didn't do what he said, they would be killed—dead!"

Once it was clear that the story had killing in it, they were hooked. I told how the Seleucid army was the most powerful in the world, with swords and armor and even elephants, and if they didn't like you, they would order the elephants to sit on you, squashing you like a pancake. "And that's why we eat potato pancakes for Kchanukkah, to remind us of all the people who got squished.

"The Seleucids put up this big honking statue right in the middle of town and said it was God, and made everyone bow down to it or be killed. None of the Jews wanted to bow down, because Jews don't bow down to statues. But they didn't want to be killed either, so most of them did it. Except for this one old guy named Mattathias, who went right up to the statue and knocked it over! The head fell off and rolled in the gutter and everyone cheered, and that began the revolution! Mattathias gathered his children, including Judah the Maccabee and his brothers, to fight for their freedom. During the daytime they hid out in caves and, at night, while the Seleucids were sleeping, Judah snuck up and hit them with his hammer—wham!"

They ate it up, and wanted more, so I told them about the oil.

"But that wasn't all! After the Maccabees won the battle and went back to the temple, they found the Seleucids had left it a super-gross disgusting mess, filled with garbage and pigs' blood. The Jews cleaned and cleaned until it was beautiful. When it was good as new, they needed to light the giant menorah, so they looked for the sacred oil. But the Seleucids had broken every single jar of it, except for one tiny jar they had missed. It was hardly any oil, but the Jews lit it, and it burned and burned! For eight days and eight nights, just enough for the Jews to get more oil. It was a miracle!"

That part didn't go over so well. The class was kind of quiet.

"Wait a minute!" said Arnold Pomeroy. "That's supposed to be a big miracle? That they had just enough oil? So what?"

Arnold Pomeroy could be kind of a jerk even then, but he had a good point. I never saw what was so special about the oil either. But I wasn't about to let Arnold Pomeroy ruin my story, so I embellished.

"Well, Arnold, I guess you don't know how cold it gets at night in the Judean desert."

"How cold?" he asked.

"Really cold. So cold that if that little light burned out, they would have all frozen, like Popsicles, and died!" Once I got back to talking about death and freezing, they got interested again.

"But that tiny flame *didn't* burn out! Instead, it got bigger and bigger, night after night for eight nights until it was a giant bonfire! They were saved! It was a miracle!"

The class actually cheered at that one. Someone even shouted "Right on!" Then I brought out the dreidels and told them how the letters Nun, Gimel, Hey, and Shin— which you already know about—actually stood for four words that summed up the whole story: "*Nes Gadol Haya Sham*," Hebrew for "A Great Miracle Happened There."

"And that," I said, "is why Chahnnukkah is so different

from Christmas. We don't just celebrate for one night ..." I took a long, dramatic pause. "We celebrate every night for *eight* nights."

A different silence fell over the class, and that's when I knew I had them. I could see Arnold Pomeroy working out the math, multiplying Christmas times eight in his mind, then slowly raising his hand.

"But what about presents? Do you really get presents every night?"

I took my time before answering. "Chhhanukah," I finally said, "is a bonanza!"

Now, what I told Arnold Pomeroy wasn't *exactly* a lie. I never actually said we got presents for all eight nights. Or at all, for that matter. As Mr. Culpepper would say, I *implied* it—and he just *inferred* it. But I didn't lie.

The truth is that in my family, we don't get any presents. We never have. That's because we're broke, and we've been broke for a long time. I know people say that Jews are rich, but that's a stereotype and isn't true. It's especially not true for my family. My mother has a part-time job, editing manuscripts for a company that makes educational film-strips. She's good at it but doesn't make very much money. And my dad hasn't had any regular work for a long time. Every month I watch him do different tricks with the bills—

like sending the check for the gas company in the envelope to the water company and the water company check to the telephone company and the telephone company check to the gas company. They all think it's an honest mistake, so they call, and then he gets them to call each other, and it can take a couple weeks for them to figure it out, which gives him time to come up with money somewhere, or get the next check from welfare.

I didn't want to tell Arnold Pomeroy what really happens on Khanukhaya at our home, but I'll tell you. Each year, after lighting the candles on the first night, when other families get presents, we get a story. But it's not a warm, feel-good bedtime story. It's more of an *explanation* as to why there are no presents that particular year. It's like every year they keep meaning to get us presents, but it never quite happens. Last year "The Explanation" was about how hard it was for engineers to find work since the collapse of the aerospace industry, and the year before that about the government making a mistake with the welfare checks. I dread The Explanation, because not only do we not get presents, but I feel guilty for wanting them. It always ends with my mom saying, ". . . but you know we get you things you really need, like clothing." And that's true, so we nod.

It's hard to be mad at my parents. They have it tough. You can't buy presents if you don't have money. And money really isn't the important thing. "Money, shmoney," my dad always says, "as long as you have your health."

He's right. And that would be great, *if* he had his health. But he doesn't. He and my mom take turns going to the hospital. It's like that sign I saw in a store window: "Sleep Fast— We Need the Pillows!" Between the two of them, they are in and out of the hospital as often as our car is in and out of the shop.

The hospital is my least favorite place in the world. For one thing, hospitals have a gross smell that comes from being so clean. And when you're there, it's all about waiting to see the person you're visiting, then waiting for them to get out. I hate waiting.

But I could take the smell, and even the waiting, if it did any good. The real problem is that it's pointless. You go to the hospital, and what do you see? Sick people. And the longer they're there, the sicker they get. That's how it is with my mom and dad: Each time they go in, they come out worse.

I would say that my mom's problems are more like our current car, the Dodge Dart—so far we've had to replace the starter, the gas pump, and the radiator—while my dad's are more like our old car, the Rambler, which was falling apart from the time we got it and finally had to be towed away in several pieces. You can see my dad's problems just by looking at him. A lot of older people have arthritis, but he's had it since he was young. It's not the usual kind that you just complain about, but a special kind called "ankylosing spondylitis," which is Latin for "curled up like a pretzel." His fingers are all knobby and twisted, almost like claws. You wouldn't know it to look at him, but when he was my age, he was a great violinist—a child prodigy, everyone says.

Now he can't even pick things up, at least not little things. Last week I got up in the middle of the night to go to the bathroom, and I saw him sitting at the kitchen table, working on another one of his inventions—a box with a button you can press, to change the TV channel. At least, that's what it's supposed to do, though it sounds impossible. He had dropped a screw onto the floor and was trying to pick it up, but couldn't. I was behind him, in the dark hallway, so he didn't see me and I didn't say anything, because I didn't want him to know I was watching. He kept trying to pick up the screw until he was almost crying. I couldn't stand it, but I couldn't stop watching either. Finally, he reached over and grabbed a screwdriver, then bent down again. I guess the screwdriver was magnetized, because it picked up the screw. I went back to bed.

Along with twisting up his hands, this pretzel-arthritis curls up his spine. He used to be tall, but now he's almost as short as Howard.

It's painful to watch my father walk. He uses a cane, and sometimes two, and tilts to the left. With every step he takes, there's this loud clicking sound, like someone snapping their fingers, and then a grinding sound as his hip bone pops back into place. It makes me cringe, but I'm used to it. What's embarrassing is when other people see him. Like last week as we walked into Thrifty's Coffee Shop—which takes credit cards—there was this little boy about three years old, staring at my dad. First his face was curious. Then it sort of scrunched up, afraid. He pointed to my dad and started to cry.

But my dad looked right at him, then did this kind of move with his head, tilting it back and forth like Charlie Chaplin. He made a funny face and a clicking sound—with his mouth this time—and the boy actually started to giggle. It was like my father was only *pretending* that he couldn't walk very well, like he was putting on a show.

That's what my dad does best: He makes people laugh. He's always telling us how important it is to laugh, especially at things that aren't funny. "Like the circus clown," he says, "who may be sad, but still laughs—and that's better than crying."

Kenny came home with my mom all excited about his new model airplane kit. And when my dad finally got home, he was whistling, which was a good sign, as it meant his meeting with Forentos about Omni-Glow must have gone well. My dad and I cooked the latkes together, and they came out perfect. Then, no one fought during dinner, which was practically a miracle in itself. After eating the latkes we gathered around the menorah, just like a normal Jewish family, and turned off the living room light. I checked outside. No snow yet, but it sure felt like it was coming.

As the youngest, I got to strike the match and light the shammes, and we sang all three blessings for the first night. Then my mom started to clap and sing "Maoz Tzur"— "Rock of Ages"—which is the traditional song you sing after you light the candles. We got two lines into it and realized we couldn't remember the words, which is our own tradition.

We stopped, and there was a long silence.

My mother finally said, "How nice to be together for the first night of Hanikah!"

I nodded, seeing no sign of a box that would hold a top hat. I looked at my mom, waiting for The Explanation. Something wasn't right. I could tell from the way she was talking, like everything was so wonderful.

"Aren't the candles lovely?" she said.

This much cheeriness meant something was definitely wrong. Kenny and Howard must have known it too, because they sat there silently, waiting.

"Why the long faces?" said my father. "It's Chhanukkah! You're supposed to be Chhhappy!"

I saw no box, or bag, or anything that looked like a present, and realized I had been a fool to expect one.

"We have some news," my mother finally said. She didn't have to say another word. From the look on her face, I knew exactly what we were getting.

Chopped liver.

THE SECOND CANDLE:
In the Land of Shriveled Dreams

Monday, December 13

My childhood isn't supposed to be like this.

I say *isn't* but at this point I may as well say *wasn't*, because it's pretty much over. My bar mitzvah is next June. That is, next June I will *become* a bar mitzvah. Just to clarify, I won't *get* bar mitzvahed. Cantor Grubnitz made that painfully clear back in September, on the first day of Hebrew school.

"I want each of you to tell me the date you will become a bar mitzvah," he said. Then, noticing there were girls in class, he added, grudgingly, "Or bat mitzvah."

A bunch of us raised our hands and began calling out dates.

"Excuse me, Cantor Grubnitz," said Ernie Maitloff. "What if you're not sure when you're getting bar mitzvahed?"

That was all it took to set Cantor Grubnitz off. For a moment he just stood there, staring at Ernie. Cantor Grubnitz has a blue vein on his forehead that gets bigger when he's angry, which happens a lot. I think it might be a gorgle, like when someone says, "Calm down, or you'll bust a gorgle!" Now it was twitching.

"If you don't know, then I'll tell you. You'll never *get* bar mitzvahed. You know why? Because it's impossible. You *become* a bar mitzvah."

Ernie had hit a nerve. Evidently, you can *get* a joke, *get* lost, even *get* busted. In fact, you can do all of them at the same time. But you can't do them while you're *getting* bar mitzvahed, because no one *gets* bar mitzvahed.

Instead, you *become* a bar mitzvah. I know that sounds bizarre—like a little kid suddenly turning into a big party with balloons and music and chopped liver sculptures. But to become a bar mitzvah actually means that you are "a child of the commandments." Just what *that* means, I have no idea, but it only happens after you've survived dozens of torture sessions with Cantor Grubnitz. Then you stand up in front of the whole congregation and sing so everyone can hear your voice cracking. Afterward everyone says mazel tov and congratulates you on becoming a man—which you're really not. You've just become a bar mitzvah.

As far as I can tell, there are two kinds of cantors. The cool kind are guitar cantors. Some even have long hair, and play songs that everyone can sing along to, like "Blowin' in the Wind." You might not think of that as a Jewish song, but it was written by Bob Dylan, who is Jewish, so it counts.

Cantor Grubnitz is the other kind of cantor: an opera cantor. You don't sing *with* him. And you don't sing *against* him, because you'd lose. All you can do is sit there and listen. I think the idea is that his voice is so loud that God will hear it and do what he says. My mom thinks his voice is beautiful—then again, she likes everything, or at least says she does. Maybe it's because she's able to hear him. I don't think his voice is beautiful at all. He can take a service that already goes on forever and stretch it out even longer by holding the notes.

But it's when he's alone with us kids that he lives up to his title—cantor—because he's always telling us what we *can't* do.

"You know what's wrong with you kids today?" he said after chewing out Ernie. He didn't wait for us to answer. "I'll tell you what's wrong. All you want to do is sit around with your transistor radios and your 'rock and roll' music."

Any one of us could have pointed out that transistor radios were from way back in the 1960s, and that what kids today actually want to do is sit around and listen to eight-track tape players, which somehow let you choose between four songs playing at the same time! They're amazing. No one knows how they work. You can switch back and forth between the Beatles, Bob Dylan, the Beach Boys, and the Carpenters. But no one was going to say that to Cantor Grubnitz. He's scary.

"So there will be no transistor radios in class," he went on. "That's not why you're here. You're here to learn your Haftorah portions. Is that clear?"

"But Cantor Grubnitz," said Ernie, who wasn't smart enough to keep quiet, "I have another question." Everyone calls Ernie "Meatloaf," on account of his last name, Maitloff. That is, everyone except me. It's not that Meatloaf is such a bad name to call someone. But I never make fun of anyone's name—especially anyone's *last* name. That's not a matter of nobility, just survival. You wouldn't make fun of anyone's name either, if you had a last name like mine. I have no problem with my first name, Joel. It's a fine name, and sounds like Joe, which is a regular guy's name, like GI Joe. But my last name is a punch line. Guaranteed to get a laugh. You don't even need good comic timing. Teachers reading it out of the roll book the first time will try not to laugh, then when they do, will pretend they're coughing. Sometimes they'll assume there must be some right way to say the name that's not so embarrassing, and rather than try, they ask *me* how to pronounce it. But there is no other way. So I end up saying it out loud, to the laughter of the class. It's even worse when it comes up accidentally, like in Health Ed when we're talking about parts of the human body. I hate my last name, and don't want to talk about it.

Back to Ernie *Maitloff*—who said, "I think I get bar mitzvahed in February. Do I still have to memorize half the Torah?"

Cantor Grubnitz sighed. "First of all, you won't get bar mitzvahed. Second, it's not 'half the Torah.' It's your *Haftorah*. They're writings from the prophets, which is what you will chant."

"But I don't understand," said Shelly Schwartz. She's really smart, and kind of pretty. "Why don't we read from the *actual* Torah?"

"We don't want you to get it dirty," said Cantor Grubnitz, with a snort. "First, learn to chant your Haftorah and become a bat mitzvah. Then, when you've done that, you can talk to me about studying Torah.

"But I know you won't," he added with a sigh. "Because no one ever does. You kids today with your transistor radios, you don't care about being Jewish. You just want to mix in, assimilate with everyone else, and pretend you're not Jewish. Just like the Jews in Germany, before The War . . ."

Now it was our turn to sigh. Conversations always turn to what happened to the Jews in "The War." And when someone says "The War," you know exactly which war they mean.

Not the Vietnam War—which technically isn't even a war, though everyone calls it one—and not the Korean War, which was *a* war, but not *the* war. They don't mean World War I either, which used to be called "The Great War"—not that there's anything great about war in my book. But when people talk about "The War," they always mean World War II.

"What do you think happened to Jews who didn't care about being Jewish during The War?" asked Cantor Grubnitz. "I'll tell you what happened. The Nazis came and got them just the same. Took everything they had, then hauled them off to death camps. You understand? People have died for this religion of ours—and you kids can't even be bothered to learn your Haftorah portions."

There's nothing you can say or do when a teacher brings up the Holocaust. It's like this card game called bridge where you put down a special card that's called a "trump" and the game is over. The Holocaust hangs over Jewish conversations like a storm cloud. I don't know very much about it, except that some people don't want to talk about it, so when they do, they whisper. Then, once they start, they can't stop. What I *do* know is that during The War the Nazis rounded up and killed six million Jews, in Germany, Poland, Austria, Hungary, and all over Eastern Europe. You know how many six million is? A lot. I asked Mr. DeGuerre, my math teacher, who said if you counted one number every single second and never slept, it would take eleven and a half days just to count to *one* million. Multiply that by six, and you get sixty-nine days—over two months—counting one number every second without a break. But these six million weren't numbers, they were real people, with houses and families and stamp collections. And it's not like they were doing anything wrong—they were just being Jewish. Some of them were my relatives.

So, right from the first day of Hebrew school, when Cantor Grubnitz started talking about the Holocaust, I knew it was going to be a long year. In that class he also assigned us times to meet with him privately, in his office, which is filled with pictures of famous cantors and rabbis, and stinks of cigarette smoke. My day is Monday—today—which is a horrible way to start the week. At our first meeting he gave me a little yellow booklet with my Haftorah portion and a cassette tape he had recorded of himself singing it, which I was supposed to memorize.

"And don't lose it!" he said.

Since then, every Monday afternoon has been pretty much the same. I go into his office and start to sing what I've learned of my Haftorah portion. I get about three lines in when he stops me, then gives me a lecture about how I'm not singing it right and I shouldn't listen to transistor radios because people have died for our religion. Then he points at the pictures of famous cantors and rabbis and says how much more learned they are than I will ever be. Believe me, an hour of that is a very long time.

Last night, though, long after the candles had burned down and I lay huddled under the covers in my bed, I had another talk with God and came up with a plan that was supposed to change today's lesson.

"All right, God," I said, "I'm sorry I bothered you with the whole dreidel thing." It's funny, but the more you talk to God, the less weird it feels. That's especially true if you figure there may not be anyone listening, so who cares? "And I know you're really busy. So, for the record, I don't care if I get only Shins from now on, okay? And you know what? I don't need it to snow. I mean, it would be nice, but if you're only going to do one miracle for me this Kchannuukkah, make my dad's operation a success. Okay?"

That's what we found out last night, after we lit the candles and my mom said they had "news."

My brothers and I stared at one another. We don't like news. We looked back at my mother, who was smiling and nodding the way she always does when something's wrong. The bigger the smile, the worse it is, and this one was big.

"Wait a minute," my dad said. "Why the long faces? This

is great news! It's what we've been waiting for. I'm going back to the hospital!"

Now we stared at him, baffled. How going back to the hospital could be good news was beyond us.

"No, no," he said, almost laughing. "You don't understand. I've been seeing a new doctor, a surgeon named Dr. Kaplowski, at Kaiser in Los Angeles." That explained the "errands" they'd been running downtown. "And he has a whole new procedure for arthritis."

"What is it?" asked Kenny.

"Gold!" said my dad.

"Gold?" I asked. "What do you mean?"

"Yep! Dr. Kaplowski is the most skilled surgeon in all Los Angeles! He'll go into my hips, remove the arthritis, then coat the bones with gold! Real, twenty-four-karat gold—the smoothest thing there is. It never rusts, never tarnishes!"

"Why didn't you tell us?" asked Howard.

"Because he's very busy, and we weren't sure we could schedule it," said my dad. "And we didn't want to get you all excited."

"Excited?" asked Kenny.

"Yeah, this will be terrific!" he went on. "I go in on Wednesday morning. Then I'll be able to walk with no problem. Not just walk, but run! And jump! And dance!"

I could not remember ever seeing my dad run. I tried to imagine him dancing, but couldn't. The closest I could come was a memory from when I was about three, of riding on the back of this green bicycle my dad used to have, as he pedaled along, whistling. My dad on a bicycle—can you imagine? Then, when we stopped, he lifted me up and put me on his shoulders!

I've held on to that memory as tightly as I can, but every time he comes home from the hospital, more bent and broken, it grows fainter. Hospitals are where things go wrong, and the more times you go, the more wrong they get.

But that's not how my dad felt. "You know what it will be?" he said. "A miracle!"

"So," I said to God, before I went to sleep, "you heard my dad. Snow would still be nice, but the real miracle I want is for my dad. So he can walk. And dance"—then I added—"just not around me." That's when I came up with a plan I thought would seal the deal. "And in case my prayers aren't enough, I'm going to ask Cantor Grubnitz to pray too."

It seemed worth a shot. Who knows, maybe God actually *likes* opera?

Then, this morning, as I opened the door to walk to school, do you know what I saw?

Snow.

That's right. Snow.

Everywhere.

Well, it wasn't exactly snow. But it was frost, and lots of it, which is practically snow. It covered our lawn, the cars, the mailbox. Tiny icicles hung from the branches of the elm tree in our front yard, and you could feel there was more to come. I checked the barometer on our porch—still between 29 and 30, but now it looked a little closer to 30. I stepped out of the house to explore what was *almost* a winter wonderland.

Everything was covered with ice, and as I walked, I could see my breath, which I tried to blow into rings of smoke, like Bilbo in *The Hobbit*. I couldn't do it, but it was still pretty cool. Not just cool, but cold. I stuck my hands in my jacket pockets and started walking to school, picturing my father dancing and singing, like Tevye from *Fiddler on the Roof,* with his new golden joints.

Frosty as it was, it wouldn't actually count as snow until there were flakes falling from the sky. I needed to see at least one—or two, so I could compare. That's one of the amazing things about snow: Every single flake is different. Even if you have six million of them, they're all different. I walked up Kimdale Drive, looking to the sky for that first flake.

Mr. Culpepper says that if you're going to tell someone a story, you need to tell them where it's happening, and I haven't done that. Here I've been going on and on about Cantor Grubnitz and dreidels and golden hips and chopped liver and everything else, but I haven't told you anything about where I live, here in Temple City. I'm like "the butcher who backed up into his meat grinder" Mr. Culpepper always talks about, "who got a little *behind* in his work."

It's called "setting the scene," and Mr. Culpepper gave lots of examples from *Tom Sawyer,* which we're reading in class and takes place in a town called St. Petersburg on the banks of the Mississippi River.

Describing a place is no problem when it's exciting and colorful like St. Petersburg, with riverboats and haunted houses and buried treasure. But "setting the scene" is harder here in Temple City, because it is the least interesting place in the world.

Even the name "Temple City" is a cruel joke—there's no temple and no city. All right, that's not technically true. There *is* a temple, but we don't go there. It's like the joke my dad told me about the Jewish guy who gets stranded alone on a desert island in the middle of nowhere. Twenty years later a passing ship rescues him. Before he leaves, he takes the crew on a tour of the island to show them everything he's built. "Over there is my house, and that's my store, where I sell myself coconuts. Here's the school, where I would send my kids if I had any. Finally, here's one temple—and there's the other."

"Wait a minute!" says the captain. "I can see why you

have a house, and maybe a store, and even a school for kids you don't have. But why *two* temples?"

He pointed at one. "That one," he says, "I wouldn't set foot in."

So, we don't go to the temple in Temple City. When we want to be Jewish, we *schlepp* across town to another temple three suburbs over. But don't be fooled: Temple City isn't named for the temple. It's named for *Mr.* Temple, who, by the way, wasn't Jewish, because Temple isn't a Jewish name. Go figure. As far as I can tell, he was the one who came up with the money to plan out Temple City, which I figure cost a dollar and seventy-nine cents. That's how much a pad of graph paper costs at Midway Drug Store. And really, he only needed one sheet to plan our city; he probably used the other pages to plan out the other suburbs around here as well because, like Temple City, they're all squares, squares, and more boring squares.

Now, I know what you're thinking, especially if you're not from around here. That Los Angeles is Hollywood, and that's where movie stars live. That's what my cousin Abby thought, when she came here from Bethesda, Maryland, last year for Kenny's bar mitzvah. As soon as she got here she started looking around, like she was trying to find someone. When we asked what she was doing, she said she was looking for celebrities. We laughed and explained that we've been here all our lives and have never seen anyone famous, and that movie stars aren't actually real people, and even if they were, they would hang out at the beach, which is miles and miles from Temple City.

You might be wondering how my family ended up stuck here, in Temple City. I wonder the same thing. As near as I can figure, it's because of the Rose Parade. My mom and dad both grew up in Cleveland, a big, old industrial city that's so polluted that a couple years ago its Great Lake—Erie— actually caught on fire! That's bad. But that was during the summer, when Cleveland is hot and sticky. In the winter it's freezing, too cold to go outside. As kids they would wake up each New Year's Day, trapped in their houses, looking for some way to escape, and turn on the TV. And what would they see?

Thousands of people, some in shorts and shirtsleeves, standing along a boulevard lined with palm trees stretching up to the sky, in a place called Pasadena, California. Huge floats glided past, everyone on them wearing beautiful gowns or bathing suits, smiling and waving. But the most amazing thing of all was what covered the floats. Roses. Bazillions of them, something unimaginable in the Cleveland winter. Had a single rose appeared anywhere in Cleveland, it would have instantly frozen and shattered, its petals falling to the ground. Yet, there they were in full bloom. To people trapped in

Cleveland—including my parents, who hadn't seen the sun in weeks—Southern California was paradise. Though their TVs could only show the rose-covered floats in black-and-white, my parents saw them in every imaginable color—and in those colors, the dream of a new life.

A lot of people have dreams they never follow—but not my dad. He told me how he and my mom decided to get married and move out west, where they would buy their very own bungalow set on a hillside surrounded by orange trees. Every orange you ate would remind you that you were living the Pasadena Dream.

By the time I was born, at the rear end of the 1950s, that dream had all but faded away. It turns out my parents hadn't been the only ones to see the Rose Parade. Millions of people came to Southern California, filling up Pasadena and spilling down into the San Gabriel Valley. They started new suburbs, and suburbs of *those* suburbs—including Temple City. And they all drove cars, clogging up the freeways and filling the valley with a gray muffin of smog.

And what about the Pasadena Dream? I've only ever glimpsed it. I remember one day when I was about five years old, this winter storm came through and washed away the smog. The next morning, the weather suddenly turned hot—you could actually see the steam rising from the ground. The desert was blooming! I looked up to the north, where there's usually just smog, and saw mountains sharp and purple against the sky. Actually purple, like the song about purple mountain majesties! I'd never seen anything so beautiful. And you know what was at the top of the biggest mountain, which is called Mount Baldy? Snow. Crisp and white, like you could reach across the sky and touch it.

That's when I started praying for it to snow *here*, in Temple City. I don't know where you are. You may live somewhere where it snows all the time, like Cleveland. Or Chicago. Or Buffalo. Maybe you've been slogging through a long, hard winter, filled with sleet and slush and rain and all that stuff that won't stop the postman but makes everyone else miserable. But that's not the kind of snow I'm talking about. I'm talking about the kind of snow that falls silently at night, so you awake to a world transformed. The kind you look back upon years later with a warm glow, recalling how wondrous your childhood was. Like the snow I read about in a poem by Dylan Thomas, *A Child's Christmas in Wales,* where he couldn't remember whether it snowed for six days and six nights when he was twelve, or for twelve days and twelve nights when he was six. *That's* what I mean: magical snow.

Of course, that's Christmas snow, which is goyisha, but what's wrong with that? Dylan Thomas wasn't Jewish, but Robert Zimmerman liked his poetry so much, he borrowed his name. That's how he became Bob Dylan. And do you know who came up with the idea of a "White Christmas" in the first place? I'll tell you who. Irving Berlin, the songwriter. Yep, Jewish. In fact, I looked him up in the *Encyclopedia Britannica,* and his real name was Israel Isidore Beilin. You can't get more Jewish than that.

So I got to thinking, why not Khanuyakah snow? Like the kind that falls in Chelm. That's one of my favorite places in the world, even though it doesn't exist. It's the mythical Jewish town of fools in Poland. My mother told me about it. She said that she used to hear stories about it from her father—my grandpa Izzy. He died five years ago of cancer and I only ever met him a couple of times, but he was sweet, and funny. When I was younger I used to ask her to tell me the stories, but she never quite did. Instead she told me about Grandpa Izzy, and what a great storyteller *he* was.

Then one day, Mrs. Molatsky, the librarian at our temple, told me about a book called *Zlateh the Goat* filled with stories about Chelm. I know Zlateh sounds like a weird name, and it is, even for a goat, but it's my favorite book. It's by this author named Isaac Bashevis Singer, with drawings by this other guy named Maurice Sendak, and it's great. One of the stories is called "The Snow in Chelm." It's about how one Hahnukkah the elders are sitting around stroking their beards—as near as I can tell, everyone in Chelm has beards—wondering what to do about the fact that they don't have any money. Then they look out the window and see that, while they've been talking, snow has fallen, and it shines and sparkles in the sun. They decide it's not just snow, but actually silver and pearls and diamonds—the answer to all their woes! They'll be rich!

But there's a problem. If the people of Chelm walk in the snow, they'll trample the diamonds and jewels. So they decide to send a messenger to tell the Chelmites not to walk on the snow. They all agree, but then there's another problem: The *messenger* will trample the snow. Oy! They think some more and come up with a brilliant plan: The messenger should be carried on a table by four strong men, so his feet won't touch the snow.

In the kitchen they find Gimpel the errand boy, and have the four cooks carry him all over town, knocking on everyone's windows, telling them not to walk on the snow. They visit every single house to deliver the message. Then the sun rises, and what do they see?

A trampled mess.

That's when they realize their mistake. Even though Gimpel's feet didn't touch the snow, the boots of the four big cooks did. How could they not have seen that coming? So they come up with another plan—that next year when it snows, they won't make the same mistake. Instead, they'll get *eight* big men, who will lift up an even bigger table, to carry the four cooks as they hold the table with Gimpel.

That's the kind of snow I'm talking about. Funny snow. Magical snow. Khanuyakkah snow.

My footsteps didn't crush any snow, but they did make patterns on the lawns I crossed, which was fun. I bent down and tried to scrape up the frost, so I could get enough for a snowball, but it kept on melting. By the time I got to Mr. Culpepper's trailer, I was shivering and my hands were freezing. I took my seat but kept looking out the window for those first flakes as he told us about Tom Sawyer.

"So there was Tom, stuck whitewashing the fence, on a Saturday no less, madder than a mule chewing bumblebees." Mr. Culpepper's from Alabama and has all kinds of funny expressions. "And the other kids come by and say, 'It's too bad you have to whitewash the fence, on account of it being such a beautiful day and all.' But Tom is smart, and he just keeps painting and says, 'Only special people get to whitewash the fence.' First they think he's joking, but then they get pulled in, and next thing you know, they're begging him to let them paint the fence.

"You see, that's human nature, to want what you don't have. And Tom's friends are not too smart. Take Ben Rogers, for example. A nice enough guy, but not really the brightest bulb in the chandelier. You could also say he's 'not the sharpest tool in the shed.'"

The whole class looked up, because we knew Mr. Culpepper was starting to *digress*. That's a vocabulary word that means "to get way off track when you're talking about something," which I guess I'm guilty of too. For me, it's the best part of his class. He'll go on saying all kinds of funny things, before he finally says, "... but I digress."

"You could also say," he went on, "that Ben Rogers is 'a few bricks shy of a load.' Or, maybe 'the light's on but nobody's home.' Or, 'if his brains were dynamite, he couldn't even blow his nose.'"

Denise Scalapino raised her hand. She always raises her hand.

"You could also say 'the elevator doesn't go to the top floor,'" she offered.

Mr. Culpepper was quick. "That's right. Or 'the cheese slid off his cracker.'"

"How about 'a couple cards short of a deck!'" someone said. That got us going. "'A few sandwiches short of a picnic,'" said Billy Zamboni. "'He checked out of the Brainy Hotel a long time ago,'" said someone else. "'He could throw himself on the ground and miss!'" Ideas were flying fast and furious.

"How about 'dumb as a bag of hammers'?" asked Mr. Culpepper, who had clearly played this game before. "Or 'he fell out of the stupid tree and hit every branch on the way down.' Or, more poetically, 'somewhere a village is missing its idiot . . .'"

I was about to say "'A couple snowflakes short of a blizzard,'" when Arnold Pomeroy shouted, "I know! I've got one!" He paused, then said, "He's 'a couple meatballs short of spaghetti!'"

Arnold says stuff like that. Funny, but not on purpose. We all waited to see how Mr. Culpepper would respond, knowing that everything we'd been saying about Ben Rogers actually described Arnold.

"Spaghetti," said Mr. Culpepper, stroking his beard like a Chelmite. "Hmmmm. That may be the most . . ." Then he stopped, because the room had begun to shake.

In an instant I was under my desk.

Ever since the earthquake last February, whenever there's a rumble of any sort, I duck under my desk and cover my head. That's what you're supposed to do in an emergency, whether it's an earthquake or the Soviets dropping a nuclear bomb. The most important thing is not to let the top of your head touch underneath your desk, because you might get gum stuck in your hair. That's what happened the first time I did it, during a drill in second grade. This time, as I was hiding under my desk, I heard Mr. Culpepper say, "Well, look who's here! Good morning, Mrs. Gabbler!"

I turned toward the back of the room. Luckily, everyone else was looking there too, so I snuck out from under my desk without anyone noticing. Mrs. Gabbler is neither an earthquake nor a nuclear bomb, but she's still pretty scary. Because Mr. Culpepper's room is actually a trailer, it shakes when anyone comes in, and Mrs. Gabbler isn't just *anyone*. She's the vice principal, and almost as tall as Mr. Culpepper. It's her job to get us in trouble. She wears a metal whistle on a string around her neck, and walks all over school with a little ruler, marked at *exactly* three inches—that's the longest a boy's hair can be. It's also the farthest a girl's dress can be above her knee. Girls have to wear dresses—that's the rule. If a girl comes to school in pants, or a boy's hair is too long, she calls their parents to take them home. And no one at all is allowed to wear patches, like the hippies do, with peace signs and anti-war slogans. If you do that, you get suspended. It's called the Bixby dress code. Everyone hates it.

"Well, well, class, we have a visitor," said Mr. Culpepper. "To what do we owe the company of your pleasure, Mrs. Gabbler?"

She didn't know what to make of that, so she glared at him through the mean-librarian glasses she wears. Mr. Culpepper and Mrs. Gabbler do not like each other at all. Whenever she comes to class, you know there's going to be trouble.

"Good morning, students," she said.

"Good morning, Mrs. Gabbler," we all responded. When I say her name, I have to remember not to call her Mrs. Gobbler, which is what Mr. Culpepper calls her when she's not around. Then someone makes the sound of a turkey and we all bust out laughing. "You will no doubt all remember the earthquake last February."

Of course we all remembered—not just the day, but the exact minute: February 9 at 6:53 a.m. Back then I shared a room with Howard—before I moved to the den—and I figured he had gotten out of bed in the middle of a bad dream and was jumping up and down. That may sound strange to you, but it wouldn't be if you knew Howard. He gets really mad. He doesn't have a gorgle—yet—but if he did, I bet it would bust.

"It's okay, Howard," I said. "It's just a dream!"

But it wasn't. He was in his bed, as freaked out as I was. All the windows rattled and his bookshelf fell off his desk.

"It's an earthquake!" Howard announced. "Get under your bed!"

I did. It was full of dust bunnies, as well as a tennis shoe I had been looking for. Then, after what seemed like forever, the quaking suddenly stopped.

Walking to school that day with my friend Brian was like something from a dream. Everything was super-quiet, and then, suddenly, the ground would move and we would both say, "Did you feel that?"

"Yes, Mrs. Gabbler," said Mr. Culpepper. "How kind of you to remind us of the earthquake, in case we had forgotten. But why, pray tell, do you bring this up now, in the middle of my lecture on *Tom Sawyer?*"

She cleared her throat, which she does a lot. I think she has something stuck there. Then she went on. "Students, you may also recall that we had to cancel school because of the earthquake."

We remembered that too. When Brian and I got to school, there were firemen walking around, and Mr. Newton, the principal, told everyone to go back home. It's hard to know what to do with a day off when you haven't planned for one, so Howard, Kenny, and I sat around nervously watching reruns of *Gilligan's Island* and *I Dream of Jeannie* on TV, looking at one another every few minutes, saying, "Was that one?"

"You may also recall," Mrs. Gabbler continued, "that we took a second day off as well, which is why I am coming to you today. Bixby School has received word from the State of California that we were not supposed to take off that second day, and that we must schedule one more day of school this calendar year in order to receive funding for next year. Therefore, we will be holding school on

Monday, December 20—exactly one week from today."

It took a little while for this to settle in. And when it did, we did not like it. The first day of vacation! Everyone started to grumble.

"Now, children, I know you weren't planning for this, and your families will have to delay their travel plans. But you must treat this as a regular day of school. Attendance will be mandatory, and tardiness will not be tolerated. And, of course, the Bixby dress code will remain in full effect."

No one was happy to hear this, and she knew it.

"However," she went on, "you will be pleased to know that we have decided to make next Monday a special day of celebration, with a wonderful surprise. Therefore, instead of having the Christmas assembly . . ." Here she stopped, corrected herself, and stared right at me. "Rather, instead of having the *winter holiday* assembly we had planned for this Friday, we will be having it on Monday."

It's never good to have the vice principal stare at you. When it happens, you're supposed to sit there and do nothing, which is exactly what I tried to do. Except right then I had to sneeze, probably from trying to make snowballs out of the frost. And just at that moment, Ricky Romero, who was sitting behind me, whispered, "Gobble, gobble!" Suddenly I had to laugh *and* sneeze. I tried to do neither, but it didn't work. Instead, both came out at the same time—as a honk. Loud, like a goose.

Everyone laughed—except Mrs. Gabbler, who glared at me.

"Joel," she said. "Could you please come to the principal's office today after school?"

I could hear voices saying "ooooooohhh" and "busted!" It's bad enough to get called into the principal's office, but on top of that, I was thinking about Cantor Grubnitz. If I didn't get home on time, I would miss the carpool, and if you think Cantor Grubnitz is mean on a normal day, just try being late.

"Um . . . I'm . . . um . . . busy. I can't come today."

"You can't come today? Why not?" she asked.

"Because I have to . . ." And then I mumbled, "For my . . . um . . . bar mitzvah."

"Your what?"

It's not like I wanted the whole class to know about my going off to secret Hebrew lessons after school. But I couldn't lie—I was already in trouble—so I said it again. "I have bar mitzvah practice."

There was a long pause as she digested this. "All right, then," she said. "Be there first thing tomorrow morning. Before school."

After school, Brian was waiting for me at the crosswalk.

"I heard you got busted for honking at Mrs. Gabbler! That's wicked! Why did you do it?"

Since the start of seventh grade, Brian and I don't see each other much in school, as I'm in the advanced classes, but we still walk home together when we can.

It's kind of a strange friendship. We met in third grade, not long after his family moved here from Montana. I had been avoiding him because he was so big; even then, he looked dangerous. One day as I was crossing the street to go home I saw him standing on the other side, staring at me. The closer I got, the bigger he looked.

"Hey you!" he said. "I have a question." I thought there might be trouble and got ready to run.

"What?" I said.

"Do you like swamp water?"

"What?" I asked.

"Swamp water," he said again. "My new neighbor, Mr. Glasser, works right here, at Jack in the Box." He pointed behind him. "He said if there was no one around, he would give me swamp water."

"What's swamp water?"

"It's a combination of everything from their soda machine plus a secret ingredient—I think it might be pickle juice. It's great!"

Whatever it was, that sounded a lot better than getting beat up, and ever since, that's been our after-school routine: swamp water, and sometimes French fries, as we walk home.

"So, you think you'll get kicked out of school?" he asked, squeezing another packet of katshup as we walked. He'd gotten to Jack in the Box before me and already had fries. We walked quickly so I wouldn't miss my carpool.

"It wasn't on purpose. I couldn't have done it on purpose if I'd tried. It was just a sneeze. But it came out as a honk."

"I heard it was like a Mack truck! The whole classroom shook! Far out!"

"The classroom always shakes—it's a trailer."

"You think you'll get thrown out of school?" he asked again. "That'd be uptight and out of sight!"

"No, it would be a total bummer."

I didn't think I'd get thrown out. As far as I knew, honking at the vice principal wasn't a capital offense. But maybe that was one of those things they explained on some day I'd missed school because of a Jewish holiday. "Whatever you do, don't honk at Mrs. Gabbler. She'll have you executed."

Once I got home, I didn't have time to think about it. I grabbed my little yellow book just in time to get the carpool. Nothing interesting happened in the carpool, so I won't tell you about it. It's with the third and fourth graders, who have Hebrew school on Monday. Sometimes we laugh and joke, but today I spent the time reviewing the three verses of my Haftorah portion that I was supposed to be able to sing by that week, like Tom Sawyer was supposed to memorize lines of scripture. But while Tom managed to fake his way out of doing it, there was no way I was going to escape. I actually *had* been studying, but I was *so* nervous about asking Cantor Grubnitz to pray for my father that I couldn't remember the words.

When I got there—a minute before 4:00—he was standing outside his office, waiting for me.

"You were almost late," he said. "Go inside and sit down. And don't touch anything. I'll be right back."

Cantor Grubnitz must have needed a cigarette. He doesn't smoke in front of us, though the smell of it on his clothes is so thick that he might as well. I think he smokes in his office when he's alone, because over the years, smoke has covered the glass on the pictures of the famous cantors and rabbis, making their eyes yellow like they have some kind of disease. They say that kissing someone who smokes is like licking an ashtray. I've never kissed anyone—and don't see it happening any time soon—but I guess if I wanted to know what it felt like, I could lick an ashtray. Sounds disgusting.

Much as I hate smoking, my dad hates it even more. Sometimes we'll be in the nonsmoking section of Thrifty's Coffee

Shop and there will be people in the smoking section, way on the other side of the restaurant, puffing away. The smoke doesn't know where the smoking section ends, though, and floats over to us. Then my dad will ask me, really loudly, "Is someone smoking in here?" He can't turn his body well to see, so he says louder, sniffing, "Joel, I can't see. What's that smell? It sure smells like someone's smoking!"

It's kind of embarrassing to me—but much more so to the smokers. One by one, they all end up putting out their cigarettes.

"So?" said Cantor Grubnitz when he came back. "Why are you just sitting there? You should be studying."

"I *have* studied. A lot," I said. That was true.

"We'll see. Start from the beginning."

"Okay. But first, can I ask a question?"

"What is it?"

"Well, I was thinking about praying."

"Praying? *You* were thinking about praying?"

"Yes. And wondering, well, if you could . . . um, pray for something."

"Pray for something?" Cantor Grubnitz was getting impatient, which was just a notch away from mad. "And what is it you think is so important that I should bother God?"

His gorgle was starting to throb and I still wasn't sure how to ask.

"Well, it's . . . um . . ." I realized it was kind of hard to explain. "Well, you see, there's . . . my father is having this . . . uh . . . he's going to be getting some gold . . ."

"Gold? You want me to pray for *gold*? No. You don't pray for gold or money or diamonds. Those are wasted prayers. It's selfish, taking up God's time from all the important work he should be doing. No. You pray for God to accept you for the wretched being you are. Not for gold. Do you understand?"

"Well, um . . . it's not really . . . you see . . ."

"This is just your way of stalling, isn't it?" he said. "Because you haven't studied, have you?"

"No, really, I have."

"Let's hear."

I opened my booklet and began to chant. It was the best I'd ever done, but two lines into it, he stopped me.

"I'll tell you what your problem is," he said. "You're tone deaf."

This evening, my dad was in a bad mood. No matter how excited he says he is about the operation, I think he's worried, and it came out during dinner.

My dad slurps when he eats. Loudly. Tonight we had turkey soup and his slurping was even louder than usual. It drives my brothers and me crazy—I don't think my mom hears it—but we all react differently. Tonight was classic.

Kenny, who has really good hearing, was clearly getting irritated, and finally said, "Dad, could you please try not to slurp so loudly?"

"What?" said my dad. "You want me to slurp quieter?"

"Actually, I don't want you to slurp at all," said Kenny.

There was silence for a minute—except for the slurping, which was no better—so Kenny said, "Can't you at least try?"

"You shouldn't tell Dad how to eat," said Howard. "It's disrespectful."

That's what set my dad off. Because even though he doesn't like Kenny telling him how to eat, there's something about the way Howard talks—like he's the boss of everyone—that drives my dad crazy.

"Don't tell Kenny how to talk to me!" said my dad, slurping more soup. "It's none of your business." Then to Kenny he said, "And I can slurp if I want to. It's how I show I enjoy my food." He slurped another spoonful.

"I'm trying to help you," said Howard.

"Stop slurping!" shouted Kenny.

"I don't need your help!" shouted my dad.

I've seen variations of this same fight every night for years, and I hate it, even more than I hate the slurping. Once it starts, my mom can't do anything to stop it. She just sits there trying to smile, looking more deflated by the second. So the next thing I know, I find myself saying something funny, telling a joke or a story.

"Hey!" I said. "Knock, knock!"

They all stopped. So did the slurping.

"Who's there?" said Kenny.

"Doris," I said.

"Doris who?" asked Kenny.

"Dor-is locked, that's why I'm knocking!" It wasn't a great joke, but they laughed. "Hey," I said, "let's light the candles! And after," I added, turning to my dad, "how about playing One, Two—Bango?"

This is a tradition for my dad and me. It started one day when I was eight years old and he told me to set up the card table because he had something special to show me. The table has a red vinyl top, wooden legs, and matching chairs, and was a wedding gift. Evidently that's what everyone got as wedding gifts in the 1950s, along with waffle irons and toasters. My parents got a toaster too, but it's broken, so about half the time it forgets to pop up. It's really more of a toast incinerator. You have to stay there and watch it, because if you get distracted, ten minutes later you start smelling smoke, then run over and find that your toast is, well, toast.

The card table is broken too, but we still use it. One

leg doesn't stay locked into place, so whoever is by that corner needs to make sure not to bump it, or the whole thing will fall over. I always sit there so my dad doesn't kick it by mistake, when he swings his legs around to get up or sit down.

After I set up the table that first time, my dad brought out one of those big, round empty cardboard ice cream containers you can get for free from Baskin-Robbins. Inside was a checkered plastic cloth with big black and white squares, and all these giant, hollow plastic black and white chess pieces. I had seen chess pieces before, but these were really neat, because the castles looked like real castles, and the knights like horses, and the bishops looked like the cantor and rabbi, with their pointy hats. There were pawns too, who looked like real soldiers, afraid of being captured.

My dad showed me how each piece moves.

"Always keep an eye out for the knight," he said. "It's the most interesting piece, because if you're not paying attention, it sneaks up on you. Watch this!" He moved a knight two steps forward and one to the right, saying, "One, two—bango!" Hence our nickname for the game. Then he showed me something he learned to do when he was young called "the knight's tour," where the knight moves sixty-four times around the board, landing on every single square exactly once. I could see why my dad liked the knight.

I had played checkers before, which was okay, but chess was something else entirely. Every chance we got, I would spread out the plastic and set up the pieces. At the start of each game, my dad grabbed one black and one white pawn, hid them behind his back, and said, "Right or left?" I would choose one and that would be my color.

When you play chess, there are a bazillion possible moves, and every one you make leads to even more possibilities. Even the biggest computer can't think of all of them. They actually tried it with this giant computer, and smoke started coming out of it, like our toaster.

My dad is good. That's because he sees things other people miss. While I'm trying to think through all the possibilities for this, that, and the other, he'll just kind of squint and tilt his head, then make a back-and-forth sound through his teeth, not quite whistling, just pondering. Then he comes up with some brilliant move, which is part of some complicated plan, and the next thing I know, I'm about to lose my queen. Sometimes he'll give me a warning or let me take back a move—but he always wins in the end. Hard as I've tried, I've never won a game.

"All right," said my dad, who had slurped enough for the evening. "Joel's right—let's light the candles." It was like changing a channel on TV. They stopped fighting, and I set up the candles—a white one as shammes, with a bent off-white one and an ugly olive-green one behind it. We lit the candles and sang the blessings and as much of "Maoz Tzur" as we could remember. When we finished, Howard announced, "I have to study," and went to his room.

"I'm going to work on my new model airplane," said Kenny, looking hopefully at my dad. "Maybe after the game you can help me work on it?" He's always asking my dad to help him, but Dad never does. I guess it's really hard for him to pick up all those little parts.

I set up the table and the pieces and I got white, which meant I got to move first. Things were going really well. There's a whole point system in chess, and I was three points ahead. More than that, I had a surefire plan to capture one of his castles. A castle is a valuable piece—five points—and it would have left him in real trouble.

Just as I was about to make my move, the phone rang. My mom answered it, and I could hear her trying to figure out who was calling. Then she came rushing into the den for my dad, looking excited.

"I think it's Mr. Forentos," she said.

"Forentos!" said my dad. He got up fast—well, fast for my dad. This was big, because Forentos knows everybody with money in Los Angeles, and had been lining up the investors for Omni-Glow. Whenever he called, it was with news about this one or that one, and how much money they were going to invest. No one had put up any money yet, but we were getting close. My dad hobbled to the kitchen as fast as he could, and I heard him pick up the phone and say, "Hello dere!"

While he was in the kitchen I noticed something on the chess board that was amazing. I could take the castle, like I said. But if I forgot about the castle—even though it's worth five points—I could make another move, with my knight, who had been sitting around doing nothing. That move would put my dad into check, and when you're in check, you have to do something—you don't have a choice. Then there would be only one possible square where my dad could move his king and be safe. But once he made that move, there was another move I could make, with my queen, that would put him into check *again*. Once I did that, the only *possible* move he could make was to block me with his bishop. But I could take his bishop with my queen, and he would be in check *yet again*, from my rook, who had been hiding behind her. Then the only thing he could do was to take my bishop with his king. That's when I would swoop in with my queen for the final blow. He would be trapped—checkmate!

I couldn't believe it. I went over each step in my mind again. It was perfect. There was nothing he could do—and no way I could lose.

As I went over my plan a fifth time, I could hear him talking to Forentos.

"Well, sure, but that's what he said last time . . . I see . . . And now . . . But what about what's-his-name, Jenkins? You said he was . . . Oh. I see. All of it? But what . . ." Then there was a long pause, while my dad didn't say anything. I could tell it was bad. Finally he said, "So that's it? It's over? But what about . . ."

There was an even longer pause, and then my dad hung up the phone.

"What did Forentos have to say?" asked my mom, a moment later. She was excited, and clearly hadn't heard a word.

"Well, I don't think we should count on Forentos," he said. "Everything takes time—and there are plenty of fish in the sea."

"Oh," said my mom. "I see." I could hear the disappointment in her voice, followed by my father's footsteps walking slowly back to the den, then a very long sigh.

That was it. I had no choice. My dad may pick on Howard. And he may slurp loudly. But he is *not* a loser.

I took one last look at the board. Then, with my right foot, I kicked the bad leg of the table. For a few seconds it hovered there, on three legs. Then, almost in slow motion, it tilted, and fell. The board and pieces tumbled to the floor.

"What happened?" said Kenny, looking up just as my dad walked in.

"I—I must have bumped the leg of the table."

My dad looked at the pieces all over the floor.

"Too bad," he said, shaking his head. "It was a good game."

Beyond him, in the living room, I could see the menorah. The candle next to the shammes had melted into it and both had burned down into a puddle of wax. Only the ugly green one remained.

THE THIRD CANDLE:
The Difference Between
My Grandmother and Houdini

Tuesday, December 14

This Kchanauakh was supposed to be about miracles. No miracles so far—just chopped liver. Make that Chopped Liver Royale.

It's strange how you can worry about something you *think* is going to happen, but then, what *actually* happens turns out to be much worse. This morning I woke up believing I was in trouble for snort-honking at Mrs. Gabbler. Now I'm wishing that's *all* it was. That I'd gone into Mr. Newton's office and he had given me a lecture: "I am afraid, Joel, that honking at Mrs. Gabbler is a very serious offense—and it calls for serious punishment."

Then he would have pointed to the paddle, hanging by a leather strap from a nail in his office. "We're not allowed to use this anymore—except in extreme cases. Like this one."

He would have taken it down and—whack! It would have hurt, but it would have been over.

Now, instead, I get to spend the week dreading something far worse.

Thanks a lot, God.

Walking to school this morning, I wanted nothing more than to be invisible. And sometimes I can *pretend* I'm invisible. But not today, on account of the frost. Or, rather, the *lack* of frost.

One of the great things about frost that I didn't mention yesterday is how it gets everywhere, even on the windows of cars. Today, although it was really cold—and still between 29 and 30 on the barometer—there wasn't any frost, so I couldn't avoid seeing my reflection in the car windows I passed. And I did not like what I saw.

At this point, I'd better tell you what I look like, especially if we're going to spend all of Chanyukah together. Mr. Culpepper says that along with "setting the scene," it's the writer's duty to "vividly describe the main character early on." That's me, and I should have done it sooner, but I wasn't sure you'd stay. It's not that people start to cry when they see me, like that kid did in Thrifty's when he saw my dad. But I am seriously funny-looking. To define something by its antonym—like *miracle* and *chopped liver*—I can tell you about Chris Carter, who came to our class at the start of this year. Tall, straight brown hair, big smile, perfect mouth and nose—an All-American boy. That very first day you could see girls whispering, and though you couldn't hear, you knew they were saying, "He's cute!"

If you can picture Chris Carter, then imagine the opposite. That's me. I am not "cute," and never will be.

First, I'm short. That, in itself, isn't so bad. But I also have braces, and everything about braces is crummy. When you smile, the first thing people see is a mouth full of metal. Sometimes bits of food get stuck in them, unless you're really careful and brush after every single thing you eat. That's what Howard does. And he tells us about it. We'll be driving in the car somewhere, or even talking to other people, and he'll suddenly announce that it's time for him to brush his teeth.

Dr. Snitkopff wants me to do that too. He's my orthodontist, and he's evil. But we go to him because he lets us pay on credit. That's because he doesn't care about the money—he's in it for the pain. In addition to all the metal he glues in my mouth, with sharp edges and wires sticking out, he gives me little rubber bands I'm supposed to put on every single day, just so. If I forget to do it, even once between visits, he knows. The moment I sit in the chair he opens my mouth, and says, "So, have you been wearing your rubber bands?"

Have you ever noticed that dentists always wait until your mouth is wide open to ask you questions? That's what Dr. Snitkopff does.

I try to nod and say, "Uh-huh."

"We'll see," he says, and out come the needle-nosed pliers, twisting and tightening until I confess (which is also hard when you can't talk). I manage to utter, "Weh, ho uh ha hi," which is supposed to mean "Well, most of the time." He doesn't care. The pliers twist.

So I'm short, with braces, and I also wear these really ugly glasses. Both Kenny and Howard had to get glasses when they got to fifth grade, so I could see the writing on the wall. Actually, I *couldn't* see the writing on the wall, and that's why I had to get glasses. I held out as long as I could, pretending I could see the board, but finally, last summer, the doctor did an eye test, said my vision was terrible, and gave me a prescription.

I wanted contact lenses. Those are round pieces of glass that are shaped exactly like your eyeball, so you put them in and they just stay. I know it sounds impossible, but they make you see perfectly. No one even knows you're wearing them—unless you lose one.

That's what happened to Larry Arbuckle. We were all in the schoolyard playing football, when suddenly he called out "Stop! Nobody move!" Everyone froze, and he explained that his left contact lens had popped out. We all got down on our hands and knees to look for it, very slowly so that no one would accidentally crush it. Contact lenses are really, really expensive—one hundred dollars each! That's two hundred dollars if you have two eyes, which is a lot of money to pay to look like you don't wear glasses. We crawled around for a long time, not finding it, until I heard Eddy Mazurki say, "Uh-oh." He said it in a bad way—not that there's a good way to say "Uh-oh." And we all knew what happened to *that* hundred-dollar contact lens.

I knew my parents wouldn't go for contact lenses, so I had a Plan B. Wire frames. Silver. That's what hippies wear, like John Lennon, who's a Beatle. It's possible to wear wire-framed glasses and look cool, so when I was at Kaiser with my dad, looking at all the frames, I pointed to a pair on the top shelf that would have been totally boss. They were mostly flat on the top and rounded on the bottom, called aviator, like a pilot might wear. They were groovy enough to look like you were wearing them just because you wanted to. But the tag said eighty-nine dollars. My dad shook his head.

"No, wire won't be sturdy enough."

Then he looked over the rack and picked out a pair on the very bottom. Not solid black, not horn-rimmed, not even tortoiseshell. They were brown at the top and gray at the bottom with a wire running through them, ugly as could be.

"Try these," he said. I did. They looked like something *he* would wear. In fact, they were. Exactly the same as his. And Kenny's. And Howard's. I was cursed.

He nodded. "They look good. You look distinguished."

Let me tell you something. There is not a seventh grader in the world who wants to look "distinguished." I was already "distinguished" enough being short, and Jewish, with braces. But these were only $19.95, so that's what I got.

That's who you're dealing with. Short, with braces and ugly glasses—totally "distinguished." *But wait—there's more!* as they say on those TV commercials. Let me tell you about my hair, or rather, my ears.

Every boy in my class wants to have long hair, as close to three inches as possible. At the very least you want it over your ears, because ears are funny-looking. Have you noticed that? Even the most beautiful person in the whole world has funny-looking ears. Sure, women can put on earrings, but all that does is announce to the world, "Look, I have something pretty hanging from my funny-looking ears!"

I don't like to think about my ears, and can usually avoid it. But as I walked down Kimdale Drive to whatever awaited me in Mr. Newton's office, I saw my ugly ears reflected in every car window. It's not that my ears are uglier than everyone else's, but they do stick out, especially now. That's because of this one barber at Dave's Barbershop. We go there for haircuts because it's only $2.25. There are three barber chairs and you get whichever opens next. One time when I was in second grade, I got Ralph, who asked me what kind of haircut I wanted. I was about to say the same thing as always: "A regular boy's haircut." It's not too short, and it grows out pretty quick.

But I had been thinking that I wanted longer hair. In fact, I didn't want a haircut at all. My mom had just taken me because Kenny and Howard were going at the same time. So I told him I'd like it "a little longer than a regular boy's haircut."

That was the wrong thing to say. Ralph tilted his head and said, "What, you want it longer in front?"

"Yeah, longer in front."

"Then you want it shorter in back."

"I guess so."

"Then you want a crew cut."

"What's that?"

"Well, it's longer in front and shorter on the sides. Like in the Navy."

My dad had been in the Navy, making radios during The War. I'd seen a picture of him, wearing a sailor's cap, but his hair was really short. So I said, "Just give me a regular boy's haircut. As long as possible."

"I'll tell you what," Ralph said. "Why don't you try a crew

cut?" Then he added, "And if you don't like it, we can bring out the hair stretcher we keep in the back room."

Hair stretcher? That sounded really cool, like one of my dad's inventions. I told him to go ahead.

I was such an idiot. A crew cut, it turns out, is really, really, *really* short. It's almost like a butch, which only leaves about a quarter of an inch all over your head, but in the front it's about a half-inch, and sticks straight up. He used an electric razor; it took him two minutes. As soon as he finished and showed me in the mirror, I shook my head and asked him to bring out the hair stretcher.

"What?"

"You know. From the back room."

There was a pause, then he started laughing. "Hey, Bill," he said to the other barber, "you seen the hair stretcher?" Soon everyone in the shop was laughing, and I went around for the next month looking like a complete dork.

But that wasn't the end of it. Since then, whenever we go to that barber shop, Ralph makes jokes like, "Let's get that hair stretcher ready!" I try to avoid him, but when I end up in his chair, he always cuts my hair as short as he can get away with. That's what happened last week. Not a crew cut, but close. I look ridiculous.

And that's how I felt when I walked into Mr. Newton's office. It was really early, forty-five minutes before the start of school. Mrs. McGillicuddy, the secretary, was typing something. "I'm here to see Mr. Newton?" I said.

"What did you do?" she asked, without looking up.

"I . . . um . . . I'm not sure."

"Well, he's not here yet," she said. "You'll have to wait."

Sitting in the principal's office, waiting, is not something I'm used to doing. I'd never been called into the principal's office, except for one time, in fourth grade, when I was in Miss Baker's class. It was December of 1968 and she was teaching us how to write letters. Richard Nixon had just been elected president.

"He is now the president-elect," she explained, "and our class is going to write letters to congratulate him on his victory and say how glad we are that he will be running the country."

Except I wasn't glad at all. He only won because Robert Kennedy had been assassinated and Gene McCarthy was too good a guy to be president. But I didn't want to fool with Miss Baker—who'd been a sergeant in the Women's Army Corps—so I wrote the letter as instructed. But I also wrote a second one, saying what I really thought—that if I was old enough to vote, and if America had been attacked by Soviet nuclear bombs so that he was the only one left in the entire country, I still wouldn't have voted for him.

At the end of the day, just as Miss Baker was standing

by the door, I snuck up to her desk, where there was a big envelope with all our letters, and switched mine. I would have gotten away with it too, because she read and graded them all before she put them in the envelope. But then in February, we got a reply from the White House. Miss Baker opened it up, all excited, and read it to the class. President Nixon promised to serve the country well, with the support of the American people. He thanked the children of Bixby School for their good wishes, then added, ". . . even Joel, who would not have voted for me."

That was the only other time I had been called into the principal's office, and questioned by Mr. Newton, who seemed more confused than angry. In the end, Mrs. McGillicuddy used Wite-Out to cover up the part about me. It looked funny, though, because Nixon's stationery is beige, and Wite-Out is white. They framed it anyway and hung it on the wall behind Mrs. McGillicuddy's desk. Now, as I looked at it, I began to wonder if I had been called in because the Secret Service had finally tracked me down. Part of me knew that was a crazy thought, but you never can tell with Nixon. And it doesn't take much to feel guilty when you're sitting in the principal's office, especially when you're Jewish.

It's like this joke my dad told me about two Jewish guys walking down the street in Nazi Germany. They see a Gestapo soldier following them, and one turns to the other and says, "What do I do? I don't have any papers!" The other thinks a moment, then says, "I have papers. I'll run away and he'll follow me. You walk home like everything's fine."

So the one guy takes off running and, sure enough, the soldier chases him. He runs and runs, until finally the soldier catches him. They stand there, huffing and puffing, until the soldier can speak.

"Give me your papers!"

The man takes out his papers and hands them to the officer, who examines them, surprised.

"But they're all in order!" he says.

"Yes, they are."

"Why were you running?"

"My doctor told me to run five miles every day."

"I see," says the Gestapo officer, still trying to catch his breath. "But why didn't you stop when you saw me running?"

"I thought maybe you had the same doctor!"

I sat there, the clock ticking away, with just fifteen minutes until the first bell. If Mr. Newton didn't come soon, I would be late for Mr. Culpepper's class, which would call more attention to me—the last thing I wanted.

I started to squirm and thought about Houdini, the greatest escape artist *ever*. He could escape from anything: straitjackets, prison cells, every kind of handcuff ever made, even locked safes! He had this one trick, his grand finale, called the Water Torture Cell. He would have members of the audience lock him up in all kinds of chains and handcuffs and ankle cuffs. Then they would turn a crank that pulled the heavy chain around his feet until he was suspended by his ankles over this big glass box, filled to the top with water. They would lower him into it, headfirst, water splashing everywhere. You could see him there, upside down, with bubbles coming out of his mouth, so you knew the clock was ticking. In fact, there was a giant clock onstage, counting the seconds. There were also firemen at the back of the theater, dressed in yellow raincoats, with big axes, so that if anything went wrong, they could rush up to the stage and shatter the glass to save him.

Once the top was locked, they would close a curtain around it. All you could do was watch the clock and wait. And wait. And wait.

After a minute or so the audience would start getting restless—many had naturally started to hold their breath as soon as Houdini went into the water, and one by one, they gave up. After about three minutes, they would begin talking to each other. You could feel the worry in the air. Four minutes. Five minutes. Six. Seven.

Their talk would grow into grumbles, even shouts.

"Something's wrong!"

"He's not getting out!"

"Do something!"

But the clock kept ticking. Eight minutes. Nine. Ten.

Everyone would be standing up, shouting for someone, anyone, to do something. Twelve minutes. Fifteen. Seventeen. Finally, when the whole crowd was going crazy, the firemen at the back of the auditorium would rush up with their axes to break the glass. They would pull back the curtain around the Water Torture Cell—and it would be empty!

The audience would gasp. Even the fire captain would take off his helmet to scratch his head in wonder. Then he would turn to face them.

It was Houdini!

The crowd went wild.

Here's what no one knew: Houdini had actually escaped really quickly. It took him less than two minutes to get out of the Water Torture Cell. That, in itself, is amazing.

A lesser showman would simply have escaped and immediately said, "Ta-da!"

But not Houdini. He waited until the time was right. And you know what he did during that time? He read.

That's right. He sat backstage, reading a book. Maybe he was studying science or math. Or maybe he was learning yet *another* language, after Hungarian and English.

Almost every picture you see of Houdini has him wrapped in chains. But when I picture him, he's sitting backstage, listening to the crowd freak out as he turns the pages of his book before putting on his raincoat and helmet, then heading down the secret passage to the front of the theater.

But that's not even what I like best about Houdini. The coolest thing, I think, is his real name. Houdini was a stage name he took after Robert-Houdin, a French magician in the 1800s. Houdin was good, but he was no Houdini.

You know what Houdini's *real* name was?

Erik Weisz. That's right. And that explains why he would sit there and study. Houdini was Jewish. Not weakling Jewish, like me, but super-duper strong Jewish.

Here's the weird thing: Erik Weisz was actually the name of this kid at our temple who became a bar mitzvah when I was a little kid. (He didn't *get* bar mitzvahed, because even Houdini couldn't do that.) The bar mitzvah of this Eric Weiss—spelled differently but pronounced the same—was something of a legend. He was right in the very middle of chanting his Haftorah portion when his voice cracked. It didn't just crack—it actually split in two. One moment he had a super-high voice, the next, a baritone.

Of course, you're not supposed to laugh when you're sitting there in the synagogue, especially during someone's bar mitzvah. We all knew that. But it turns out there's nothing quite so funny as a whole sanctuary full of people trying not to laugh.

Actually, there is one thing funnier. That was Rabbi Buxelbaum, who was also trying not to laugh as he watched all of *us* trying not to laugh. To Rabbi Buxelbaum's credit, he managed not to laugh during the service, though there were tears running down his face.

Of course, everyone felt bad a month later when Rabbi Buxelbaum died of an embolism—that's when part of your brain pops. Nobody mentioned Eric's Haftorah, but you've got to wonder what happens to laughter that gets stuck in your brain. Maybe Eric had something to feel guilty about. But me, what had I done but laugh and sneeze?

"Joel?"

I looked up to see Mr. Newton standing at his door, waiting.

"Mrs. Gobbler told me to come see you," I said.

"You mean Mrs. Gabbler?"

"Gabbler. Yes. Mrs. Gabbler." That was dumb.

"Right. Come in." He motioned for me to sit in a brown metal chair across from his desk. When I did, it wobbled. "So?" Mr. Newton said. "Have you given it some thought?"

I nodded. It seemed the only thing I could do was apologize.

"I've given it a lot of thought. And . . . all I can say is . . . I'm really sorry."

"I see," he said. He looked disappointed. "May I ask why?"

"Well, I guess . . . doing that is, um, wrong."

"Wrong?" He still didn't seem satisfied and I had no idea what else to say. He took a deep breath. "I'll certainly respect your decision," he finally said, "but I have to tell you it would really mean a lot to us. To the whole school. I think it would make other students feel better. You know, about being here on Monday."

What? When? I was confused, and starting to sweat.

"The way we'd imagined, it would be to start with some songs, Christmas carols." He corrected himself. "Rather, *holiday* carols. And then you'd come up. Along with your family. Monday *is* the last day of the holiday, right?"

I stared at him, baffled.

"Are you talking about the assembly?" I asked.

"That's right."

"You want me to be onstage at the assembly? Why?"

"To light the candles. And tell the story of Chaanukah," Mr. Newton said.

"Lighting candles? With my family?"

"Yes. I'm sorry, I thought Mrs. Gabbler had talked to you about it. You see, last week at the faculty meeting, we were discussing the winter holiday assembly, which had to be moved to Monday, and what would make it special. Several of your teachers mentioned how when you were younger you used to tell the story of the holiday each year in class. So we'd

97

like to ask you to do it this year, at Monday's assembly, for the whole school. And we're inviting your family as well, to light the candles in the, uh, menorah, I think you call it? That way the whole school can see how the Jewish people celebrate." There was a long pause while I took that in. "So, what do you think?"

What did I think? I thought of Houdini in the Water Torture Cell, stuck, out of breath, unable to escape, the minutes ticking away . . . But I just sort of nodded.

"Great!" he said. "Oh, and by the way, don't tell any of the other kids." He winked. "We want it to be a surprise."

The first bell rang.

"You'd better get to class," he said.

Tell anyone about it? Was he out of his mind?! Like I would walk up to someone and say, "Hey, guess what? I may *look* like a dork, and you may suspect I actually *am* a dork, but on Monday I'm going to stand up in front of the whole school with my dorky family and prove it!"

No, this secret would die with me, hopefully before Monday. I made it to class on time and, luckily, no one asked what had happened in the principal's office. In fact, all day long no one said anything, which was great, until last period— Home Economics. It's supposed to be a class just for girls, but this year, as part of Women's Liberation, they decided to let girls take Wood Shop and boys take Home Ec. The good part is we get to eat. So far we've learned to make pancakes and cookies, and today, Mrs. Hernandez was teaching us to make deviled eggs.

"Once you've hardboiled the egg," she said, "the trick to peeling the shell is to roll it gently on the table."

I was doing pretty well until a voice behind me said, "Hey, Joel—what happened in the principal's office?"

It was Amy O'Shea.

"Nothing, really," I lied.

"Did Mrs. Gabbler say anything about what's happening on Monday?"

"What? Why?" I smashed my egg. How did Amy know? "Um . . . no," I said. That, at least, was true. *She* hadn't said anything. But *he* sure had.

Evidently I hadn't cooked the egg long enough either, because there was gooey yolk all over my hand.

I'd better tell you about Amy O'Shea. You wouldn't think someone who looks like me would have a girlfriend. And you'd be right. Magicians don't have girlfriends—we have assistants. Mine is Amy O'Shea.

I've known her since first grade, though we never talked much, because, well, she was a girl and I was a boy. Also, she always sat in the back of the classroom. Some kids sit there because they don't want the teacher to call on them.

That's not the case with Amy; she knew the answer to every question. She was back there so she could practice drawing horses. Even in first grade she was really good at it. She knew all their muscles and had these special techniques of perspective that made her pictures look three-dimensional. Since then, she's gotten better and better. Her horses look like they're going to come to life and run off the page.

Then, at the start of sixth grade, two things happened to Amy. One is that she suddenly got beautiful. Like too-beautiful-to-even-imagine-talking-to beautiful. I mean, she had never been homely, like me. She always looked like, well, Amy. But when we came back from summer vacation, all the boys said, "Wow! Have you seen Amy?"

The other thing that happened was she became a radical. She ran for student council, and made speeches about all the things she wanted to change at Bixby, like abolishing the dress code and having better food in the cafeteria. She won the election, no problem. She's the most popular girl at Bixby—and every boy has a crush on her.

You're probably wondering how someone as pretty and popular as Amy O'Shea would end up spending time with a dork like me.

Here's what happened: One day last spring I went in after school to see Mr. Winters, my sixth-grade English teacher. Amy was there too, cleaning the chalkboard.

I was there to show him a card trick I'd just made up. It started like every other card trick.

"Okay, Mr. Winters, pick a card." He did. "Now, don't show it to me. Just put it back in the deck, and shuffle it."

This was all pretty much standard. Then the routine kicked in.

"Now, the problem with being a magician," I said, "is that no one trusts you. Like, you just picked a card from this deck, but you probably think it's already hidden somewhere, or up my sleeve. Am I right?"

"I wouldn't be surprised," he said.

"So I'd like you to check. Just look through the cards—don't show me—and make sure your card is there."

He looked, then looked again. "Hold on," he said, then frowned. "It's not here. Where did it go?"

"What will you give me if I tell you?"

"What do you want?"

"To change my grade on the spelling test. From a C+ to an A."

I'm pretty smart, but spelling is one thing I cannot do. I can learn all the rules, like "*i* before *e* except after *c*, or when sounding like *a* as in *neighbor* or *weigh*." The problem is that sometimes the rules don't work, with words like *weird*, which is a weird word. In those cases, you're just supposed to memorize the way it goes, but my mind always mixes up the letters.

"Joel, I can't change your grade," Mr. Winters said.

"All right, then. Trick's over." I gathered up the cards and turned to go.

"Wait a minute," he finally said, leaning in close. "All right. Where's my card?"

"Hmmmmmm," I said. "You don't trust me, so how do I know I can trust *you,* and that you'll actually change my grade? Change it first—then I'll tell you."

He sighed, then opened the grade book. There was his card—the seven of spades. He smiled and gave me an A+.

As I walked out of the classroom, quite pleased with myself, Amy followed.

"You put the card in the grade book before you did the trick," she said. "It was while he was stacking up the textbooks, wasn't it?"

I didn't say anything. "Then you made him choose it," she went on. "Only it was another seven of spades. You had it on the bottom of the deck. Then, when he put it back, you hid it in your hand—and while he looked through the cards, you slipped it into the back pocket of your pants." She pointed. "Which is where it is now. Right?"

Normally I hate getting caught in a trick. But she was amazing. I took the card from my back pocket.

"But don't worry. He has no idea how you did it. He also didn't notice that the card he picked had a blue back—and the back of the one in his grade book was red."

Right again. I had borrowed a seven of spades from another deck. Next thing I knew I ended up walking with her all the way from Bixby School to the stable where Daisy, her horse, lives. That's right, she actually has a horse, who she cares for every day after school. Don't get the idea she's rich, any more than I am. She just loves horses so much that she worked every weekend—mowing lawns, babysitting, and cleaning out garages—to buy one. Horses are expensive to keep—and they eat *a lot*. That's why Amy was cleaning the chalkboard. The janitor's supposed to do it, but he never does, so Mr. Winters pays her to do it each day with a lunch bag filled with Quaker Oats, which she gives to Daisy. She loves that horse—and all animals.

"We shouldn't eat animals," she said. "They have feelings. That's why I'm a vegetarian. In fact, I'm circulating a petition to get the cafeteria to offer a vegetarian choice for lunch. Better than that gross stuff they call 'Farmstyle Stew,' whatever it is. Will you sign it?"

I nodded. She was right: The stew was disgusting. Nodding was all I *could* do, because I couldn't speak, too astounded that I was actually *walking* with Amy O'Shea.

She had lots of big opinions. She hated the fact that girls weren't allowed to wear pants at school: "Don't you think it's unfair? Boys get to wear pants, and there are all kinds of things you just can't do wearing a dress, like run and climb. All because of Mrs. Gabbler, who thinks we should be 'lady-like.' Who wants to be 'ladylike'? Not me. I want to be free! And patches. Why can't we wear patches on our clothes? What are we supposed to do when they wear out, throw them away?"

But her biggest feelings were about the war in Vietnam. "America shouldn't even be there," she said. "Nixon should end the war and bring the soldiers back. Then Tommy could come home." That's her older brother. He's nineteen and in the Army, somewhere in Vietnam. She loves him and is really worried about him. Talking about him seemed to upset her, so she changed the subject, asking me about magic and how long I'd been doing it.

That's the one thing I can always talk about, and when I told her about the birthday parties I did on weekends, her eyes lit up.

"You get paid? How much?"

"Fifteen dollars a show," I said proudly.

"That's pretty good," she said. "But I bet you could charge more if you had an assistant. It would be more professional." She thought for a minute, then said, "You could charge twenty-five dollars."

She was right. Having an assistant puts a magician into a whole different league, like Mister Mystery, who has the lovely Linda Lee. He makes her float in the air and cuts her in half and everything.

"Let's say you pay your assistant one-third of what you make—that's eight dollars and thirty-three cents. That leaves you sixteen dollars and sixty-seven cents, which is more than you're making now, and you would do a much better show."

And, just like that, I had an assistant, who happened to be the most popular and smartest and prettiest girl in all of Bixby School. The next week she came over to my house to practice. I thought it would take a long time to teach her the tricks—how to set them up, what to bring out and when. But she got everything the first time.

A couple weeks later we did a show at the Temple City Library, where Mrs. Molatsky works, and this guy from the *Temple City Times* wrote an article about it—on the front page! Suddenly everyone was calling for birthday parties and Cub Scout meetings, and we were charging twenty-five dollars, just like Amy said, sometimes thirty, and, once even forty! My mom was driving us to shows almost every weekend, sometimes to two shows on the same weekend! I make sure to pay Amy right after each show, so she can buy food for Daisy. The rest pays for my magic lessons, and whatever's left over goes to my family, though I don't want her to know that.

At Amy's suggestion, I had business cards printed up

at Quik-Copy. They're really cool, fluorescent red with a top hat on them, and the name "Joel Edwin." It had been Mister Mystery's idea to use my first and middle name as a stage name, instead of my last name. "That way," he said, "your audience will laugh at your jokes instead of, well, you know . . ."

Everything was going great until one afternoon, the middle of the summer, after a show at the Rosemead Library. Amy and I had packed up my magic suitcase and were just hanging out with Herrmann—she's my rabbit—waiting for my mom to come pick us up, when all of a sudden I realized that I liked her. Really liked her. Like, *liked her* liked her. Like, I didn't know what to do about it. Suddenly, I had a secret—and I sure couldn't tell her.

Amy's really smart, and beautiful, and talented, but nobody's perfect. As observant as she is, she misses some things that are really obvious. For example, she has somehow failed to realize what a total dork I am. And I don't want to push it because we've got a good thing going. If she knew I *liked* her, that would be the end of that. So I've managed not to say anything. With us, it's strictly business, and always outside of school. In school, we don't talk, which is why it was so weird—wierd?—that she had come up to me in Home Ec.

"Look, Joel, I need to talk to you about Sunday." She

seemed really upset. "I can't come . . . I'm really sorry."

"Uh. Okay," I said. "No problem. I'll be fine."

That was an outright lie. This was really bad news. Sunday's magic show was supposed to be our biggest yet! If there was ever a time I'd need an assistant, it would be on Sunday.

"I'm really sorry. It's just that . . . I'll be in San Bernardino. With my father."

"Your father?"

She nodded, and I could see she was on the verge of tears. "He and my mom separated. He moved out two months ago."

"I'm sorry—"

"I guess it's better. They're not fighting so much. But now he lives in San Bernardino, and I spend one weekend a month with him. He and my mom had to switch around the schedule, so now this is his weekend—he's picking me up Friday after school, and will bring me back on Sunday night. And that's why I can't come." She wiped her eyes. "Will you explain to Herrmann why I'm not there? And don't let her drink too much water before the show."

I didn't know what to say, so I just looked at my egg, which was a gloppy mess.

"But I'm still planning on coming with you to Mister Mystery tomorrow after school. My mom will drive me there from the stable, and if you want, she can give you a ride home."

"Hey, everybody!" called out Arnold Pomeroy. "Look at Joel's egg! Guess the yolk's on him!"

Mrs. Hernandez came over, muttered something about boys in Home Economics, and gave me another egg.

"Try again," she said. *"Gently."*

Another one of Mr. Culpepper's funny sayings is "Time is nature's way of keeping everything from happening at once."

That may be so, but it doesn't always work. Now I've got two huge things coming up—the assembly on Monday, which I don't even want to *think* about, and Sunday's show, which I've been thinking about for weeks.

This afternoon I spread out all my magic tricks on the floor of the den—my bedroom—to decide which ones I could do without an assistant. I sat on the floor beside Herrmann's cage and looked over my list.

"Well, Herrmann," I said, "looks like it's you and me on Sunday. Amy can't come."

Herrmann looked a little sad, but she's a rabbit, and always looks a little sad.

"The problem is that all the best tricks are the ones with Amy—and you. But, don't worry, I still plan to bring you. We'll make it work."

The first trick to go was the arm guillotine. It's a cool one, you've probably seen it before—it looks like you're going to slice off someone's arm, but in the end they don't get hurt, even though the guillotine blade *does* go right through a carrot. When I do it with Amy, we have a whole comedy routine, and she feeds the carrot to Herrmann. I suppose I could do the trick with a volunteer from the audience, but there's always a chance that they'll freak out. And even if *they* don't, my grandmother *definitely* will.

I'd better tell you about my grandmother. It's another one of those antonym things. Imagine a grandmother who is soft and nice, baking cookies, sending birthday gifts, and saying things like, "Well, isn't that lovely?"

My grandma Anna is not like that. At least, not now. When I was a kid, she would babysit for us and sing Yiddish songs. I had no idea what they meant, but they were sweet. She also used to tell me funny things she had learned in English class when she came to America, like a poem that began "If wishes were fishes . . ." But her accent was so thick that it came out "Eef veeshes vere feeshes."

"Then what?" I would say. "What if wishes were fishes?"

She would shrug, then say, "Eef eefs and ands vere pots and pans . . ."

I never did figure out how the poem went, but I liked it. And I liked her. She would have our family over for dinner and make the best blintzes, these Jewish sweet-cheese-filled pancakes. Every time she saw me she'd say how much I looked like my father when he was young, call me *bubala,* then pinch my right cheek. It drove me crazy. Why always the right one? I think it made my face lopsided.

But then everything changed. She started to put strange things in the blintzes—once I found gravel—so we couldn't eat at her house anymore. We still went to see her, but she would get really upset, yelling at my mother. Since then she's gotten a lot worse. Now I would happily let her pinch my right cheek as much as she wanted, if she would go back to being the grandma she was when I was young.

Most of the time now she's just really mad, screaming mad. Usually it's about the gas men—whoever they are— who she says are coming to throw gas at her. My dad says it's not her fault; it's because something terrible happened to her before she left the old country. But that was sixty years ago, and he has no idea what it was.

She used to live in Pasadena, which isn't far from here by car, maybe seven or eight miles. But then, about a year ago, she got so worked up about the gas men that she walked all night to our house, and when we went out in the morning, we found her asleep on the porch (which is not very comfortable—it's coated with AstroTurf, which looks like grass but is actually prickly plastic). We didn't know what to do, so my dad woke her up and drove her home.

A month later, she did it again. Then again a couple weeks after that. We never knew when we were going to wake up and find her on the porch. The funny thing is that when she was sleeping there, she looked so peaceful. We learned not to wake her up suddenly, because that's when she would start screaming.

"The gas men! They're following me! They're throwing gas at me!"

I once made the mistake of trying to argue with her. "Grandma," I said, "that's not possible. You can't throw gas!"

She paused for a second, then started shaking her head. "Shah! Where's your father? And your mother—what's she doing to him?"

The biggest problem with my grandmother is that she's convinced my mother is trying to kill my father. She used to call over here about fifteen or twenty times a day, and when we answered the phone, she would start to scream. "Your mother! She puts poison in his food! Don't let him eat it!"

We weren't supposed to tell her where my father was working. But she found out anyway, and called there again and again until she reached his boss. Then she told *him* all about how my mother was trying to kill my father. After that happened a couple of times, he lost his job.

I know that sounds crazy, but to *really* understand how crazy it is, you'd need to know my mother. The only way

she'd be dangerous is if you could poison someone with nice-
ness. She never gets mad, even when she should. If holding
in laughter can cause an embolism, can being too *nice* make
you bust a gorgle? That would be bad. I couldn't understand
how she put up with my grandmother saying those horrible
lies.

"How can you stand it?" I asked her once.

"Oh," said my mother, "life is difficult for her. She's—not
well."

"Yeah? I get sick too, but I don't call people murderers!"

"We have to be understanding," she said. "She's suffering.
Because of what happened when she was leaving Poland."
There it was again. "Besides," said my mom, "when she starts
to scream, I just do this." My mom reached a hand to her
hearing aid. There was a short squeal as she turned it off and
smiled weakly.

My grandma hadn't come over for a while, but then, one
morning last summer, I found her on the porch, right in
front of the door. I could have gone out the back door, and
probably should have. But I figured I could jump over her
no problem.

Big mistake.

I actually *did* make it over—I'm sure I didn't touch her.
But a few seconds later, she woke up and started to scream,
so loudly and for so long that the neighbors called the police.

That had happened a few times, and the officer who usually came was pretty nice about it. My dad, who can charm anyone, explained that she was upset because she lost her cat—which wasn't true, as she never had a cat. The officer managed to calm her down, saying they'd find the cat, and gave her a ride back to Pasadena in his police car.

This time, though, there was a new police officer—with a crew cut—who didn't buy the cat story. What's more, as he came toward my grandmother, she started screaming at *him,* calling him a Cossack and a whole bunch of other things in Yiddish, saying that *he* was the gas man. He didn't like that at all. He looked so mad, I thought he was going to handcuff her, but instead he backed up to his car and radioed the police department. About ten minutes later this big white van pulled up. Four huge guys got out—and one of them was carrying something. You know what it was?

A straitjacket—exactly like Houdini's! It even had leather straps. The big guys held her arms as they slid on the jacket and fastened the straps. As soon as they did, she stopped screaming and stood there with a confused smile on her face.

"See that?" my dad said. "She's fine. All calmed down. She was just upset about her cat. So, why don't we take off the jacket and—"

"Stand back, sir," the officer said to my father.

I watched my grandma, mesmerized. I knew that Houdini

would have escaped from it in a couple of minutes, or less. I knew exactly how he would do it too. He could dislocate his left shoulder, which is the first thing you have to do to escape from a straitjacket. Although there are lots of things dislocated about my grandmother, her shoulder isn't one of them. I knew she wouldn't escape.

Eventually they took her to the Los Angeles County Sanitorium. *Sanitorium* is one of those funny words, because it should probably be called an *In*sanitorium. I never went there, but my mom and dad did, several times, and came back *haggard,* which is a vocabulary word for "looking exhausted and unwell, especially from fatigue, worrying, and suffering." When I asked my mom about it, all she said was, "Well, the wallpaper is nice."

That's how I knew it was *really* bad. If there's even a tiny speck of good somewhere, my mom will find it. So if wallpaper was the best she could do, that meant it was horrible. I think it actually made my grandma a lot worse, being around all those crazy people. They only let patients make phone calls once a week, on Sundays, when she would call us five or six times. Whenever I answered, I tried to bring up subjects that wouldn't upset her, but it wasn't easy.

"Hi, Grandma! How's the food in the sanitorium? Are you making friends?"

"Shah!" she'd say. "Where's your father? What's she doing to him?"

"I hear the wallpaper is really nice. What color is it?"

"Poison! She gives him poison!"

Eventually I would have to hang up, and because there was only one phone, she would get in line and call again. After about a month, and several trips to the courthouse, my dad arranged to have her moved to the Jewish Home for the Elderly and Infirm of Greater Los Angeles.

A week after she got there, we all went to visit. I don't know what the sanitorium was like, but I can't imagine it was much worse than this. All the people were sitting around a big room, in green plastic chairs. A bunch were arguing, some were asleep, and some were just chewing. A radio was playing really loud classical music, I guess to drown out the other noise.

The whole place reminded me of this Jell-O parfait they advertise on TV. We've never had it—my dad says it's goyisha food—but the commercial makes it look pretty cool. It's a powder you mix with boiling water, then put it in a special glass that's swirly and shaped like an ice-cream cone. Somehow, it makes three layers—foamy on top, creamy in the middle, and see-through at the bottom. I have no idea how it does that, but the exact same thing had happened to the air in the Jewish Home.

The top layer was all smoke, mostly from cigars. The bottom layer smelled like cleaning fluid, with just a hint of throw-up. And the middle layer was pure noise. Not just any noise, but *kvetching*.

If you're only going to learn one Yiddish word, I suggest *kvetch*. It means complain, but in a Yiddish way, which is a high art. I only know a little Yiddish, but it was clear that everyone there was trying to outkvetch each other.

On the far side of the room, sitting all alone, was my grandmother. Not screaming, not sleeping, not chewing, not even kvetching—just sitting. When we gave her the flowers we'd brought, she stared at them but didn't speak.

It was so horrible that I didn't want to go back a second time, but my dad said, "It's a *mitzvah* to visit the sick." People think *mitzvah* means "good deed," but it actually means "commandment," something you *have* to do, so I went. And it's a good thing I did, because on that second visit, as we walked in, something *amazing* happened.

"Gladys?" said a woman at the counter. "Is that you?"

"Esther?" said my mom. "What are you doing here?"

It was the third Esther, who is neither Chopped Liver Esther nor Esther Nestor, but Never Stops Talking Esther. She looked at my brothers, then at me.

"You're the baby, aren't you?"

"I used to be," I said. "When I was small." I get that a lot, and don't generally like it, especially when it's followed by that grabbing of the cheek thing, which makes me feel like a chipmunk. But that didn't happen this time. Instead she said, "Wait a minute! You're Joel! Aren't you the one who does magic shows?"

I nodded.

"I read the article about you in the *Temple City Times*. It said you're a professional magician!" Her eyes lit up. "Wow—a celebrity right here in the Jewish Home for the Elderly and Infirm!"

People heard her talking and started to gather around. "Look!" she said. "This is Joel, Gladys's son! He's a real live magician!" A couple of people applauded, even though I hadn't done anything. "Can you show us a magic trick?" she asked.

I always have something with me, ready to impress whoever asks. I pulled some sponge balls out of my pocket—red and fluffy. I put one in my hand, one in hers, picked up a pen from the counter to use as a magic wand, and waved it over both our hands. I opened my hand to show that the ball had disappeared. Then she opened her hand, and she had both of them! More people had wandered over and they applauded. I made one ball disappear—and pulled it out from under Esther's clipboard. Then I did it again, but this time pulled it from the ear of an old man standing next to me. Everyone loved that.

"Hey," she said, "this gives me a great idea. Why don't you come do a performance for us?" Before I could answer, she said, "Ever since I started working here last month, everyone asks me, they say 'Esther, why don't you bring in a magician to do a magic show for us?' And I say, 'I don't know any magicians.' But, now, just like that, here you are! It's magic!"

She brought a calendar down from the wall and turned some pages to December. "I know!" she said. "Let's do it for Hannuukkah! Our celebration is Sunday afternoon, December nineteenth, in the social room. The kitchen will serve latkes for lunch, then we'll light the candles, and then you! It'll be wonderful! How much do you charge?"

I had no idea what to say. This was way bigger than a birthday party. Could I charge forty dollars? Fifty? I gulped and was just about to speak, when she said, "We have one hundred dollars in the entertainment budget. Will that be enough?"

My heart nearly stopped. One hundred dollars?! All I could do was nod.

And the best thing of all was right then, my grandmother came up to me. Only she wasn't the screaming grandmother. She was the nice grandmother. She put her arm around me and said, "This is my grandson Joel—he's the baby." She squeezed my cheek. "He's a wonderful magician!"

"Don't I know it!" said Esther. "Not only that, I've just

hired him to do a magic show for us at our annual Cha-
nukka party!"

My grandmother didn't say anything; she just reached
over and squeezed my cheek again. It was the happiest I'd
seen her in years.

I put the arm guillotine away. "A magic trick is only good if
it works for your audience," Mister Mystery had said at my
first lesson. "The most important thing is not the trick. The
real magic is in you, the magician."

Since that lesson, I'd been working hard to make myself
as magical as possible.

"Hey there, ladies and gentlemen, boys and girls, children
of all ages!" I said to the mirror in the hallway. "I know why
you're here. It's because you believe in—" And this is the
important part. The pause. That's what really nails it. You
don't rush; you take your time. But not too much time—
just enough to look slyly to one side. When Mister Mystery
does it, he actually winks, usually at some beautiful woman
in the audience. It's not just charming, it's misdirection;
they'll look at your face instead of your left sleeve, where the
bouquet of spring-loaded feather flowers is hidden. Then
they're amazed when you pull it out and say, "—magic!"

It's in those first few moments onstage, Mister Mystery
says, when you win them over. "You know how long it takes

an audience to decide if they love you or hate you? Thirty seconds. You need a fast and flashy opening, Joel, to show them you are confident and in complete control. After that they're in the palm of your hand."

Taking my glasses off, I looked in the mirror, working on my smile. "Hey there," I said, winking at myself. "How you doin'?" I was just getting it, the perfect magical look. "I know why you're here. It's because you believe in—"

"Hey, Joel?" my dad called from the other side of the house. "Could you give me a hand?"

I put the flowers away and went to my parents' bedroom, where my father stood in his boxers and a T-shirt, with some clothes and about thirty bottles of pills on his bed. About as unmagical as you can get.

"Oh, good. Can you bring down my suitcases? The big one and the little one."

"All right," I said. The attic is above my parents' closet, and that's where the suitcases live. Getting them down is tricky, and takes someone small, so it's my job.

I got the old yellow high chair from the corner of the kitchen and used that to climb to the upper part of the closet. From there I pushed open the square trapdoor that leads to the attic, and climbed up. It's filled with dust and a lot of junk, as well as the suitcases my parents have had since they moved to California, which I brought down.

Packing clothes for the hospital is easy, as you don't need to wear much, just those robes they give you that leave your tushy sticking out. The hard part is packing my dad's medicines. He's always taking pills, some for pain, some for vitamins, and some for who knows what. The problem is that he needs help reading the labels. As bad as my eyes are, they're the best in the house, so he calls me when he can't see. He picked up a bottle, squinted at it, lifted up his glasses, and squinted again.

"Can you read this?" he asked.

"A-ce-ta-min-o-phen," I said.

"Good—put it into the small suitcase. And how 'bout this one?"

"Ascorbic acid."

"Good," he said. "Vitamin C. For healing. Put that one in too. And this one?"

"Prednisone."

"Ah! That's what I was looking for," he said.

"Should I put it in?"

"Nope. Put it on the top shelf in the bathroom, so high up that I can't reach it. I've been taking it for years, and Dr. Kaplowski told me to stop taking it at the beginning of last week, or he couldn't do the surgery. I haven't touched it since, but want to be sure I don't bring it along by mistake. All right, how about this one?"

We went through the bottles until the little suitcase was filled.

"What's the big suitcase for?" I asked.

"The Neck-O-Matic, of course!"

"You're bringing it to the hospital?" I asked. "Why?"

"Are you kidding?" he said. "Not just bringing it, I'm going to sell them the design! Last week I told Dr. Kaplowski all about it, and he's really interested. This is the perfect opportunity!"

It was a crazy idea. "But, Dad," I said, "that doesn't make any . . . It's not—"

"Don't worry," he said. "There's a patent pending, so it's protected." A couple months ago my dad wrote to Washington, DC, to apply for a patent for his design. "Let's set it up," he said, "one more time before I go."

I wanted to go back to practicing my magic, but my dad made it sound like his last meal on death row so I dragged the box with the Neck-O-Matic from the corner of the bedroom. It was really heavy, so I had to slide and kick it all the way to the door that leads to the bathroom. I opened the box and took out the neck brace, which looks like something you'd wear if you had whiplash, then the pulleys and rope, which I looped over the chin-up bar in the doorway. There was also a heavy-duty blue plastic tray that said DRIFT-WOOD DAIRY on it. It's supposed to hold milk cartons, but my dad uses it to hold bricks for the Neck-O-Matic. That's what was in the rest of the box, which is why it was so heavy. I set up the pulleys like he'd shown me, and the tray, which is held up at each corner by a rope and has to balance just right so the bricks don't fall off. My dad took his place in a chair under the chin-up bar, made sure everything was right, then fastened the brace around his neck.

Even though I've helped him with the Neck-O-Matic for years, it still creeps me out. If you were to walk into the room, you would think I was helping my dad to hang himself. It's supposed to relieve pressure on his neck and back by slowly separating his vertebrae. That's the problem with ankylosing spondylitis—it turns your spine into one solid bone. I don't know—maybe the Neck-O-Matic really works. My dad thinks it does, and he's the one being stretched.

When the rope was tight, he motioned with his hand for me to put in the first brick, then another, then a third. The hand motions are key, as you can't really talk while you're in the Neck-O-Matic. He grimaced for a moment, breathed out, then relaxed, a look of calm spreading over his face. A moment later, he motioned for me to put on another brick. There was the grimace, then the sigh, then the hand motion again. Finally he signaled for me to stop, which I did. Then he gave me the other hand motion, which meant it was joke time. That's the only part of the whole business I like.

For the Neck-O-Matic to work, my dad has to sit there, not talking, for twenty minutes, which is like a Guinness world record for him. To pass the time, I tell jokes.

"So this guy goes into a job interview," I said. "And the first thing he notices is that the man interviewing him has no ears. He doesn't say anything, of course, and the interview goes well. At the end, the interviewer says, 'Well, you seem like just the man we're looking for. I like your spirit, your drive. There's just one final question—do you notice anything unusual about me?'

"The guy thinks about it, then decides to be honest.

"'Well, in fact I did notice something. You don't have any ears.'

"'That's true,' says the interviewer. 'Thank you for coming in—we'll keep your application on file.'

"Right away, the guy knows he blew it. The next candidate comes in, and the same thing happens. The interview goes well and, at the end, the interviewer says, 'You seem great. Just one question—do you notice anything unusual about my appearance?'

"He thinks about it, then says 'Well, as long as you're asking, I can't help but notice you don't have any ears.' The same thing happens—he doesn't get the job."

My dad motioned for me to add another brick, which I did, then went on.

"As the second guy leaves the office, he sees a third guy waiting, and says, 'Look, pal, I just blew this interview—I'm never gonna get the job. I don't know why, but I'm going to do you a favor. The guy who's going to interview you doesn't have any ears. And he's kind of sensitive about it. So, if I were you, I wouldn't mention it.'

"The third guy goes in, and the interview goes well. Then, at the end, the interviewer says, 'You seem like just the man we're looking for. Let me ask one more question—do you notice anything unusual about my appearance?'

"The guy pauses for a moment, then says, 'In fact, I do. Unless I'm mistaken, I believe you wear contact lenses.'

"The interviewer gets all excited. 'Yes! That's right! Well, we can really use someone with your observational abilities. That's terrific! Tell me, how did you know?'

"'Well,' says the guy. 'It's obvious. If you had any ears, you'd wear glasses.'"

My dad busted out laughing. That was good and not good. Good because it's good to laugh, and my dad always says laughter is the best medicine. But not good because if you laugh too much while you're wearing the Neck-O-Matic, it yanks the rope, which starts the tray of bricks bouncing up and down, and one of the bricks could fall on your foot. If that happens, laughter is the worst medicine.

I adjusted the bricks in the box, and tried to figure what to tell him next. Usually I can make a story out of whatever happened in school, but I didn't want to tell him about getting called into Mr. Newton's office, or anything about the assembly. All day long I'd pictured the scene of my family and me, looking pathetic as we huddled around our menorah. The only consolation was that my father wouldn't be there, because he'd be in the hospital recovering from his surgery. That, at least, was lucky. Having him at the assembly would be a disaster. Everyone would howl with laughter at the way he looked and walked.

I switched to waiter jokes, which are funny, but not brick-on-your-toe funny.

"So, two guys go into a restaurant and both order iced tea. 'And be sure the glass is clean!' says one. A few minutes later the waiter comes back with the iced tea and says, 'Which one ordered the clean glass?'"

Tonight when we lit the candles, we were all in a pretty serious mood, with surgery early the next morning. But not my dad. He looked happy as could be—maybe even a little taller, after the session with the Neck-O-Matic.

"You'll never guess who called today," he said, the moment we finished the blessings, even before we tried to sing "Maoz Tzur." We all looked at him. "It was the principal of Bixby School!"

"Mr. Newton?" said Kenny. "Why?"

"Well," my father went on, "let me tell you the whole story. Bixby School has to have an extra day on Monday. And to make it special, they're going to have their holiday celebration."

"That's what they call it now," said Howard, "because when I was there we kept complaining about mixing church and state. But all they did was change the name. It's still just a Christmas assembly."

"Ha!" said my dad. "That may have been true then. But not this year! And do you know who will be the star of the celebration?"

Kenny and Howard looked baffled.

"We will!" he said.

I couldn't believe it. My dad knew the whole time.

"That's right. Joel will be telling the story of Hanikkah to the whole school! Mr. Newton said that they've never celebrated the holiday before. They want to have our whole family there, onstage, lighting candles! Can you picture that?"

I could, even though I'd been spending all day trying not to.

"How wonderful!" said my mom. "We'll be making Bixby School history! I think I'll wear my blue dress." Then she began to hum "The Horrible Song."

"Absolutely!" said my dad. "And I'll wear my bow tie."

"But, Dad," I said, "you won't be able to come, will you?"

"Are you kidding?" he said. "I wouldn't miss it for the world! As soon as Mr. Newton called, I telephoned Dr. Kaplowski and told him I had an important event on Monday. He said not to worry, that the recovery should be quick—and that by Monday, I'll be dancing! Picture that! Me with my new golden hip joints, dancing around the menorah!"

With that, he started singing "If I Were a Rich Man," like Tevye from *Fiddler on the Roof,* my dad's favorite song from the whole musical.

I was mortified. It was bad enough that the whole school would be watching my family do our Jewish thing in public, but picturing my father dancing made it far worse. Everyone would look at me and think: Now I get it! *That's* why Joel is such a dork.

My father was oblivious, singing and trying to snap his fingers—"Yabba-dabba-dabba-do!"—sounding like a cross between Tevye and Fred Flintstone.

"Please, God," I whispered, "whatever you do—don't let my father come to the assembly on Monday."

THE FOURTH CANDLE:
A Tiny Shred of Something to Believe In
Wednesday, December 15

It took forever to fall asleep last night. Every time I closed my eyes, I saw my dad on the Bixby School stage, and heard the deafening sound of laughter. Then, this morning, I woke up early from a dream and couldn't get back to sleep. I was standing with my father on top of a hill, in the fog. We were both wearing our pajamas. He had invented a special kind of kite that flew without wind. My job was to hold the kite. At first it was going great—there was no wind, and the kite took off. But then it carried me up, high into storm clouds, with lightning. I called to my dad, but no sound would come out of my mouth. I could hear him, though, shouting, "This is great! They'll love it!" as I was carried higher into the sky. "We'll be rich!"

That's when I woke up. It was still dark outside, but I got out of bed and ate a bowl of Chex, then went back to my room. It was really quiet, a quarter till six in the morning. My mom and dad were heading to the hospital early, and would be up soon.

"Hey, Herrmann," I said. "You awake?"

I took her out of her cage and sat her on my lap. "How you doin'?"

She scrunched up her nose, which is what she always does.

"Me, I'm not so good," I went on, "but thanks for asking. I had this dream about a kite. And a storm. And my father."

I told her all about it. She didn't seem particularly interested, but neither of us had anything better to do, so I kept on.

"I'm also kind of worried because he's going to the hospital today—again. For another operation. To put gold in his hip joints."

Even as I told Herrmann about this, I began to wonder how they do such a thing. Do they have liquid gold they somehow squirt in? If so, how hot does gold have to be to melt? Do they use a needle? Herrmann wasn't interested. She crawled off my lap and began to hop around the room.

Herrmann is actually my second rabbit. I named the first one Houdini, but he escaped. I should have seen that coming. Even so, I'm not entirely sure how it happened. The rabbit cage is in a corner of the den, and when Houdini was here, it was surrounded by newspaper several feet around the cage. That's because Houdini was a boy rabbit. When I picked him at the pet store, I didn't think of something that every magician should know: Boy rabbits can learn to pee standing up in their cages. Or at least Houdini did. I think he used to play a game with himself to see how far he could get. Hence the newspaper.

Rabbits are supposed to be cute, and Houdini definitely was. He was an albino except for a little black spot on his left ear. After a while, though, adorable turns to boring. Rabbits in stories always seem to be doing interesting things, but not Houdini; he spent his time mostly eating, sleeping, pooping, and peeing. Some life.

Aside from his magic career, the most interesting thing about Houdini the rabbit was an experiment we did together last year for the sixth-grade science fair. If you've ever had a rabbit, you know that you feed them little food pellets. They also poop little pellets. My hypothesis—as we're supposed to say in science—was that there would be a one-to-one ratio of food pellets in to poop pellets out. I asked Mrs. Skurvecky—who was my science teacher last year and again this year—if anyone had ever done that experiment before. She said no one had, as far as she knew, and that there was probably a good reason. Still, I decided to spend a week testing it, counting out the food pellets, counting up the poop pellets. It was going well for the first couple days, though my hypothesis was off—it looked like the ratio of food in to poop out was *two*-to-one. Then I discovered that he was eating his poop pellets whenever he got a chance. That threw a monkey wrench into my research—in addition to being disgusting—so the results were inconclusive.

While the poop pellet experiment kept me interested, I think Houdini was pretty bored. Sometimes I left the cage open for him to run around the room—after he'd finished peeing on the newspaper. One day, though, I got called away to set the table for dinner. The sliding door at the back of the den was open and he must have hopped outside. It shouldn't have been a problem, as the yard is fenced in, but when I went to find him, he was gone. I called out to Kenny and we looked all over, but there was no trace of him. Houdini had vanished.

It was a complete and total mystery. I suppose a bird, maybe a hawk, could have swooped down, plucked him up, and flown off. Or maybe he found some opening under the fence, slid through, and made a break for freedom. That seemed nearly as dangerous as the hawk, given all the cars on the street.

Then again, rabbits are lucky. At least their feet are supposed to be. That's what the man at the school carnival told me in fifth grade when I managed to knock down two out of three metal milk bottles with a baseball. The prize I won was a rabbit's foot, which, for some reason, had been dyed pink, and hung on a little chain. The lucky rabbit's foot idea didn't make much sense to me, as the rabbit missing this one didn't seem very lucky at all. Then again, Houdini had four feet, all attached, so maybe he really was lucky. And maybe, just maybe, he did break through some hidden hole in the fence, hopped quickly between the moving cars, then found a secret tunnel behind the tall grass that led to an enchanted meadow where he now lived, running free. At least, that's what I'd like to believe.

But what I know for sure is that he's gone and now I have Herrmann. I got a girl—for obvious reasons—and named her after another magician, who was also great but not an escape artist. When she's not in her cage, I never let her out of my sight.

"You're not leaving me, are you, Herrmann?" She looked up at me and did that nose scrunch thing. "That's right, you're staying here with me. And don't worry about my dad either. He'll be fine. You'll see. He'll come back from the hospital with gold joints in his body, running around just like you."

Just then I heard arguing from my parents' bedroom, then shouting.

"No, Bob!" my mom was yelling. "We can't take it! We'll be late!" My mom only raises her voice when she gets really, really, *really* frustrated. "They said to be early—and there's already going to be traffic!"

"Don't worry," my dad said. "We'll take the access road and

avoid the traffic on the on-ramp. That'll save ten minutes."

"But it's too heavy! I can't carry it," she said. "And neither can you." It drives me crazy when they fight. "Bob, this is an operation, not a business deal."

"But it's the perfect opportunity," he said. "It'll be great! They'll love it!"

He sounded just like he had in my dream. I stomped to their room and knocked on the door. When my mom opened it, she looked like she'd been crying. My dad looked terrible too. I mean, he never looks very good, but now his face was puffy, and his body was stiff as he rested against the closet in his torn robe, T-shirt, and boxers. Beside him was the suitcase with the Neck-O-Matic, which he had apparently been trying to push.

"Oh, Joel," said my mom. "You're up—"

"You want the stupid Neck-O-Matic?" I said, totally losing my cool. "All right. Fine." I walked into the room, grabbed the suitcase, and started to drag it. With all the bricks, it was really heavy.

Even as I did it, I felt guilty. This was the time to be especially nice to my parents, and I was being a brat. But I couldn't help it. I kicked and pushed it through the kitchen, toward the front door, scraping the floor, knocking over a chair.

"Joel, really, you can leave it . . ."

I rolled it over, out the front door. By now, Kenny and Howard were both up, watching me. "See?" I said, shoving it down the stairs. "No problem." I kept rolling it over and over until I got to the car. I couldn't lift it, but Kenny came out in his pajamas, with the keys, and opened the trunk. With a heave-ho, we lifted it up and in.

"There's your Neck-O-Matic!" I said, slamming the trunk shut.

"But how will we get it out?" my mom asked.

"There are orderlies at the hospital," said my dad. "That's their job, to help with luggage. Big, strong guys. They can put it on a wheelchair..."

They came out to the car, my dad hobbling to the passenger seat, my mom on the verge of tears as I gave her the keys. Just before they left, my dad said, "You're not worried, are you, Joel?"

I shook my head and said sarcastically, "Why should I worry? You've got the Neck-O-Matic."

"You're just upset now," said my dad. "But it'll be all right—I'll be back. With golden joints!"

"I'll call from the hospital when the operation is over," said my mom.

I didn't say a word to Kenny or Howard; I just ran to the den and slammed the door. Herrmann and I looked out the window as they drove off.

"Nothing to worry about," I said to her. "They'll love it. It'll be great."

I think I'm getting a gorgle.

When I left for school a while later, the air was crisp. There was no frost on the ground, but the sky was gray and cloudy, and the barometer on the porch still read between 29 and 30, pushing toward SNOW. But as I walked down Kimdale Drive, the day got hotter with every step. By the time I got to school, the last bit of fog had burned off. The little kids were all at the far end of the school, near the cement factory, packed into the giant sandbox, digging like crazy. One of them was running around screaming, "Look, everyone, it's true! I found a dime!"

The other kids gathered around to see, like it was the most amazing thing in the world, then went back to digging.

This whole sandbox thing began two years ago, when I was in fifth grade. Howard was in Mr. Culpepper's class and he came home one day looking very serious, saying there was something he couldn't tell us, and we shouldn't ask him about it. Then he went to his room and closed the door, like he always does. Howard's usually pretty bad at keeping secrets, but he kept this one.

We had no idea what it was until the next week, on Monday morning, when Brian and I got to school, and found the main yard deserted.

"Whoa!" said Brian. "What happened? Did someone drop an atomic bomb?"

Brian always says things like that. But it was weird. Not atomic bomb weird, but weird just the same. Then I looked and saw that all the kids were at the sandbox way down at the far end of the playground. We went to see what was going on, and everyone was digging.

"It's wicked cool!" said Eddy Mazurki.

"What happened?" I asked.

"Didn't you hear?" he said. "Over the weekend there was a robbery! At the Bank of America, down the street. Because the thieves were being chased by the police and they didn't want to get caught with the money, they buried it—right here in the sandbox!"

"Look!" shouted Debbie Henderson. "Thirty-five cents!"

Everyone gathered around to look at her coins. Sure enough, there was a quarter and a dime.

"Where did you find it?" someone asked.

"Right there!" she said, pointing.

A moment later, we were all digging. Every few minutes, someone would shout out, and we'd rush to see what they'd found. Usually it was pennies or nickels, but Billy Zamboni found a half dollar.

The bell rang, and we went off to class, though no one wanted to. At recess, almost all the kids were at the sandbox, digging for coins. At lunchtime the eighth graders showed up—including Howard. They weren't digging—they just stood there, on the basketball court, watching us and laughing.

It turned out that Mr. Culpepper had been teaching Howard's class about rumors. That was the secret. They had made up the story about the bank robbers, and told just a few kids. Those kids told more kids. And now, here we all were, digging.

When you think about it, the story is ridiculous for all kinds of reasons. For one, since when do bank robbers steal *coins*? Even if they did, and were being chased by police, why would they stop to hide the money in the Bixby School sandbox? And if they *had* buried it, why would the coins be scattered all over the place?

It made no sense at all. But here's what made it work: We found money. Real money. Why? Because it's a sandbox, and kids have been losing their lunch money there for years. But when someone finds a quarter, you don't stop to wonder whether it's true—you just dig.

As the week went on, the digging got out of hand, with kids fighting over who got to dig where, until Mr. Newton finally called a school assembly to tell us that there had been no bank robbers, there was no buried treasure, and to stop digging. Then Mr. Culpepper stood up onstage and told us about how his class had started the rumor as an experiment, and ended by saying, "So, you see? You can't believe everything you hear."

We all felt pretty dumb. "You're not actually stupid," Howard explained to me later. "Just *gullible*. That means you believe something without questioning."

"I know what the word *gullible* means," I said. "Or at least what it's *supposed* to mean. Because it's not even a real word."

"What?" said Howard.

"That's right. I read this book on language. It's actually slang."

"Really?"

"Yeah, from sailors, who saw seagulls and were fooled into thinking there's land nearby when there really wasn't. But it's not a real word—that's why it isn't in the dictionary. If you don't believe me, look it up."

Off Howard went to find the dictionary—*he's* the gullible one. And, eventually, the digging stopped. But here's the strange thing. Even though the whole school now knew it wasn't real, every few months kids would start digging again, getting all excited about the stolen loot. And when the teachers explained the whole thing to them, they just nodded and kept right on digging. Because, in their minds, being told it was a rumor made it even *more* true, and they figured the teachers were just saying it was a rumor so they could dig up the money and keep it for themselves.

This morning I watched them dig for a while, amazed at the crazy stuff people believe. But here's the craziest thing of all: As I sat there watching, knowing it was completely ridiculous, part of me wanted to dig too.

It's like the story I read about the Chelmite lying in the grass one summer day, taking a nap. But he can't sleep because there are kids nearby, making noise. So he says, "Hey, children! Did you know there's someone at the other side of Chelm giving away free apples?"

The kids get all excited. "Free apples?" they say, and run off. With the kids gone, the guy goes back to sleep. A few minutes later, though, he hears people running past, talking about free apples, and he chuckles. Then he hears more people. Suddenly, everyone is running to the other side of town, talking about free apples. Finally he can't help himself. He jumps up and runs to the other side of town, saying, "Free apples? Sounds crazy! Then again, who knows?"

I wonder if that's how it is with God. And prayer. And miracles. Like it's all just this big rumor that makes no sense at all. But then, once in a while, someone gets what they're praying for. So we go on believing, because what else are we going to do?

Quietly, as I watched the kids dig, I said a little prayer.

I couldn't help it. No one heard me—except God, if God was listening. "Hey, God," I said, "look, I was a real jerk to my parents this morning. So I'll tell you what. Forget the snow. A heat wave is fine by me, just as long as my dad's surgery turns out okay. So he can walk. And maybe even dance. That's the only miracle I'm looking for. All right?"

As always when talking to God, I felt silly. Then again, who knows?

This close to vacation, the teachers have given up trying to teach us anything. Especially Mr. Kunkle, our social studies teacher, who we see first thing on Wednesday, and who never seemed all that interested in teaching us anything in the first place. Even at the start of the year he seemed like he was running on fumes, reading long portions of the textbook while kids went wild.

"Class, as you are well aware, we will be having an extra day of school this coming Monday," Mr. Kunkle said in his deep voice I can only describe as *soporific,* which is a vocabulary word that means "puts you right to sleep." He speaks slowly, and three or four words is all it takes. He could be a great hypnotist.

"This additional day will provide us all with an opportunity to review some of the fascinating topics we have covered during the course of this semester . . ." I was already tired from last night, and the room was stuffy. I could feel my head starting to droop. "So, please open your textbooks, sit quietly, and review chapter seven."

I opened my textbook to chapter seven, which we'd already read, all about the evils of Communism and the Soviet Union, and how everything they say is "propaganda." It made me wonder if there was some kid in the Soviet Union reading from a textbook that says how evil everything in the United States is, and how everything *we* say is propaganda.

Tired of chapter seven, I turned back to chapter four. It's the only part of our textbook—or any textbook I've ever had in school—that mentions Jews. There's a grainy black-and-white photo of the entrance to Auschwitz, a Nazi death camp. There are guards with guns, and people are passing under a sign in German. The caption says: *This is the entrance to Auschwitz, one of many Nazi concentration camps. The sign above the prisoners, "Arbeit macht frei," translates to "Work Will Make You Free," which was not true. During World War II, six million Jews were killed by the Nazis, many in death camps such as this.*

I looked at it for a long time and must have drifted off, because I was seeing the dream from this morning, only now I was under the gates of Auschwitz, holding the kite string. In the sky high above me was my father, holding on to the kite, shouting, "It'll be great! They'll love it!" I jolted awake, thinking how at that very moment he was somewhere in the hospital, maybe strapped to a table, being rolled down the hall to an operating room, with surgeons looking over him, sharpening their scalpels, cutting him open, and pouring in gold. Maybe the gold was already in his body, and maybe he was starting to move around, like the Tin Man in *The Wizard of Oz*.

At recess everyone was talking about the assembly, and what the surprise would be. Mary Wigglesworth said she heard that the PTA was going to give everyone snow cones, like they sell after school on the last Friday of the month, but these would be free. Someone else said it would be cotton candy, and Arnold Pomeroy said they were both wrong, that it would be free corn dogs for everyone, as many as we could eat, and he could eat about fifteen of them, with ketschupp and mustard.

Billy Zamboni said it wasn't about food at all—that he'd heard there would be a visit from a real TV star, the actress who plays Jeannie on *I Dream of Jeannie*. But Tim Stevenson said it would be the guy who plays Darrin on *Bewitched*. Then people started talking about which Darrin it would be, because there had been two different actors playing the part in the series, and when one left the show, they just stuck in the other like no one would notice. Someone else said they would *both* be there, but Davie Miller said he'd heard there would be two even *bigger* TV stars: Sonny and Cher! And they would be singing at the Bixby winter holiday assembly!

I was relieved when the bell rang and we went to science class with Mrs. Skurvecky, who turned off the lights and showed us a film about how plants grow, which sent me right back to sleep. I woke up when the lights went back on, with just a few minutes to the end of class, and she said we could talk quietly until the bell rang, so I went up to her.

"Do you have a question, Joel?"

"Yes, Mrs. Skurvecky. Do you know what temperature gold melts at?"

"Well," she said, "I'd have to check to be sure, but I think it's pretty hot—around two thousand degrees."

Wow. That was really hot. A picture flashed in my mind of a doctor holding a beaker filled with melted, bubbling gold, pouring it into my dad's sliced-open hip joint.

"Is something the matter, Joel?"

"No, nothing."

"Are you sure?" she said. "Why do you want to know about melting gold?"

"Because, well . . . I'm just curious."

The bell rang, and I was out the door. A minute later I was across the street and running down Kimdale Drive.

On Wednesdays after school, the timing is really tight. I need to run home, feed Herrmann, grab my magic suitcase, then run to Baldwin and catch bus number 259, which is supposed to arrive at 3:37. That gets me close enough to Oak Grove Boulevard to jump out at 3:52. That's just long enough to get to Mister Mystery's apartment for my lesson at 4:00. If it all works right, I get there with three minutes to spare.

Today I ran even faster than usual so I could check the Phone-O-Matic. I made record time, getting home by 3:20. I fed Herrmann and sure enough, the tape reel was spinning around, its loose end whipping all over the place. This is another one of my dad's inventions. He's always waiting for important phone calls he doesn't want to miss, even if no one is home, so he built a machine with Howard's old Erector Set. When the phone rings, it sets off a doorbell buzzer that triggers a motor that turns these gears that lift the phone receiver off the hook. Then he has two tape recorders hooked up, with a lever from the Erector Set rigged to push the button on one and then, thirty seconds later, on the other. The first one plays a recording he made about the Phone-O-Matic, saying that the caller should talk to it even though it's a machine. Then the first tape recorder clicks off and the second one turns on and records the person's voice.

I stopped the tape from going round and round, then found scissors to cut off the end, which gets shredded from all that spinning. Once I did that, I ran it through the tape heads and rewound it.

That's the unfinished part of the Phone-O-Matic. It can only take one message at a time. It turns out that while it's easy to get the Erector Set to press a button to record, it's hard to get it to stop and reset. Someone *had* called, and I hoped it was my mom saying the surgery was over and everything was okay. But when I reached the beginning and pressed PLAY, there was a garbled sound, some clicks, and then silence. That could have meant that the caller didn't understand the Phone-O-Matic and hung up. I played it again. Too garbled to hear. It could have been my mom calling. Because she doesn't hear very well, she's never quite sure what to do when she calls the Phone-O-Matic. She's supposed to leave a message, but sometimes she gets flustered and hangs up. Whatever happened, there was no message. I wrote a note for Kenny and Howard: "No news yet." Then I reset the Phone-O-Matic. It was 3:31. I grabbed my suitcase and ran out the door.

I got to the bus stop, sat down, and pulled out my watch. It's my dad's old one that he gave me when the band broke, so I keep it in my pocket. It read 3:35. Perfect. Right on time. I stopped to catch my breath. Then waited.

And waited.

And waited.

Jews don't believe in hell, at least not the kind with flames all around and devils poking at you with pitchforks. There is some idea of Gehenna, where the sky is made of copper and the ground is made of lead, but it's not like if you're bad you get sent there after you die.

I asked Rabbi Buxelbaum about it once, before he died, when I was in second grade at Sunday school, and we had Meet the Rabbi Day. He told us all about being a rabbi, then asked if we had any questions. I raised my hand.

"What happens after you die?" I asked.

"After you die?" he said. "They put you in the ground. But Judaism is not about what happens in the next life. It is about making the best out of this one."

Maybe so, but that still left me wondering about this hell business. After a lot of thought, I've decided that we don't actually need some imaginary hell, because we have RTD buses.

RTD stands for "Rapid Transit District," but everyone calls it "*Rancid* Transit District," because the buses are both slow and disgusting, crawling along block after block of ugly streets the color of smog. If it was up to me, I would never ride another RTD bus. I would have a car—a red

Sunbeam Tiger, like Maxwell Smart drives on *Get Smart*. Or a Corvette Stingray. Even a VW Beetle. Anything but a bus.

But the bus is the only way I can get to Mister Mystery's. That isn't his real name, by the way; it's a stage name. His actual name is Sheldon Greenberg, and that's one of the cool things about him: He's Jewish! But not awkward-out-of-place-homely-looking-like-me Jewish. No, he's *suave*, a vocabulary word that means "charming, confident, and elegant." He always knows exactly what to say and do. Nothing ever knocks him off balance—though sometimes he pretends to be surprised, like when he's doing The Cut and Restored Rope, and he invites a volunteer to cut a rope into two equal pieces. Only they're not equal; one is longer. So the volunteer tries again, and again, but the more they cut it, the longer it gets. Then Mister Mystery will say, "Hello!" and the audience laughs. Why? Because they know he's in complete control.

That's what magic is.

I've been learning to do it on Wednesday afternoons in his apartment. I've got to tell you about this place. I've never been anywhere like it. It's clean. It's perfect. He knows exactly where everything is. When I went for my first lesson, we sat at his desk and he opened a drawer filled with manila files, each one neatly labeled. He took one out, opened it, and handed me a sheet of paper—a list of magical effects I'd be learning.

Just producing the list was magical. It read:

1. FORCING CARDS
2. MAKING COINS APPEAR AND DISAPPEAR
3. SPONGE BALLS
4. CUPS AND BALLS
5. CUT AND RESTORED ROPE
6. THUMB TIP
7. LINKING RINGS

The last one was actually an illusion I had seen him do at our temple, where he performs each year on Purim.

"But the real magic," he said at that first lesson, "is not in the tricks." I nodded, knowing that I could never be as cool as him. "The real magic happens in their minds. But only when we make it happen—like this." As he said "this," a John F. Kennedy half dollar appeared at his fingertips. He asked me to hold out my hand so that he could give it to me, but when I did, the half dollar had vanished.

"You see?" he said. "People want to believe in magic. In miracles." He leaned in closer to me. "And you and I? We let them." So saying, he reached into my right ear. I felt something funny—and it was the coin!

"That's why we magicians never reveal our secrets—except

to other magicians, of course. Because they understand this. But to the audience?" He shook his head. "Even if they beg. Because as much as they think they want to know the secret, what they really want is to *believe*."

What *I* really wanted to believe, as I sat there at the bus stop on Baldwin, was that the stupid bus was coming soon, even if it was already fifteen minutes late. Finally I saw it, way down the street, taking its time. I checked my watch again: 3:52.

When it finally arrived, I jumped on, as though that would make it go faster, and I put my quarter in the fare box and looked around. The bus was practically empty, so I could have sat in the seat marked RESERVED FOR ELDERLY AND HANDICAPPED. But I didn't. I sat in the one right behind it and thought about how much I hate buses.

You know why? Because buses are for losers. This one was really hot. I pressed the button by the window that said PRESS TO OPEN, but it wouldn't budge.

"They don't open," said the driver, looking at me in his mirror.

"But it says press—"

"They're fake windows," he said, shaking his head. "To save money."

The sign above his head read CLIMATE CONTROLLED, so

I said, "Well, then, could you turn on the air conditioner?"

He shook his head again. "It's broken."

Great. I looked out the window that didn't open, and you know what I saw? Cars. Nice cars. Shiny cars. Mustangs. Alfa Romeos. Corvettes. All filled with smiling people, zipping along. And I was stuck on the bus. Waiting. Forever.

The minutes ticked by. I thought of my father, in the hospital, and wondered whether he was out of surgery. Maybe he was already walking. Dancing? The doctor had said it would be quick, but this quick? Who knows. Maybe. Time does strange things when you're on a bus.

Then I thought of Amy O'Shea, who was probably already at Mister Mystery's apartment, waiting. She had been asking about Mister Mystery since she learned I was taking lessons, and about a month ago I asked him if she might come to one, which he thought was a great idea. But when it came time to ask her, I was nervous, like I was asking her out on a date.

And now I was late. Really late. The bus stopped at a red light. Then it stopped at a green light. Someone got on and, by the time they did, the light was red again. It was like we were moving backward through time, and I'd be stuck on this bus forever.

When the bus finally got to Oak Grove, it was already twenty minutes late. I ran the last three blocks to Mister Mystery's apartment and arrived drenched in sweat and coughing from the smog. I rang the bell. His voice in the speaker said "Hello!" that way he always does, then he buzzed me in and I ran up the stairs.

"It would add a whole new dimension!" Amy was saying to Mister Mystery as I entered. She was standing up, talking, while Mister Mystery sat at his desk, nodding.

"Hello, Joel," said Mister Mystery, turning to me. "Have a little trouble getting here? Not a problem. I was just hearing Amy's thoughts about your act." I nodded, realizing how much more I was sweating now, even though I was inside, with the air-conditioning on. "She has some great ideas!"

"I was just saying how we could do a routine to music," she said. "It would be really professional—and we could charge more!"

"She's absolutely right," said Mister Mystery. "Music would put you a notch up."

"Maybe the ABC blocks," she said. "It's a good trick, but not much of a routine." She turned to Mister Mystery. "Do you have any music we could use?"

Amy was right about the ABC blocks. You stack three up on a stick, then cover them with a square box. Then, by magic, the B block is transported to a hat your assistant is holding. It's a cool effect, but doesn't have much of a story.

"I like the way she thinks," said Mister Mystery. "One step ahead."

He walked to the entertainment center, slid open a door, and there was a turntable. He thumbed through the records on the shelf, then chose one. "This might be the perfect magical music: Herb Alpert and the Tijuana Brass. Do you know them?"

Of course I did—they're on the radio all the time. And Herb Alpert—you guessed it—is Jewish.

He placed it carefully on the turntable. "And this may be just the song you're looking for. It's called 'Tijuana Taxi.' Let's try it!"

Amy nodded, then opened up my suitcase and took out the ABC blocks, which she set up on Mister Mystery's magic table. I hadn't brought my hat, but Mister Mystery had his, which he handed to me. I slapped it against the back of my wrist, and it popped open. So did Amy's eyes as I handed it to her.

"You have to get one of these!" she said.

Mister Mystery lowered the turntable's arm. There was the music, and suddenly Amy was dancing around, having a great time.

I just stood there watching her. I had no idea what to do. I don't know how to dance. I'm not talking about the fox-trot or waltzing. I'm talking about regular old dancing, the kind of dancing around that you're just supposed to *know* how to do, like Amy was doing. She looked as natural as could be, holding the hat, putting it on her head, then looking back at me. And I just stood there, staring, feeling like a complete idiot.

"C'mon, Joel!" said Mister Mystery. "Have fun with it!"

I have to do something, I thought, so I tried waving my arms around, because that seemed like part of it. Even as I did, though, I felt stupid, like I was drowning on dry land. And I couldn't very well lift the blocks and show them— which is the first part of the trick—while I was flapping my arms, so I stopped and started to shake my legs around instead. Now I looked like the guy in a film we'd watched in science class, who was having an epileptic seizure.

"Hello!" said Mister Mystery, standing by the record player. He lifted the arm and the music stopped. "Perhaps we should try it again—a little slower, shall we? Joel, maybe just start by listening to the music. Then close your eyes and feel the beat."

The music began and I did just what he said, closing my eyes, hoping that Amy was closing hers too, so she wouldn't see me. But with my eyes closed, I began to see pictures. My dad in the Neck-O-Matic. My parents driving off to the hospital. A beaker of bubbling liquid gold. A kite over the gates of Auschwitz.

I shook my head, trying to get the pictures out of my mind.

"That's good," said Mister Mystery. "Let your head sway back and forth. Now let your body move with the music." I tried to bring up happy pictures. My father healthy and out of the hospital. "There you go!" he said. "Good. That's it!"

Yeah, I thought. This is good. I imagined my father with his new gold joints, a huge smile on his face. As I did, I could feel my arms floating over my head. I snapped my fingers. I took a step. Then another.

Suddenly I opened my eyes and found myself stamping around the room, singing. "If I were a rich man! Yidel-didel-deedle-didel-deedle-didel-deedle-di! All day long I'd biddy-biddy-bum . . ." I was doing the Tevye! It was crazy, but I couldn't stop. Neither Amy nor Mister Mystery was moving. They just stared at me. Mister Mystery's face had this look of genuine astonishment—something I'd never seen before. And Amy looked like she was either going to laugh or cry.

I froze, suddenly realizing how idiotic I looked. What had I been doing?

Mister Mystery stopped the music. "Well," he finally said, "that was . . . um . . ." It's the only time I've ever seen him at a loss for words. Finally he said, "That was really something."

His intercom buzzed, meaning the next student had arrived. Without saying a word, I repacked the ABC blocks. Amy returned his hat, which he took with a little nod. Then we left, in silence.

Amy's mother was in the car waiting for us, and we climbed into the backseat, me with my suitcase on my lap. I scooted away from Amy and looked out the window.

"Hello, Joel," said Mrs. O'Shea. "Good to see you."

"Yes, Mrs. O'Shea. It's good to see you too." I sounded like a zombie. I could feel my embarrassment spilling out and filling the car.

"How was the magic lesson?" asked Mrs. O'Shea.

"Oh, fine," said Amy.

Neither of us said another word, all the way to my house. It was just a ten-minute drive, but it felt much, much longer. The whole time, I kept wishing I was on the bus.

As soon as I got home I knocked on Kenny's door, then Howard's, and asked if Mom had called. They both said no. Just then, the phone rang.

"I'll get it," said Howard. "In case it's bad news."

By the time he got it, the Phone-O-Matic had already lifted up the receiver and started playing its recording.

Hello dere! How you doin'?

"Turn off the machine!" Kenny said.

"Hello? Hello?" I could hear my mom's voice. "Who is this?"

This is Bob talking, but I'm not really here.

"Who is this?" said my mom again.

"It's Howard!" he shouted into the receiver. "We're unhooking the Phone-O-Matic!" My mom's hearing is especially bad on the phone. "Hold on a moment!" he said loudly.

"Can you hear me?" my mom shouted back.

Kenny finally turned off the machine, and Howard managed to pry the receiver out of the holder and put it up to his ear.

"This is Howard," he said loudly. There was a pause. "My day was fine. Is the operation over? How is Dad?"

There was a long pause. And then a longer pause. Howard kept saying "Uh-huh."

"What's happening?" Kenny whispered. "Did the operation work?"

Howard shushed him and went on with the uh-huhs. There must have been about ten of them, then Howard said, "But don't the doctors . . ." and then "When?" and a bunch more uh-huhs. It was driving Kenny and me crazy.

"Just tell us how Dad is!" I whispered, and Howard shushed me.

"Oh, hello, operator," he finally said. "I see. Well, then, good-bye."

Then he hung up.

"What did Mom say?" Kenny asked. "How did the operation go? Is he all right?"

"No," said Howard. "They didn't do the operation."

"Why not?" I asked.

"They couldn't. Because Dad had a bad reaction to a medication."

"What medication?" asked Kenny. "What are you talking about?"

"It's called prednisone."

"But he stopped taking it over a week ago!" I said. "He had me put it on the top shelf in the bathroom so he wouldn't take it by mistake!"

"Yes, that's true," Howard said. "But that wasn't good, because he's been taking it for so long. His body had a reaction to him stopping, so they couldn't do the operation."

"So he's coming back home?" I asked.

"No, he's not," said Howard. "Without that medicine, his body shut down."

"Shut down?" I asked. "What do you mean?"

"His body went into shock. Like he's asleep, but they can't wake him up."

"They can't wake him up?" asked Kenny, starting to cry. "Is he in a coma?"

"Yes," said Howard. "But Mom said the doctors told her

not to use that word because that makes it sound bad. They think he'll wake up later."

"When?"

"They don't know. Then the operator came on the phone and asked her to put in fifteen cents and she didn't have any change, so she had to get off. But she said she'll call us later. And that we should eat the TV dinners in the freezer."

"But he'll be fine, right?" said Kenny. "I mean, this is temporary, isn't it?"

"Not exactly," Howard said. "The doctor said he'll 'probably' wake up. That means he might not." Howard let this sink in. "Comas aren't good. He might die."

I did not want to hear that, and started to cry too. I thought about how mean I'd been this morning with the Neck-O-Matic.

"But don't worry," Howard said. "He probably won't."

We stared at the phone, waiting for it to ring, but it didn't. So we stared at the Phone-O-Matic, but it didn't do anything either.

"I know!" said Kenny. "Let's listen to Dad's voice on the Phone-O-Matic!"

We all agreed that that was a good idea, so Kenny set it up. I went to the next room to dial it from the other line. It rang a couple times and then there was a loud click. Soon I heard my dad's voice.

"Hello dere! How you doin'? This is Bob talking, but I'm not really here. But don't hang up, because you're talking to me through the magic of my new invention, the Phone-O-Matic—patent pending! It's hooked up to two tape recorders, one you're hearing right now with my voice and the other I'll listen to when I get home. Now it's your turn to talk—go ahead and try it—and don't . . . be . . . frightened!"

There was a loud click as one tape recorder turned off, and then another as the second recorder turned on. It seemed like I should say something, so I said, "Hi, Dad. This is Joel. We just wanted to hear your voice. Bye."

I went back to the kitchen. "Maybe we should light the candles," Kenny said. Howard and I nodded in agreement. "And let's put the TV dinners in the oven, like Mom said." We agreed with that too. "And then, as long as we're having TV dinners, we should watch TV, while we wait for her to call. It's Wednesday—*Star Trek* is on."

"No," said Howard. "We shouldn't watch TV. We should pray."

"Let's pray first, then watch TV," said Kenny.

"No," said Howard. "We should just pray."

They turned to me to cast the deciding vote. I didn't know what to say. The idea of the three of us praying together was weird. Then again, it seemed that not praying might make God even madder. I'd been thinking all day about the little prayer I'd uttered last night asking God not to let my dad come to the assembly. He certainly wouldn't, if he was in a coma. Or dead. I didn't want my prayers to kill my dad, the way Eric Weiss's prayers may have killed Rabbi Buxelbaum. We had to do something.

"How about this," I finally said. "Let's light the candles— and say *those* prayers—then watch TV." That seemed the safest way to go, since *Star Trek* is, believe it or not, a Jewish show. Even though Gene Roddenberry isn't Jewish, the two other writers are. And the actors are Jewish. Captain Kirk—Jewish. Chekov—Jewish. And Mr. Spock—especially Jewish. You can tell because when he holds his fingers in the Vulcan greeting, he's actually making a secret Jewish symbol, called the sign of the Kohanim, the priestly class of Jews who descended from Moses's brother Aaron. It's the letter Shin—same as on the dreidel. Except on the dreidel it's bad, but here it's good, because it stands for one of the eighteen names of God. Yep, God has eighteen names, but they're actually nicknames, because God's *real* name is top secret, and no one can pronounce it, but if you *could,* you would have magical powers. When Leonard Nimoy—who plays Mr. Spock—was a kid in temple one day, the rabbi did the blessing of the Kohanim, which comes at the end of the service. Everyone is supposed to look down, but he looked up—and saw the rabbi holding his hands that way. It stuck with him, and he thought to himself, If I ever play a Vulcan on TV, I'll make that my special sign!

So watching *Star Trek* seemed to be as good as praying, or maybe better, because praying doesn't seem to work, at least when I do it.

"All right," said Howard—who also likes *Star Trek,* and kind of looks like Mr. Spock. "That's what we'll do. We'll light the candles, then pray, then eat our TV dinners while we watch *Star Trek.*"

We put our TV dinners in the oven—I got turkey, my favorite, with the foil you fold back while it cooks so the apple-cranberry cobbler gets browned. Then we set up the menorah, lit the candles, and said the blessings. Howard got out the prayer book from his bar mitzvah and announced there was a prayer for healing, which he read aloud. Kenny and I said, "Amen," but Howard wouldn't leave it there. He looked up and said, "God, you should wake up our father. So he doesn't die."

That added-on part didn't seem like much of a prayer to me. For one thing, I know that whenever Howard tells me to do something—even if it's something I already want to do—it makes me feel like doing the exact opposite. But Kenny and I said "Amen" again and nodded in agreement, then we took our TV dinners out of the oven and sat down to watch *Star Trek*. I was hoping it would take my mind off my dad, and it did—for a while. It was a great episode: Captain Kirk and Mr. Spock travel back through time so they can change history to prevent The War. As I watched it, I kept thinking that I wanted to travel back in time—to last night, in my parents' room—and say, "Dad! Take these pills! Otherwise you'll go to sleep and maybe not wake up!"

Even the *Star Trek* episode backfired, because they only succeeded in *delaying* The War, so the Nazis developed their own atomic bomb and won! It was horrible. They were trying to figure out how to fix it when the phone rang. We all ran to get it, but Kenny got there first, picked it up, then kept saying, "Uh-huh . . . uh-huh . . . uh-huh. I see."

When he finally hung up he said, "Dad's still asleep. They hope he'll wake up tomorrow. Mom's staying at the hospital tonight. She'll call in the middle of the night if he wakes up."

We sat thinking about that a while, then went back to watching TV, but by then, *Star Trek* was over. We never did find out how Captain Kirk and Mr. Spock stopped the Nazis, and finally, Kenny and Howard went to bed.

When I got to my room, I reached under my bed, where I have a shoe box with all my impromptu magic tricks, which are the ones you can do at a moment's notice. I sifted through and found my lucky deck of cards, the ones with the blue backs. Herrmann was up too, running on her wheel, so I sat next to her cage, took out the jokers, and shuffled the cards.

These are regular cards—not marked in any way. I stared at the back of the first card. "Red," I finally said, then put it to one side. The next card: "Also red," and put it on top of the first. Then the next: "Black," and started another pile.

This isn't a magic trick—though there is one that looks just like it, called Out of This World, where you choose a volunteer and they guess the color on the face of each card without looking. One by one, they go through the whole deck and, lo and behold, get every single one right. They're shocked, convinced they have psychic powers. I saw Doug Henning, this hippie magician with long hair who dresses in rainbow clothes, do it on *The Merv Griffin Show*.

But this isn't that. This is about real magic. I have tried this again and again over the past couple of months, counting each time to see how many I got right, then writing down the number on the inside of the top of the shoe box. By the simple law of averages, I should get about half the cards right. The more I do it, the closer I should get to the average of twenty-six. But here's the thing: My average is *twenty-nine and a half*. And one time I actually got thirty-eight right—my record. There's no explanation for this besides magic. And if I can believe in magic, I can believe in God.

I counted the cards. Twenty-seven right, twenty-five

wrong. Not very good, hardly better than average. But I decided to stop there. Because I *really* want to believe in magic. And I want to believe that rabbits' feet are lucky, and that Houdini the rabbit made it to that enchanted meadow, that there actually is buried treasure in the Bixby School sandbox, and that somewhere, on the far side of Chelm, someone is giving away apples.

And even if none of that is true, I really, *really* want to believe my dad will wake up.

THE FIFTH CANDLE:
Shlemiels and Shlimazels

Last night, I couldn't fall asleep. Every time I closed my eyes, I saw either red or black playing cards, then looked up to see that the red ones were held by Captain Kirk, with a sly smile on his face, while the black ones were held by Mr. Spock, who never smiles but just says "Highly illogical," which the whole business with the cards was. Whenever I opened my eyes, I saw the ceiling of the den, which is covered with glow-in-the-dark paint and phone dials and bits of tape, all the rejects from Omni-Glow.

I decided to try reading myself to sleep, and pulled out *Zlateh the Goat*. I turned to my favorite story, "The First Shlemiel," which is about—you guessed it—the first Shlemiel. That's another one of those great Yiddish words. It makes your mouth feel like it's chewing on a bagel. When I was a little kid I asked my dad what it meant. He thought for a moment, then looked it up in *The Joys of Yiddish*.

"It says 'a shlemiel is someone who falls on his back and breaks his nose.'"

That didn't make much sense to me, so he added his own explanation. "The shlemiel is the one who spills the soup. And the one who the soup lands on—that's the shlimazel."

Now I had two words I didn't understand, so he explained. "A shlemiel is someone for whom everything goes badly. Everything he tries fails, everything he touches breaks."

"Okay," I said. "Now I get it. So what's a shlimazel?"

"A shlimazel," he said, "is a shlemiel who's down on his luck."

Since then I've been trying to sort it out—and hoping against hope that my dad, while he may *look* like a shlimazel, and *act* like a shlimazel, isn't *actually* a shlimazel. Because shlemiel stories have happy endings, but shlimazel stories never do.

"The First Shlemiel," which I've read a hundred times, explains that there was a first shlemiel, who lived in the village of Chelm with his wife, his baby, and a rooster who slept under the bed. Shlemiel was really lazy, and wanted to do nothing more than eat and sleep, so Mrs. Shlemiel did all the work, selling vegetables in the marketplace. One year, for Chaannakah, she made a pot of delicious jam to have on their latkes. Jam may not seem like a big deal to you, but it was a rare treat for the Shlemiels. The problem was that she didn't want Shlemiel to eat the jam, and she knew that if she simply told him not to eat it, he'd end up eating it—because he was a shlemiel, and that's what shlemiels do. The house was tiny, and there was no place to hide it, so she came up with a plan. As she was going to work she said, "Shlemiel, I have three things to tell you, very important."

"What's that, Mrs. Shlemiel?"

"First, whatever you do, don't let Baby Shlemiel get hurt."

"Of course, Mrs. Shlemiel! I won't let the baby get hurt. What else?"

"While I'm away, don't let the rooster out of the house! If you do, he'll run away."

"Of course!" said Shlemiel. "And what's the third?"

"Last night, while you were asleep, I stayed up and made a pot of poison! It's up there on the shelf." She pointed to the jam. "Whatever you do, don't eat the poison!"

"My dear Mrs. Shlemiel," he said. "You need not worry about me eating the poison. I may be a shlemiel, but I'm no fool!"

With that, she went off to work, sure he wouldn't eat the jam.

And what do you think happened? Everything that wasn't supposed to.

When Baby Shlemiel took a nap, Shlemiel went to sleep too, and began to dream. But in his dreams, he wasn't just Shlemiel—he was Shlemiel the King! King of Chelm, king of Poland, king of the world! How did such a shlemiel become king? In this case, he had a magic dreidel, and whenever he spun it, it landed on Gimel, so he won, and won, and won, until he was so rich, they made him king.

Wonderful as his dream was, it was just a dream, and right in the middle of it, the rooster woke up and began to crow. To Shlemiel, who was asleep, the crowing sounded like a bell—and in Chelm, when there's a bell, it means one thing: fire! He jumped up to see where the fire was, and knocked over Baby Shlemiel's crib. Baby Shlemiel fell on his head and started screaming. When Shlemiel heard the screaming, he was sure there must be a fire, so he ran to the window and opened it up. But there was no fire outside, just falling snow. Then the rooster flew out the window—gone! Shlemiel tried to call him back, but it was pointless—like looking for last winter's snow, as the old saying goes. Meanwhile Baby Shlemiel was still screaming, so Shlemiel picked him up and sang him the Shlemiel lullaby.

Finally Baby Shlemiel went back to sleep. But now he had a big bump on his forehead.

Oy! thought Shlemiel. *I've done everything Mrs. Shlemiel told me not to do! I let the baby get hurt—and now he has a big bump on his head. She told me not to let the rooster out of the house—and now the rooster's gone. Everything I do is wrong. I'm just a shlemiel.*

He was so miserable that he decided such a life was not worth living. And do you know what happened then? That's right. He ate the poison, which, of course, was actually jam. But he didn't know that, though he did think it was surprisingly delicious for poison. He finished it off, then he lay down to die. But he didn't die—he drifted off to sleep, dreaming he was Shlemiel the King.

That must have been when I finally fell asleep, because the next thing I knew it was morning. I heard Howard and my mom talking in the kitchen.

"What else did the doctor say?" asked Howard.

"Well, there were three of them," said my mom. "Dr. Kaplowski kept shaking your dad, saying that he should wake up any minute. But Dr. Robbins said he wasn't so sure, that he knew of cases where patients go into shock and never wake up. Then the third doctor, whose name was Hardy, took out a safety pin and stuck it in your father's arm to see if he'd respond."

"Did he?" asked Howard.

There was a pause. "Well, not exactly. But . . . I'm sure he will soon."

I got out of bed and went into the kitchen.

"Good morning, Joel. How did you sleep?"

She looked more tired than I'd ever seen her. "Fine," I lied. "Dad's still in a coma?"

"Well, the doctors don't like to use that word. They prefer to say he's asleep, just not waking up. Dr. Hardy says he might even be dreaming."

"Dreaming? That's good, right? So when the dream ends, he'll wake up?"

"That's what the doctors hope. Maybe some time today. But they also said that the longer he sleeps . . ." She stopped herself, and changed the subject. "Joel, what would you like for lunch today?" I could see she was packing some food in a paper bag—cottage cheese and rye bread and bologna. "Should I make you a sandwich?"

This was freaky. She hadn't made my lunch for three years.

"When are you going back?" I asked.

"Pretty soon. I just need to get a few things."

"We should go with you," said Howard.

"No," she said. "There's nothing to do at the hospital but wait. Besides, you shouldn't miss school."

"But we're not doing anything in school," I said. "We haven't done anything all week. We should go to the hospital to be with Dad."

That's what I *thought* I should say, so I did. But I sure didn't want to go. Like I've told you, hospitals are my least favorite places in the world—next to buses. The only thing worse would be a combination bus and hospital, a "buspital," so you could be stuck in a waiting room *and* traffic at the same time.

"Or maybe I should just stay home," I said. "And wait for you to call." But that didn't feel right either. What would I do? Sit around and watch reruns of *The Beverly Hillbillies*? Pray during commercials?

Kenny came in from his paper route. "Is Dad out of his coma?" he asked my mom.

"No," said Howard, answering for her. "He's still asleep. And don't call it a coma."

"But he *will* wake up," said Kenny. "Right? From the thing that's not a coma?"

"We can't be sure," said Howard, settling into the role he loves, boss of the family. "So we all have to keep praying. I'm going to bring my prayer book to school and pray during recess."

"That's right," said my mother. "You should go to school, like normal, and try not to worry. I'll bring the telephone numbers of the school offices, and lots of change this time, and the moment your father wakes up, I'll call from the pay phone."

With that, she took her bag of food and drove off. Kenny and Howard rode their bikes to school. I fed Herrmann.

"There's nothing to worry about," I lied. "He'll be fine."

I stepped outside to the tiniest hint of a chill in the air. Really, it would only feel cold to you if you had just been sitting by a fire and then went outside wearing no clothes at all. It wasn't a winter maybe-it'll-snow chill, but rather a summer enjoy-this-tiny-hint-of-coolness-while-you-can-because-it's-going-to-be-hotter-than-hell-today chill.

That's why I was so surprised when I looked at the barometer and saw that the needle was still between 29 and 30, right on the edge of SNOW.

I realized the stupid thing hadn't budged since I'd started checking on the first night of Qchanukkah. I don't know what it read before then, because I'd never bothered to look at it. I thought maybe the needle was stuck, so I tapped the glass cover. No movement. I tapped harder. Nothing. I hit it. Nothing. Finally I pounded it with the ball of my hand—and it shattered. A big shard of glass cut right into my palm, and the next thing I knew blood was running down my wrist onto the AstroTurf.

I got so mad, I kicked the wall, which was stupid, because now my foot hurt along with my hand. Trying not to drip blood everywhere, I went back inside, washed off my hand, found the hydrogen peroxide in the bathroom cabinet, and poured it onto my palm. It burned like crazy, but it's what you're supposed to do so you don't get an infection. Then, with my other hand, I tried to put on a Band-Aid, but it wouldn't stick. There's some kind of surgical tape you're supposed to use, but we didn't have any, so I got cotton balls and masking tape and wrapped it around, which made me look like a mummy in progress.

When that was finally done, I went back outside to clean up the broken glass, and used the hose to wash the blood off the AstroTurf. I looked at the barometer needle up close and saw it was completely rusted, bent back and actually stuck to the cardboard where the numbers were written. It hadn't barometered anything in years. Luckily, the needle hadn't punctured my skin when I'd broken the glass, because then I could get lockjaw, which is what happens when you get cut with a rusty piece of metal. Then you can't speak or eat because your jaw is stuck and you end up in the hospital waiting to die. Maybe they'd put me in the bed next to my dad.

Staring at the broken barometer, I realized what a complete idiot I had been for ever thinking it would snow. Or believing in miracles. Or in God. Or anything.

Walking to school, I was angrier than I'd ever been, at everyone and everything, even my dad. That felt really bad, because if he did die, I would feel even worse than I already did for asking God not to let him come to the assembly, which is probably what put him into a coma in the first place. Just my luck, the only prayer of mine God has ever heard.

I was angry at my mom too, which was mean *and* impossible. I can't be mad at her, because she's so absurdly nice. I was *definitely* developing a gorgle, and could feel it starting to throb.

I kicked a rock, which flew across Kimdale Drive. That felt good, so I looked for another, bigger rock, and kicked it too, as hard as I could. Big mistake. Because it wasn't actually a rock, but a hunk of cement, sticking up from the ground. It didn't move at all, and now my toe hurt so much, I was hopping around on one foot.

That's when I figured out who I was the *most* mad at.

God.

That's right, God. What had I done other than say I didn't like chopped liver, and just this once would appreciate a miracle instead?

"Oh," says God. "You don't like your plate of chopped liver? Well, then, have some more. In fact, have a lot more. Don't forget, you little shlimazel, I rained plagues down on Egypt, and I can rain chopped liver down on you. Here's a bucketful! Don't you realize I'm God almighty? I can unleash a flood of chopped liver upon you, the likes of which the world has never seen! I made every living creature, every cow and chicken and goose, and I can chop up *all* their livers and bury you in it, so that every breath you take is chopped liver, deep and dark and disgusting, and all you can do is beg! And you know what you'll beg for? Chopped liver! You'll say, 'Oh, God, sorry I wasn't more grateful for the chopped liver I had! If you'll just give that back to me, I'll eat it all and lick the plate! I'll eat a whole Nixon's head of chopped liver—and every other president too—a Mount Rushmore of chopped liver, and never ask for another miracle!'"

I was just about to kick another rock but stopped myself, as I was already limping. When I finally arrived at school I noticed that the big sign in front had been changed. Since the beginning of the year it had said JOIN THE PTA! but now it read MONDAY DECEMBER 20! WINTER HOLIDAY ASEMBLY! MERRY XMAS!

I stood there on one foot, staring at all the exclamation points. It was like the first one was supposed to make you forget that you had to come to school on a day when you should have been on vacation, the second was to keep you from noticing the missing *s* in *assembly,* and the third was to make it all sound exciting. And the word *Xmas*—how do you even say it? Do you pronounce the *x,* like *X-ray*? If it's *Christmas* without the *Christ,* is it okay for Jews to say? Christians talk about Jesus Christ all the time but aren't supposed to say it when they're mad. That's why Larry Arbuckle's dad shouted "Jesus H. Christ!" when he was using a wrench to hammer a nail and accidentally hit his thumb. Adding the *H* makes it somehow okay.

There are all kinds of games religions play with themselves. We Jews have plenty. Like my family keeps *kind of* kosher, mostly by not eating bacon. We do eat something called Bac-Os Bits, which *look* like little pieces of bacon and *taste* like bacon and may actually *be* little pieces of bacon. I suppose I could check, but if I did, and found they *were* bacon, I would have to stop eating them. And I really like bacon, so I try not to think about it.

Everyone who knows anything about kosher knows that pigs aren't kosher. But it turns out lots of things *are* kosher that you'd never want to eat—like locusts, which are completely kosher, boiled, baked, or fried. I haven't tried them, but I bet they're crunchy. But no matter how many kosher locusts you eat, it doesn't make up for eating pig—or shrimp, which is also not kosher. Unless you eat it in a Chinese restaurant—like the one we go to, called Five Wonderfulness—where it somehow doesn't count.

As I was looking up at the sign, thinking about Bac-O-Bits and Jesus and Chinese food and trying *not* to think about my dad, lying in the hospital in his shock dream that we weren't supposed to call a coma, I spotted Amy on her bike, down

177

the street, headed right toward me. She was the *last* person I wanted to see, or rather, the last person I wanted to see *me*, after the world's most embarrassing magic-turned-dancing lesson. I limped around the corner and down the hallway to the basketball court, where I found a four-on-four game in progress, with no one waiting to play, which was good. That meant I could stand on the edge of the court, hoping no one else showed up.

I like basketball a lot. The problem is that I'm no good at it. I know all kinds of things about the game, and can name all the starting players for the Lakers: Jim McMillian, Gail Goodrich, Happy Hairston, Jerry West, and Wilt "The Stilt" Chamberlain. But it's one thing to understand the game and another entirely to play it, especially for me. I'm short, and neither dribble nor shoot very well, which is what basketball is all about. The best I can do when I get the ball is try to pass it to someone else. If I do get stuck with the ball and end up taking a shot, I have to hope that it hits the rim, at least. If it doesn't, everyone shouts "Air ball!" When that happens, you have to chase the ball and hand it over to the other team. I've thrown plenty of air balls. Only once have I ever made an actual basket, and that was just dumb luck. And now, with my bandaged hand and hurt foot, I would be even worse.

Not wanting to be seen by anyone—especially Amy

O'Shea—I stood behind the pole that holds up the basket, concentrating as hard as I could, willing myself to become my new favorite superhero. Silently, slowly, unseen, I transformed into Normalman. His superpower? You guessed it: He's normal.

He looks normal, with a regular boy's haircut, no distinguished-looking glasses or braces, and a last name that doesn't embarrass teachers when they say it. He's tall, good-looking, and strong, the sort of guy girls look at and say, "He's cute!"

Normalman never goes around feeling like he's too awkward to live. He has a normal family in a normal house, and a dad who stands tall and healthy and has no big schemes, just a normal job with a normal paycheck. Normalman and his dad have a great time. On weekends they go out and throw the football around, just like normal fathers and sons.

Normalman has all kinds of special powers. He's popular and fits into any group. He knows which rocks to kick, and he never does things that are dorky. He can dance without looking like he's having a seizure, and even enjoys it. In fact, Normalman has a girlfriend, the beautiful Amy O'Shea. After school they walk to the soda fountain to buy root beer floats, which he pays for with money from his normal after-school job at the corner grocery store. She's amazed by how normal he is, and wants to see his merit badges—the medals he gets for being normal—though he's a bit reluctant to show them off.

"Aw, shucks," he says in his smooth, deep voice. "It's not a big deal. I'm just a normal guy." But she insists and so, with a sigh, he brings them out.

"This one is for getting a haircut that doesn't make me look like a dork. Here's one for having straight teeth. These three are a set—the first is for not *saying* stupid things, the second for not *doing* stupid things, and the third for not *believing* stupid things. Here's one I got for not standing up at a school assembly and making a fool of myself."

"Wow!" she says. "What about this one here? It's beautiful!"

"That's for not whispering a prayer that puts my dad into a coma."

"Cool! And what about this one—it's huge!" Amy says, picking up a large, shiny gold medal.

"Oh, really, that's nothing—"

"It says it's for 'life-saving.'" Her eyes open wide. "Did you really save someone's life?"

"Well, yeah, but it wasn't a big deal. Heck, anyone would have done it."

"Who was it?"

"Nobody, really."

"Please, tell me!"

"All right. It was that kid Joel. You know, the funny-looking one, short, with glasses and braces—and that last name."

There's a look of recognition, then a snort of laughter before she stops herself. "You saved his life? How?"

"Well, he was dying of embarrassment, too ashamed to be on the planet, poor guy. So I just, kind of, well, you know, saved him."

"That's amazing! But how?"

And then he smiles his normal smile. "That, I am afraid, is a secret I cannot reveal."

And you know why he can't tell? Because every superhero has a secret identity. Superman can't tell Lois Lane he's Clark Kent, Batman can't say he's actually Bruce Wayne, and Peter Parker certainly can't let anyone know he's Spider-Man. Normalman's secret? He didn't just save that kid Joel—he actually *is* Joel.

"Hey! You gonna play or what?"

"Huh?" I said. "What?"

Eddy Mazurki had shown up, meaning I'd have to play. The team that was losing got first pick, and they chose Eddy, of course. I stopped dreaming about Normalman and started looking for someone on my team I could pass the ball to if it came to me. I was glad to see Ricky Romero, who is actually *good* at basketball. My plan worked, except for the last time, when I passed to Ricky but made the mistake of being open, and he passed the ball right back to *me.* I wasn't looking and—wham!—it hit me right in the face, twisting my distinguished-looking glasses all around. They didn't break, though the part that was supposed to go over my left ear now stuck out to the side. I tucked it behind my ear and went on playing, wishing the bell would ring. Then Ricky threw it to me again while I was standing at the top of the key. I wanted to pass it back to him, or anyone on my team, but no one was open. That's when the bell rang, which meant I had to shoot, because you always have to take a shot at the buzzer. Chris Carter was right in front of me, so I tried my special shot—the overhead hook, like Kareem Abdul-Jabbar, which I can sometimes make when I'm by myself.

"He sends up a prayer!" shouted Eddy Mazurki.

The ball made a perfect arc over Chris's head, right toward the basket. And then . . . over the top of the backboard. Air ball. So much for prayers.

In the beginning of *The Phantom Tollbooth,* the narrator tells how wherever Milo was, he wanted to be somewhere else. That's how I felt, except there wasn't any place I wanted to be. I just wanted to be nowhere—and well out of sight of Amy O'Shea.

But I had to be *somewhere,* so that the office could find me if my mom called to say that my dad had woken up. They would send Mrs. Gabbler, who would come running across the playground to give me the news.

"Joel, Joel!" she would say, huffing and puffing, waving a little slip of paper. "Your dad came back to life!"

Seeing Mrs. Gabbler running was something I could scarcely have imagined yesterday, and now I was counting on it. Every time a door opened I thought it might be her. I wished I had a Porta-Phone, which is another idea my dad's been working on. It sounds crazy, like something from science fiction, but he said there's no reason that telephones have to be plugged into the wall, and that someday people will walk around carrying their telephones with them on little carts! I liked the idea, but not the name—it sounded too much like porta-potty, which is gross.

It was hard to concentrate on anything today. All I could think about was my dad in his not-a-coma, maybe dreaming of dreidels, like Shlemiel. If the dreidel lands on Gimel, he wakes up. Hay—he's half alive. Nun—he stays asleep. And Shin? Well, that would be it for my dad.

I tried to think about something else, anything else. In Home Ec, we were baking cookies shaped like trees and snowmen—all the Xmas things that aren't actually Christian. I stayed toward one side of the classroom, as far as possible from Amy, and focused on decorating my cookies.

I like Xmas cookies. And fruitcake—even though people

make jokes about it. And I love the feeling you get when you're gathered with your family around the tree, warmed by a crackling fire, roasting chestnuts and opening presents, Jack Frost nipping at your nose and Tiny Tim saying "God bless us, every one!" At least, I *think* I love all that stuff— I've never done any of it. Maybe I just like it because it's forbidden fruit—like bacon.

That reminded me of something that happened last week, when my dad was driving me to the orthodontist and we were stuck in traffic, meaning we would be even later than usual. He honked the horn—and it worked! The traffic cleared up. As we drove on, he said, "Now we're makin' bacon."

It wasn't a joke, exactly, just one of those funny things he says. Or used to say.

"What happened to you?" said Brian during recess as we ate our cookies. "All during class I was trying to tell you about the new blue Corvette Stingray I saw, and you didn't say a thing! It's like you're a zombie! You limp around like one, and your glasses are all bent up. And what happened to your hand? Did you get into a fight?"

"Yeah," I said. "Sort of."

"Cool! Who was it? Just tell me, I'll beat the tar out of 'em."

"God."

"God?" he said, shaking his head. "Are you crazy? Big mistake. You can't pick a fight with God. You're on your own."

"I didn't pick a fight—God did."

"Doesn't matter. You're never gonna win. What's it about?"

"My dad's in the hospital," I said.

"Again?" he said. "Wasn't he just there a couple months ago? What are they doing? Did they forget something?"

"They're not doing anything."

"Then why did he go?"

"He was supposed to have an operation. To get his hip bones coated in gold, which would have been great. But then he went to sleep and didn't wake up."

There was a long pause as Brian considered this. "You mean he's dead?"

"Not quite. He's in a coma, but we're not supposed to say the word."

"A coma? Oh, man, comas are bad! I saw this news program about a guy who was in a coma for twelve years! And then, when he finally woke up, he died!"

"Thanks, Brian."

"Oh, sorry."

"They think my dad will wake up sooner than that."

"Maybe it'll be like Rip Van Winkle, and when he wakes up, he'll have a beard to the floor and grandchildren!" Then

Brian got this serious look on his face. "Wait a minute. If your dad's in a coma, what are you doing here?"

"I don't know."

"Shouldn't you be at the hospital, waiting for him to wake up? Or die?"

"Probably," I said. "I don't know what to do."

"Wow. Total bummer."

Brian's loyal, but not very reassuring. The bell rang and I went off to math class.

My math teacher, Mr. DeGuerre, is a square. Really. I don't just mean the kind of square that hippies talk about—though he's that too. But Mr. DeGuerre is *actually* a square, or at least his head is. He has hardly any chin, making the bottom of his face square, and a perfect flat-top haircut. Not a crew cut, like the one I got stuck with, but a little longer in some parts, so it's perfectly level. You could rest a platter on his head and it would stay. In fact, you could probably turn him on his head and balance him that way, with no hands. Then the thin black tie he always wears—with a white short-sleeved shirt—would hang down in front of his face, bisecting it, as they say in math, into two rectangles. Today, though, he was wearing a Santa hat, which stuck up like an isosceles triangle, turning his head into an irregular pentagon—with a pom-pom on top.

"All right, class," he said, standing in front of us as he shook a cup filled with dice. "As you all know, today is Thursday. If this were a normal Thursday, we would be reviewing for the test on Friday. Given, however, that this is not a normal Thursday . . ."

That's how he talks, like a machine, if a machine could talk. The whole class was looking at the cup in his hand, and we knew what was going to happen: math dice. That's this game he invented that we usually play on Fridays after the test.

". . . and because it is so close to vacation, and it is no longer possible to get you to do any work, and because someone decided that we would have school on Monday . . ."

Even though he sounds like a robot, I like him. And I like math. I guess I like him *because* I like math. That's because math is easier than everything else. You follow a bunch of rules and you get answers that are either right or wrong. If you get a wrong answer, you figure out what mistake you made, then fix it and get the right answer. The rules don't change, like they do in spelling. Nor does it boil down to opinion or propaganda, like social studies.

Best of all, math doesn't depend on God's mood. It's not like God wakes up and says "I'm tired of twenty-three and thirty-eight adding together to make sixty-one. Today, just to mess with Joel and his family, I'm going to mix it up, make twenty-three and thirty-eight add up to *seventy*-one. Let's see how they deal with it."

Nope. Math is straightforward, and so is math dice. Mr. DeGuerre divides us into teams, and we take turns answering questions. Before each round he rolls the dice; the higher the number, the harder the question. When we get to a question that no one can answer, Mr. DeGuerre always says, "Any more guesses? Or shall we ask the Computer Who Wears Tennis Shoes?" That's his nickname for me. It's from a movie a couple years back about this guy who had a super-fast brain. As nicknames go, it's not bad—and a *lot* better than my last name. But Mr. DeGuerre is the only one who uses it, so it doesn't help much. When I answer the question, my team gets the points, which is exactly the opposite of what happens in basketball. And that's why I love math dice. Usually.

But today, as he stood there shaking the dice in the cup, my mind wandered to this poster I once saw of Albert Einstein—who was, of course, Jewish. He was also really funny-looking, with hair sticking up all over the place like he didn't care. But somehow it all worked for him. Maybe that's because he was a super-genius. In the poster, though, he looked even crazier than usual, staring right at the camera, sticking out his tongue. Printed at the bottom was something he'd said: "God does not play dice with the universe."

I liked that idea as soon as I saw the poster. I thought it meant that there was an order to things, that they don't just happen randomly. If Albert Einstein said that, and he was so smart, it must be true.

Now, though, as Mr. DeGuerre rolled the dice and asked math questions, I thought about my dad in the hospital and began to wonder: What if that's *not* what Einstein meant? What if he meant that God is actually playing some *other* game?

I had already tried playing dreidel with God—that didn't work. Maybe checkers? Or One, Two—Bango? Scrabble? Or Parcheesi, which isn't that fun to play, but is fun to say.

But those are just board games. What if God is going for bigger stakes? Maybe basketball? Toss the universe in, sometimes you make it, sometimes it hits the rim and bounces out—and sometimes it's an air ball, and we go flying through space forever. Or how about mumblety-peg? Kenny showed me that game. You play it with a pocketknife that you throw down, trying to get the point to stick in the ground. If you're crazy, like Kenny's friend Danny Jarlsberg, you throw it at your bare foot, trying to get as close as you can to your toes without hitting them. Once Danny got right between his big toe and his second toe—thwack!

I know that sounds like a crazy game for God to play with the universe, but if you look around, you've got to wonder.

I suspect this is one of those truths you learn when you

grow up. Because Howard is three years older than me, I get a preview of everything that's coming up. It's not like a preview on TV, where they say "Will Batman and Robin escape from the Joker's Spinning Wheel of Death? Tune in next week—same Bat-time! Same Bat-channel!" With Howard, everything he learns becomes a secret that he won't tell Kenny or me. But unlike TV, where you have to wait until next week, we can usually trick Howard into telling us right then.

That's how I found out what happens after you *become* a bar mitzvah and are ready to learn about certain forbidden topics. I used to think that sounded really cool, until one day a couple years ago, just after Howard's bar mitzvah. Kenny and I were working on making armpit farts, and Howard walked in, all grumpy. He's always grumpy, but this was worse than usual. We ignored him and went on making armpit farts and laughing until Howard couldn't take it anymore.

"I don't think you'd be laughing if you knew what the Nazis did to the Jews," he said.

We stopped the armpit farting.

"What?" I asked.

"When?" said Kenny.

"During The War."

"What did they do?" I asked.

"I can't tell you about it," said Howard. "You're too young. But if you knew, I'm pretty sure you wouldn't be laughing."

And he stood there, silent. But Kenny and I had figured out that the way to get Howard to tell us a secret is to pretend we already know.

"Oh, yeah," said Kenny, "I heard all about the Nazis. They killed a lot of Jews."

"Yes," said Howard. "But *how* did they kill us?"

"With machine guns?" I asked.

"Yes, but that's not all. It was much worse than that."

"I know," said Kenny. "There were showers."

"Showers?" I asked. "What?" That made no sense to me, as I had just switched from taking baths to showers, which I liked.

"That's right," said Howard. "Showers. With poison gas. And when you're older, you'll learn all about it in Hebrew school. Then you won't be laughing."

There was one of those awkward pauses, the kind that seem to fill my entire life, and then Kenny said, "So it *was* showers, right?"

Howard nodded. "All the Jews were rounded up and they had to stand in a long line. They were hungry and dirty and the guards pointed machine guns at them and shot them if they stepped out of the line. But the guards said, 'It's okay. After this, you'll get a nice, warm shower!' When everyone went into the shower room, the Nazis locked the doors. But instead of water coming out, there was poison gas!"

"Hey!" I said. "That's what Grandma's always saying! So it's true!"

"No," Howard said. "Grandma wasn't in Nazi Germany. She was in Poland, years before, where they had pogroms. That's another way they killed the Jews, dragging them through the streets by their beards. But they didn't have poison gas."

Now I was all confused. And upset. I didn't want to hear any more about the Nazis killing the Jews. But now Howard was on a roll, and there was no stopping him.

"But I wasn't talking about the pogroms," Howard continued. "I was talking about the Holocaust, and you interrupted me. We saw a movie today. It's one the Nazis made. They actually filmed what they were doing to the Jews! They were going to make a museum about how there used to be Jewish people before they became extinct!

"And in the film you can see all the things they took from the Jews. There was this huge pile of eyeglasses and another big pile of teeth they pulled out because they wanted the gold fillings. The people who were still alive looked like skeletons. There were also dead bodies—and some of them were our relatives!"

"Which ones?" I asked. "Who?"

Howard shook his head. "You don't know them. I don't either. And we never will. Because they're dead."

That was too horrible to think about.

"But, like I say," said Howard, "you're too young to know about all this. I shouldn't have even told you, but I had to, because you and Kenny were laughing all the time."

It was hard to know what to say to that. I felt like I should apologize, but I wasn't sure why or to whom.

"It's okay," he said to me. "You didn't know. Because you haven't become a bar mitzvah yet. So you don't have to worry about it. You can go on being a happy kid." And to Kenny, he said, "And your bar mitzvah isn't for another year, so don't worry."

Howard left, and Kenny and I stood staring at each other, not knowing what to do. Somehow, it didn't seem right to go back to armpit farting, given what the Nazis had done to the Jews.

Until then, I had been looking forward to my bar mitzvah, even though it meant meeting with Cantor Grubnitz. I thought that it would all build up to a party where I'd get checks—and tons of gifts!

But Howard had tipped his cards, something a good magician never does. Now I understood. Your bar mitzvah was the end of your childhood. I could picture the scene with Cantor Grubnitz standing in front of us bar mitzvah kids. "I hope you all enjoyed being children," he would say, "because that's over. And now it's time to tell you about the horror and suffering of the Jewish people."

Then he would turn off the lights and play the film. And I would watch relatives I had never known—and would never meet—standing in line to take showers of poison gas, thinking, *Wow, childhood was awful! And that was the good part?*

So maybe it's not dice or board games or basketball that God plays with the universe. Maybe it's *bowling*—and we're the pins. God steps up to the line, rolls the ball down the lane, and then . . .

"So, we've finally stumped the computer?"

Everyone was staring at me, waiting.

"Well, well," said Mr. DeGuerre. "This is a first."

On the chalkboard was a long equation filled with fractions and symbols and x's and y's. I could have figured it out. But, really, I thought, *Who cares?*

"The computer isn't even going to hazard a guess? What does it all add up to?"

"A perfect strike," I said.

Tough as it was to stay focused in math class, I had no problem staying wide-awake at Hebrew school.

For one thing, my heart was pounding because I was—yet again—late. It's not like anything important or interesting ever happens in Hebrew school, but the problem is Cantor Grubnitz, who stands out in front of the temple, smoking and looking at his watch until it's exactly 4:15. Then he snubs out his cigarette, goes into class, and closes the door, screaming at anyone who comes in even a minute later.

And you know why I was late? You got it: the bus. On Thursdays there's no carpool, so I have to run from school to catch the bus a couple blocks down in front of the 7-Eleven store. If I run fast enough, I can get there in plenty of time—the number 257 is supposed to come at 3:42. *Supposed to.* Usually, though, it doesn't. Sometimes it comes much later.

Today, I got there right on time and the bus arrived just a minute later, which was perfect. There was no traffic, and hardly anyone got on or off, so we even went through some green lights. Then, about a half mile from the temple, the driver pulled over to the side of the road and waited.

I thought another passenger was coming, but I didn't see anyone.

The light turned from green to red and back again. And again. And again.

"Why are we stopped?" I finally asked.

"We have to. I'm running ahead of schedule."

"What?" I said. "But you came to my stop right on time."

"Nope," said the driver, shaking his head. "I got there early. There was another 257 that was supposed to come but didn't."

"Why not?"

He shrugged. "I don't know. All I know is that my orders are to wait here until we catch up to the schedule." He looked at his watch. "Shouldn't be long—just another ten minutes."

Great. That would get me there just after 4:15. The temple was about ten blocks down the road, and I figured that if I ran, I might just make it. But my foot was still sore from this morning, so I ended up jog-limping all the way to the temple. When I got there I pulled out my watch: 4:18—three minutes late. Just then I heard the honk of a horn and looked up to see the stupid bus zipping past, the driver waving at me. My whole Quasimodo run had been pointless.

I peeked through the window of the classroom, where I could see that Cantor Grubnitz had already begun. He had written the four Hebrew letters of the dreidel on the board, and when he turned around to write more, I saw my chance. Opening the door quietly, I snuck into an empty desk. Just as I did, he turned back.

"So, you see," he said, "an Israeli dreidel has one letter that is different." He pointed to the board, where he had written another four letters below. "The dreidels you play with have Nun, Gimel, Hey, and Shin, for *Nes Gadol Haya Sham*—Hebrew for 'A Great Miracle Happened *There*.' The lower four letters are what you would find on a dreidel in Israel: Nun, Gimel, Hey, and the letter Pey instead of Shin, for *Nes Gadol Haya Po*—'A Great Miracle Happened *Here.*'

" 'Here' means Jerusalem, which is where the Kchkanukkah story took place. But maybe you're wondering what kind of miracles happen here, where *we* live? For example, maybe you're thinking—like I am—that it would be a miracle if once, just once, Joel got to class on time." Everyone turned back to look at me and laugh. Cantor Grubnitz picked up a pen and opened his roll book to mark me tardy. But then he stopped, put down the pen, and smiled.

"No. I've changed my mind. Today, Joel, I am not going to mark you tardy. And you know why? Because Hannuukkaahh is a joyous time, a time to celebrate. You can think of this, Joel, as my gift to you." He paused, waiting for me to say something, but I just stared at him.

"What's the matter, Joel? You don't look very happy." His smile turned to a frown. "You should be happy. And yet, you're not. Maybe you want a bigger gift? Is that it? That's the problem with you kids. You're all greedy. When I was young, we were happy to get a few pennies, maybe a handful of almonds and raisins. Then we would sing and dance and celebrate a great miracle—the victory of the Maccabees! The rededication of the temple! We have a God who works miracles! And we get to study them! So you should be happy."

I could see his gorgle starting to swell.

"You kids nowadays think it's all about the presents you get, like race cars and transistor radios."

I heard Sidney Applebaum whisper "Yes!" Since the beginning of the year the class has been playing Transistor Radio Bingo, based on guessing how many times Cantor Grubnitz will say the words *transistor radio* on any given day. Everybody puts in five cents, and the one who guesses the total wins it all. I usually like it, and once I even won, but today I couldn't have cared less.

"Or even worse than transistor radios, one student came to my office wanting me to pray for gold!" The class laughed, but no one seemed to know it was me. "Can you imagine? Praying for gold! So enough of your greed and selfishness!" he said, now looking right at me. "Be happy! It's a mitzvah!"

I had no problem not being happy for Cantor Grubnitz. He can cry in his soup, for all I care. My mom, though, is another story. This evening when I got home from Hebrew school she was as miserable as I've ever seen her. I could tell because of how cheerful she was acting.

"What's cookin', good-lookin'?" she said when I got home. That's what she always says to me. Just from her tone, I could tell my dad hadn't woken up, and there was no point in my asking her. "How was Hebrew school?"

"It was fine," I lied. "We celebrated Kchchanukkah."

"That's nice," she said, taking a carrot loaf out of the oven. That's a special recipe of hers, made with carrots and rice and eggs. It tastes better than it sounds.

"Oh, look!" I said. "You made carrot loaf! Great!"

What's even weirder than my mom pretending to be happy is that I do the exact same thing. The happier she acts, the happier I act, and it just keeps going like that, until my face hurts from smiling. I can't help myself.

Kenny, on the other hand, wears his heart on his sleeve, and as we ate dinner, there was no question how worried he was.

"Can't the doctors do something to wake him?" he asked. "Like make a loud noise? Or shake him?"

"Well, they've tried. And they're doing the best they can," said my mother. "Hopefully he'll wake up tomorrow."

"But what if he doesn't?" said Howard. "What if he dies?"

There was a long pause, and my mom looked like Howard had punched her in the gut.

"Well, we just have to hope for the best."

"And pray," said Howard. "Maybe Dad's asleep because we haven't prayed enough." He looked at Kenny and me. "I know I've prayed a lot. Maybe you two haven't prayed enough."

"I've prayed more than you," said Kenny.

My mom looked like she was about to collapse. "I know!" I said. "Let's light the menorah. Then we can *all* pray."

I found six pretty good candles, and chose the longest, a yellow one, for the shammes. My mom lit it, and the three of us took turns lighting the others. Howard read his special prayer for healing. Then, just before we started faking our way through "Maoz Tzur," Kenny discovered something on the box of candles.

"Hey, look!" he said. "The words to 'Maoz Tzur' are right here on the box! In English *and* Hebrew!"

He was right. Not only were they in English and Hebrew, but they were in *Hebrish,* which is Hebrew words spelled with English letters. I had never thought about the words before. Even though the song's about a rock, it's supposed to be about God, who always comes through, especially when things are looking bad.

Yeah, right.

"This gives me an idea," said my mom. She brought the box of candles to the den—my room—and we followed her to the corner, where we have this really old upright piano she used to play when we were kids.

"See, it even has notes!" She put the box on the music holder, opened the piano, and began to play. It took her a couple tries to get the right notes, and the piano was way out of tune. Some of the keys buzzed when she hit them, and a few didn't make any sound at all. None of us have very good voices, and we're embarrassed if we have to sing in public, so we usually mouth the words, even when we're *not* singing about Jesus. Now, though, Kenny and Howard sang out loud with my mom. I didn't feel like singing at all—especially about rocks. My foot still hurt, and the first time through I just kind of mumbled. But then something kicked in—I don't know what—and when the Hebrew came around, I sang out loud, as my mom somehow figured out ways to avoid the keys that didn't work. The third time through, we all sang as loudly as we could, so even God could hear us.

When my mom reached the end of the song, we all stopped, listening to the fading echo of the piano. Even after they'd all gone to bed, I could still hear it.

"Is that what you want, God?" I asked. "Just the four of us down here? And my dad up there, your own personal shlimazel?" I shook my head. "Send him back. Please?"

No response.

I wonder if God's in a coma too.

THE SIXTH CANDLE: Sucker Bets

For just a moment when I awoke this morning, I thought it was summer vacation. The air was hot and stuffy, and my sheets were clammy.

Then I remembered everything. No matter how hot it was, this was the dead of winter and my dad was in the hospital. I jumped out of bed and ran to the kitchen to see if there was news.

"Mom?" I called.

There was no one home. Kenny and Howard were both gone, off to school already, and on the kitchen table was a note: "Joel—Went to the hospital. Cream of Wheat on the stove. I'll call if your father wakes up. Love, Mom."

Sure enough, there was Cream of Wheat on the stove. Lumpy and cold. Outside, I could see heat lines rising from the asphalt, which gets soft on really hot days. The sky was "hazy," as the weatherman likes to say, which is a euphemism for "smoggy." Amazing to think that I'd begun this Ckhanukah believing it would snow, imagining I'd be building snowmen and making snow angels. Now it was so hot that even a *thought* of snow would evaporate.

As I picked out lumps from the Cream of Wheat, I realized what I was: a sucker.

That's someone who falls for a cheap trick. I always keep a list of "sucker bets" with my impromptu magic. They're not real magic tricks—more like a cross between an illusion and a crank phone call, like Kenny's friend Danny always makes. He'll dial a number and say, in his deepest voice, "This is the telephone company. We'll have a repairman working on your phone line for the next half hour. If anyone calls you during that time, it is very important that you do not answer the phone—or they could be electrocuted!"

Then he waits for exactly twenty-eight minutes and calls the same number. It rings. And rings. And rings. And rings. After about fifty rings, they finally pick up.

"Hello?"

And that's when Danny screams as loud as he can.

Prank calls are pretty mean, so I don't do them. Sucker bets are kind of mean too, and I only do them when I have a heckler. That's someone who thinks they know how the trick is done and shouts it out to everyone. When that happens, the only thing to do is invite them up for a sucker bet.

"Sir," I'll say, "you seem very smart. In fact, extremely smart. I know, because I can read your mind. To prove it, I'd like you to take this pad of paper and this marker, stand way over there where I can't see you, and write any word you want in big letters. Meanwhile, I'll stand over here and write something on this pad of paper. And I will bet you one dollar that, whatever word you write, I will write the exact same word."

The heckler will go for it—they always do. I put down my dollar, they put down theirs, and then they walk to the far side of the room and hide the page to be sure I can't see. I hide what I'm writing as well. Then, when they've finished, I put down my pen and say, "All right—you've written your word. Want to raise your bet?"

They'll usually go for that too, maybe even up to five dollars, or ten if the audience cheers them on. Then, when their money is on the table, you have them turn their pad over, and you see they've written something like "lasagna" or "gymnasium" or "Mississippi." They stand there with a big grin.

I smile back, and say, "Believe it or not, as promised, I have written the exact same word." That's when I turn my pad around and show them: "THE EXACT SAME WORD." The audience will laugh, and the heckler will grumble—and lose.

I have a bunch of bets like that: Tie a Knot Holding Both Ends of the Rope, Walk Through a Playing Card, and The Shell Game, which is a classic sucker bet you've probably seen. There are three walnut shells you slide around and the sucker has to guess which one has the little pea hidden under it. They think they know—but they don't. After each sucker bet I ask the heckler if they want to go double or nothing. I always win, of course, and when we've gone four or five rounds, and they're getting really mad, I always tell them, "Keep your money." Then I whisper, "But don't spill the beans."

It's one thing to get stuck on the losing side of a sucker bet. But what's worse is to fall for it again. And again. And again. Like I had this whole Kchanikah, starting with the Gimels. And the snow. And the prayers, I thought as I stepped outside and into the blast of heat. You know what I was? A sucker. Not just a sucker—a shlimazel.

I suppose that's why, halfway down Kimdale Drive, I turned around, ran back home, and reached under my bed to grab the shoe box marked IMPROMPTU. I pulled out the list of sucker bets, which I put into my backpack. If there were going to be sucker bets, I was sick and tired of being the sucker. Then I decided to take the whole shoe box, with the rope for "The Professor's Nightmare," a deck of marked cards, my lucky deck of unmarked cards, flash paper, a pair of scissors and the thingamajig for The Cut and Restored Necktie, and a bag with fifty bronze coins for a trick I've been working on for Sunday's show called The Miser's Dream.

With that, I headed to school. My backpack was heavy now, especially with all the coins. A couple years ago, Shell Oil ran a contest, which they called States of the Union, but was really their own version of the shell game. Whenever you got gas from a Shell station you also got a little white plastic package with an aluminum coin. On the coin was a picture of one of the fifty United States. The idea was to collect them and if you got all fifty, you'd get five thousand dollars! The problem, of course, was that some coins were really hard to get. Nearly impossible, we found.

But it wasn't for lack of trying. Each time we stopped for gas, my brothers and I asked for a coin for each of us, maybe another for good luck, and one for our little sister, who we explained was sick at home with typhoid fever. One guy heard that and gave us a whole box. And you didn't have to fill up the tank; you'd get just as many coins for putting in a gallon of gas, which is only thirty-five cents. So we would go from one Shell station to the next, buying a gallon here, a gallon there.

Before long we had hundreds of aluminum coins. There were tons of some—"Shoot, another Nevada!"—while others were really hard to get, especially Delaware—that single coin stood between us and five thousand dollars. So my dad, being the kind of guy he is, wondered if it was the same at Shell gas stations all over the country. Maybe, just maybe, there was somewhere with plenty of Delawares but no Nevadas. So he took out classified ads in newspapers around the country, offering to pay twenty dollars for a Delaware coin.

The ads were in the papers for a while, and then this guy in Chicago wrote to say that he actually had three Delawares! You do the math—that's fifteen thousand dollars! Enough to pay off the medical bills for my dad's last operation *and* all the loans my parents had taken out since then. My dad called the guy, long-distance, and talked to him. He was legit! So my dad airmailed him a money order for sixty dollars, and tossed in a bunch of Nevadas we had lying around.

Then we waited. Two weeks later, we got the package. We were so excited when we opened it—and out came three coins.

Connecticuts.

Connecticut? Who needed Connecticut? We had dozens of Connecticuts.

We never did win the prize. And the guy never did send my dad's money back. In fact, all we got for our efforts was one "instant winner" prize: a set of fifty bronze coins, one for each state. It seemed like a booby prize at the time. Neither Kenny nor Howard wanted the coins, so I got them. Now they jingled in my backpack, another sad souvenir of my dad.

Because while stories have happy endings, I thought, life doesn't—especially if you've ever done anything you shouldn't have, like utter the wrong prayer or lie about a little sister with typhoid fever. The best you can hope is that something turns out to be not quite as horrible as it could have been, and when that happens, you call it a miracle.

But even that doesn't happen very often. In fact, it's rarer than a Delaware coin. Because God, the great magician, evidently doesn't like heckling. And *loves* sucker bets.

When I got to school I saw that the sign had been changed. Someone must have found a bunch of extra *s*'s and exclamation points, because now, below WINTER HOLIDAY ASSEMBLY, it said SPECIAL SECRET SURPRISE!!!!!!

As I stood there puzzling it out, the bell rang, and I tried to remember which class I had first. God might not play dice with the universe, but I'm pretty sure that Mr. Newton plays dice with the schedule, because today we had classes in an order that we'd never had before, with Home Ec first. Luckily, all the girls, including Amy O'Shea, were in the music room next door, practicing Christmas carols—or, rather, "winter holiday songs"—for Monday's assembly, which I didn't even want to think about.

That left about a half dozen of us boys in the classroom, which felt like the inside of an oven. Mrs. Hernandez opened a window, but that made it even hotter. A stick of butter she had brought out for a cooking project had completely melted.

"Boys, it's too hot to cook," she finally said. "Do whatever you want, as long as you don't get in trouble."

Nobody wanted to do anything but argue about how hot it was.

"It's so hot in here," said Larry Arbuckle, "that we should turn on the oven to cool down!"

"It *is* on!" said Eddy Mazurki. "And it's not helping."

"It's even hotter than summer," said Billy Zamboni.

"No, it's not," said Eddy. "It just seems that way because it's winter and it's supposed to be cold."

"No way, Jose!" said Billy. "You just think that because the heat has baked your brain! It's so hot outside that you could actually fry an egg on the sidewalk."

"That's just an expression," said Eddy. "You can't really do it."

"Yes, you can!" said Billy.

"No, you can't!"

This went back and forth for a while, driving everyone

crazy, before Mrs. Hernandez finally said, "Enough!" She went to the refrigerator, brought out an egg, and said, "Give it a try."

Mrs. Hernandez likes experiments, especially those involving food. Earlier in the fall Jimmy Bowen came in from the cafeteria with a rock-hard grilled cheese sandwich, which everyone calls Bixby Brick-and-Rubber. Everyone was tossing it around the room like a Frisbee when Billy Zamboni said he thought we could put a stamp on it and mail it. To our surprise, Mrs. Hernandez took it from him and said, "Let's find out!"

She took a stamp from her desk drawer, made labels with the school's return address and her home address, then pasted them all on. Mary Wigglesworth agreed to put it into the mailbox near her house on the way home from school. Sure enough, a week later, Mrs. Hernandez brought it to school, the stamp postmarked and everything. Given the success of that experiment—and the fact that it was just too hot to stay in the classroom—frying an egg on the sidewalk seemed like a good idea.

"But if anyone sees you, don't say I gave you permission."

We went outside and gathered around a burning hot spot on the cement. Larry cracked open the egg.

Nothing. Just gooey egg spreading out, running downhill.

"Try again," said Billy Zamboni. "Look—it's even hotter on the asphalt!"

We grabbed a second egg from the classroom and went out to a spot on the asphalt by the tetherball pole that was never in the shade. Larry cracked another egg. Nothing.

"It needs oil!" he said. "You can't fry an egg without oil!"

We sent Jimmy back to class to get oil and another egg, then tried it again. Still nothing.

"Butter!" said Larry. "Everything fries better in butter!"

As they tried to fry eggs—almost a dozen of them—they switched from arguing about the heat to complaining about the dress code. An eighth-grade boy had been sent home because his hair was three and a half inches long, and another girl had been sent home for wearing something called culottes. It turns out they're a cross between pants and a skirt, but have too much pants in them for the Bixby dress code.

I kept out of it, listening instead to the girls practicing Christmas carols, which is what the songs are no matter what you call them, just like a coma is a coma. They sounded really good. I could just make out Amy O'Shea's voice and found myself singing along with them, under my breath.

The truth is, I kind of *like* Christmas carols, and I'm not the only Jew who does. After "I'm Dreaming of a White Christmas," they sang "Rudolph the Red-Nosed Reindeer," the Christian version of "The Horrible Song." And who wrote it? A Jew named Johnny Marks. Then they sang "Let it Snow," by Sammy Cahn and Jule Styne, both Jewish. The whole time we were out there trying to fry eggs—which never worked, by the way—the choir sang only one Christmas song that *wasn't* written by a Jew, and that was "O Tannenbaum," which is German for "O Christmas Tree." But even *that's* Jewish, because Tannenbaum isn't just a Christmas tree, it's also a name, and as Jewish as you can get. My mom has a bunch of cousins in Cleveland, half of whom are actually *named* Tannenbaum, so go figure.

When the bell rang for recess, it was too hot to even complain about how hot it was, so we all stood around the drinking fountain pouring water over our heads. Talk turned to the fact that this should have been the last day before vacation, but wasn't, and how horrible it was that they were making everyone come on Monday.

I had figured that most kids would just find ways not to come, even if attendance was mandatory. But it seemed that everyone was planning to be there, because of the "surprise" they'd been promised. The rumor mill had been grinding along.

"I heard that anyone who shows up will get their grade raised one letter in any class they want," said Billy Zamboni.

"No," said Arnold Pomeroy, "it's better than that. I saw a

stack of report cards on Mrs. McGillicuddy's desk. At the end of the assembly they'll hand them out to everyone who comes, with pencils and erasers, so we can change the grades before our parents see them. It'll be far out!"

Yeah, I thought. And they're giving away free apples too.

I spotted Amy across the way, and even though she was talking to a gaggle of girls, I was worried that she might see me, so I snuck off to this secret place I know, a little alcove behind the back door of the wood shop. The door is blocked from the inside by the drill press, so no one ever opens it.

Even though it's in the shade, it was still about a hundred degrees. I sat on a cement step and leaned back against the door, my shirt soaked in sweat. Reaching into my backpack, I pulled out my impromptu box. I took a coin from the bag and produced it from different places—my ears, my mouth, thin air—then threw it into an imaginary bucket. That's the one part of the trick I'm missing—Berg's Studio of Magic sells a silver-plated Miser's Dream bucket, with a hiding place for extra coins. But it's thirty-five dollars, which is out of the question, so I'll be using a coffee can.

I was working on rolling one coin across the back of my fingers, which is really hard, when I heard a voice say, "So, is that it? Am I fired?"

I looked up. It was Amy O'Shea. Great. The one person in the world I least wanted to see—and she looked upset.

"What?" I asked.

"If so, I'd rather you just tell me," she went on, "so I can start looking for another job. I have to feed Daisy."

What was she talking about? And how did she even know where to find me?

"So, that's it. You're firing me, right? As your assistant?"

"No," I finally managed. "Why would I do that?"

"Because . . . of Wednesday. You were so mad at me. After the magic lesson."

I stared at her, truly baffled. She was wearing a Santa hat with a giant peace button on it. It was a crazy thing to wear on such a hot day, but she looked cool as could be. Don't girls sweat?

"So I'm not losing my job?" she finally said.

"Amy . . . I wouldn't . . . No, of course you're not fired. You're the best assistant ever."

"Then . . . why have you been avoiding me?"

"Wait . . . Avoiding you? No. Why would I do that?" I may be a good magician, I thought, but I'm a crummy liar.

"You know, you're not a very good liar," she said.

How does she *do* that?

"Tell me about it," I finally said. "And I'm a rotten dancer too."

"I don't know about that," she said, cheering up. "Dancing is something you learn to do."

"Yeah?" I said. "Well, I never did."

"What you need is a good teacher—and the right music."

"Like what?"

"Not Herb Alpert, that's for sure," she said. "Kind of square, you know? I have a better song—and dance—for the ABC blocks. I can show it to you and we can do it in the act instead of that . . . um . . . other thing you—"

"Okay, okay, show me," I said, not wanting to relive the Tevye incident.

"All right, then, stand up." I did. "First, move your head forward and back like this." I did that too. "Now bend your elbows and flap your arms, like wings." It felt silly, but she was doing the same, so it was okay. "Now kick your legs out and cluck. And look, you're dancing the Funky Chicken!"

Sure enough, I was dancing—with Amy! And we were laughing. "Your feet start kickin', that's when you know," she sang, "you're doin' the Funky Chicken!"

After a few minutes we just stopped and stood there, and I realized I still had my fingers in my armpits. I was hoping she didn't notice how dorky I looked, when she leaned in close and whispered, "There's this secret . . ."

"Secret?"

"About what's happening on Monday . . ."

Oh no! I thought. How does she know? I took my fingers out of my armpits.

". . . at the assembly."

"But wait," I said. "How did you—"

"Joel!"

We both looked up. It was Mrs. Gabbler.

"There you are," she said, out of breath. "I've been looking all over for you." She gave Amy a look, then me. "There's a phone call for you. In the office."

It wasn't far from my hiding place to the office, but it felt like a long way. Even though I was running, everything seemed to happen in slow motion.

When I got to the office, there was Mrs. McGillicuddy at her desk, pointing to the phone, which was off the hook. I picked it up.

"Hello?"

"Joel?"

There was a long pause. I could hear my mom crying.

"He's awake!"

When I got to Mr. Culpepper's trailer, I was already late, but I stayed outside rubbing my eyes so no one would know I had been crying. My mom told me that she'd been sitting there staring at my dad for hours, when he suddenly woke up and asked for a glass of water, like nothing had happened. She was going to pick up a challah from Canter's Deli, then swing by the house to get Hanaka and Shabbat candles, pick up Kenny and

Howard at the high school, then zip by Bixby to pick me up.

"And we'll celebrate Shabbanukkah!" she said. That's my family's special name for the Friday night of Haanukkah, which is also Shabbat.

I still looked like I'd been crying, so I soaked my whole head in the drinking fountain, shook the water out of my hair, and went inside.

I needn't have bothered. Nobody noticed how late I was or cared how I looked. The room was complete chaos, with students running around screaming. Not only was it the last period on Friday, but Mr. Culpepper's trailer has its own separate air-conditioning, which he must have set to "refrigerate." Everyone had sprung to life, like the hanging plant in Mrs. Skurvecky's class that gets all wilted when she forgets to water it, then perks up when she finally does. The boys were literally bouncing off the walls, which were made of this spongy foam. I actually saw Eddy Mazurki take a running start, throw himself against the wall, fall on the floor, and hobble around.

"Whoa!" he said. "That's far out!" Then he did it again.

"Wicked!" said Larry Arbuckle. "Me too!"

Mr. Culpepper isn't a magician, but he'd be a good one, because he always has something up his sleeve. For a while he just stood in front of the class, cool as a cucumber, watching the pandemonium. Then his lips began to move, but we couldn't hear what he was saying. After about a minute, everyone took their seats. We had to get really quiet, and could just make out the words ". . . of course, it's supposed to be a secret."

We all stared at him. He was wearing a red-and-green cardigan and a blue tie with a snowman on it. Finally Patty Henderson raised her hand, and when he motioned to her, she whispered what everyone was wondering. "What's the secret?"

Mr. Culpepper smiled and, still whispering, said, "Well, I'm not supposed to tell you this, but I know what's going to happen at Monday's assembly."

Now the room was dead quiet, no sound but the whoosh of the air conditioner. I couldn't believe he was doing this. I shook my head, in tiny motions, my eyes wide open. I knew he could see me, but he didn't stop.

"I'm really not supposed to tell," he whispered. "But it's so tempting, especially because it involves someone here, in this very room."

How could he spill the beans? I looked around the room, pretending I didn't know *exactly* who he was talking about. My eyes met Amy's, who looked as panicked as I felt.

What the heck?

"That's the thing about a secret," Mr. Culpepper whispered. "It's no fun unless you tell someone." Now he looked right at me—and winked! "Of course, you would all have to promise not to tell a soul outside of this classroom."

Everyone nodded their heads. I was trapped. I tried disappearing into my seat, which never works. Then Amy raised her hand.

"Yes, Miss O'Shea. Would you be able to keep this secret?"

"Well, yes," she said slowly. "But first, um, I was just going to say that I really like your sweater." The class laughed.

"Thank you, Amy. It was a gift from my aunt Matilda from Baltimore, which she sent just last week." Then he lowered his voice and said, "So, once the choir finishes singing—"

"Yes, it's a beautiful sweater," she said, interrupting him. "And your tie," she went on. "It's a really nice tie. I especially like the snowman."

That was a bit much. Everyone laughed again. What was she doing?

"Thank you again," he said, looking at his tie. "I'm glad you—"

"But it looks like there's something *on* the tie," she interrupted again. "Right there"—she pointed—"just above the snowman."

"Where? What?" he said, looking down at his tie, flustered.

"It looks like a stain," she said. "Could it be gravy? Or maybe mustard?"

Everyone stared at her, then at Mr. Culpepper's tie, then

back at her, baffled. No one in the room had any idea what she was doing. Except me. Now I knew *exactly* what she was doing. And she was doing it for *me*.

It's a magic routine we do. You invite a volunteer from the audience—who happens to be wearing a tie—and compliment him on how nice it looks. But then you point out there's a stain—"Could it be gravy? Or maybe mustard?"—and offer to remove it. It doesn't matter that there's really no stain; it's below their chin, and hard for them to see. Besides, they're too surprised to think about it when you bring out a big pair of scissors—like the one Amy knows I keep in my impromptu box. She must have seen it in the alcove.

"Miss O'Shea, why are you interrupting—"

"Well...because...I just thought...maybe it's gravy. Or mustard?" she said again, hopefully.

There was a long pause while everyone stared at her. She had nothing else to say. In fact, no one in that room had anything to say, except me. I stood up.

"Mr. Culpepper," I said. "I can fix that."

Everyone turned from Amy to me.

"Joel, what are you—"

"Don't worry about that stain," I said, reaching into my backpack for the box. "I've got something here that will make your tie as good as new." I opened the box. "Ah, here it is!" I said, taking out the scissors—and the secret thingama-jig that makes the trick work.

"Whoa!" said Denise Scalapino. "What are you doing?"

"Are you crazy?" said Eddy Mazurki.

There was no turning back. I walked to the front of the class, sweating again despite the air-conditioning, and lifted up his tie, pretending to examine the spot—which wasn't really there. Mr. Culpepper just stood there, dumbfounded—the way every volunteer does—as I lifted the scissors.

"Joel, what are you doing?"

"Don't worry, Mr. Culpepper, this won't hurt a bit."

"W-wait a minute . . ." he stammered.

I folded up the middle section of the tie. "Could you hold this?" I asked. He did. You can get a volunteer to do almost anything, because they're in shock.

Then I made two quick clips with the scissors—snip! snip!—just as Mister Mystery had taught me, and held up the piece of fabric I'd cut from the middle of the tie as Mr. Culpepper stood there holding the rest of it.

The class was stunned. I waved the piece of fabric around. Mr. Culpepper stood there holding his folded-up tie, with his mouth wide open.

"And don't worry about this," I said as I rolled the fabric into a little ball and pushed it into my fist. A moment later I opened my hand—and it was gone.

"May I?" I held up the tie, rubbed the spot I'd folded, then let go. His tie unfolded, in perfect condition, onto his chest.

"See?" I said. "Good as new. And look! No stain!"

Not that there ever was one.

He stood there blinking. A moment later, the bell rang. With a whoop and a holler, the class was out the door. And so was I—my secret safe, at least until Monday.

My family is always late. In fact, my brother Kenny was late to his own bar mitzvah. They actually started without him. That's because of my dad, who always tries to fit in one more thing. In that case, it was stopping for batteries for the tape recorder so he could record the ceremony. We did get them—on sale. As far as I know, though, Kenny has never listened to the tape, and isn't likely to, as the recorder is now part of the Phone-O-Matic. But my mom is pretty much always on time, and this afternoon, as I ran out of Mr. Culpepper's class to the sidewalk, she was there, with Kenny and Howard already in the car. I jumped in like it was a getaway car, and we made a dash for the freeway to beat the rush-hour traffic.

If you've ever seen pictures of Southern California, they're probably from way over on the other side of Los Angeles, of beautiful people at the beach soaking up the sun and surfing. You can almost hear the Beach Boys singing, "Catch a wave and you're sitting on top of the world."

That's what we were trying to do: catch a wave. Not the kind in the ocean, but a wave of traffic. The idea is to time it so you're just *ahead* of the crest, pushed along by millions of cars.

Sure enough, we glided onto the freeway, the open road before us, and behind us a great mass of cars—all those who had missed the wave.

"That's great!" shouted Kenny. "We're beating the traffic! Drive faster, Mom!"

"That's illegal," said Howard, from the front seat. "We could get a ticket, or get into an accident."

The air conditioner in the Dart is broken, but with the windows open, the breeze felt cool. As I looked through the hole in the floor, the freeway passed by in a blur, faster than I'd ever seen it before.

We were "one step ahead," as Mister Mystery says. "That's what makes a great magician. Of course, your audience thinks you're *way* ahead, doing all kinds of impossible things. But, really, it's just *one* step."

Houdini was always one step ahead. His greatest trick, after the Water Torture Cell, was Metamorphosis. He would have members of the audience come onstage and lock him in handcuffs, bind him in chains, then put him into this big bag, which they would tie up and lock inside a trunk. Then, his wife and assistant, Bessie, would stand on top of it, lifting up a long round curtain that covered her and the trunk. She would hold it over her head and count "One!" then lower it. She'd lift it again—"Two!"—then lower it. Then she'd lift it one more time, but this time you'd hear *Houdini* shout "Three!" The curtain would drop to the floor, and instead of Bessie standing on the trunk, it was Houdini! Bessie had disappeared.

Then the volunteers would unlock the trunk to find the bag, still tied. Inside the bag would be Bessie, chained up exactly as Houdini had been. The crowd would go berserk.

What made the trick amazing was how quickly it all seemed to happen. But, actually, they were just one step ahead. The moment the bag was tied, Houdini escaped from the handcuffs and chains. As soon as the trunk was locked, he freed himself from the bag. And by the time Bessie lifted the curtain, he was out of the trunk. The second part of the trick worked exactly the same way except it was Bessie who stayed one step ahead as she snuck into the trunk, the bag, the chains, and the handcuffs.

And now we were one step ahead, riding the wave of traffic to Los Angeles. There we would see my dad and celebrate Shabbanukkah, and on Saturday we would bring him home to rest and recover. But no way would he ever be well enough to come to school on Monday. And without him, I might just survive the assembly—an escape worthy of Houdini.

Inside the hospital, it was even colder than Mr. Culpepper's trailer. Nurses were wearing winter coats, shivering in the lobby, which was like an echo chamber. Even though the floor looked perfectly clean, there was a guy pushing around a polishing machine to make it even shinier. He wore a Dodgers cap and sunglasses, bopping around to music only he could hear.

We took the elevator to the sixth floor, and it was just as we got out and started walking toward my dad's room that I began to feel afraid. Excited as I was to see him, I remembered how every other time he'd gone to the hospital, he had come back looking weaker, older, sicker. So I tried to picture him in my mind, on the bicycle, healthy and tall, like Normalman's father.

We opened the door to his room and found him in bed, snoring, his mouth wide open, drooling. His head was turned toward his shoulder, and he looked like a bug that had been trapped by some scientist and pinned down in a glass case. His three false teeth were out of his mouth, in a cup next to his bed. Even though he was asleep, his glasses were on his face, but they were crooked.

"He's sleeping," said my mom, "but it's just regular sleep. Not—you know . . . Bob?" No response. "Bob? Hello? I have the boys . . ."

Nothing.

"Dad!" Howard called out. "We're here! We came to visit you!"

My dad didn't say anything for a long time, and I began to wonder if he actually had woken up. But then my mom pushed on his shoulder and said again, "Bob? Wake up! The boys are here!"

A moment later he opened one eye, then looked from Howard to Kenny to me.

"Who dat?" he said. "Is dat my boys?" The other eye opened, and there was a big smile on his face. "My three sons?"

That was kind of funny, because *My Three Sons* is a TV show we sometimes watch, except that the dad and those three sons are normal.

"Hey, Dad!" said Kenny. "You're awake! Just in time for Shabbanukkah!"

"Shabbanukkah?" he said. "Shabbanukkah already? I must have been asleep. Oy, was I sleepy! I was so sleepy . . ."

"You weren't just asleep," said Howard. "You were almost dead! But you're awake now. And look!" He held up a paper bag. "We brought you the menorah and candles!"

"And Manischewitz!" I said.

"We got a fresh challah too!" added Kenny, pulling it out of his backpack. It had been under all his books, so it was smashed flat. But as we watched, it began to reinflate.

I looked at my dad, who seemed to perk up as well, happy that we were there.

Howard put the menorah on the narrow table they roll up so people can eat in bed, and Kenny jammed in six candles. Unlike me, he really doesn't care about the color or the order or which one is the shammes. Meanwhile, Howard set up the Shabbat candles. It's funny about Shabbat. When I was little we used to celebrate it every Friday night, lighting the candles, drinking the wine, blessing the challah. Then it kind of stopped. Maybe that was why God was so mad at us? That seems a bit silly, but who knows, when it comes to God? Anyhow, on Shabbanukkah, we always light the Shabbat candles.

With all the problems his body was having, my dad's mouth worked just fine, and he was chatty as could be, about his time in the hospital, the nurses, and the food. Then, suddenly, he said, "Hey, Father! Are you there?"

I didn't know who he was talking to—I thought maybe God. But then he said, "Knock-knock, you there? Father Joseph, I want you to meet my boys!" He motioned to a curtain in the middle of the room, and said, "Pull that aside, will ya, Joel?"

When I did, there was an old man with gray hair and the thickest eyebrows I've ever seen lying in bed. He was bruised and bandaged, hooked up to all kinds of tubes. Hanging above his head was a large cross. He waved at us.

"Boys, this is Father Joseph. We've spent the morning trading jokes."

Looking at Father Joseph, it struck me that whatever he was there for was no laughing matter. For one thing, he had a hole in his throat. I knew what that was: It's what can happen if you smoke and get cancer and your throat gets all messed up so they have to cut a hole in your neck for you to breathe. It's called a tracheotomy. The horrible thing is that some people with a hole in their neck keep on smoking—by sticking the cigarette right in the hole! They actually showed us a movie about it in Health Ed class, where a guy blew smoke right out of his neck. It gave me nightmares.

Father Joseph put his finger over the hole in his throat, then spoke to my dad.

"Well, well . . . three fine young men!" he said. He had a thick brogue, but sounded kind of mechanical, like an Irish robot. "How proud you must be!"

"That's right, Father Joseph," said my dad. "That's Howard, my oldest, Kenny, the middle, and Joel, the youngest. And you know my wife, Gladys."

"Yes indeed," he said. "We had quite a nice visit while you were asleep."

"Yes, we did, Father Joseph," said my mom. "How are you today?"

"Well, I can't complain, ma'am, saints be praised," he answered. That struck me as an odd thing to say, because by the looks of him, if there was *anyone* who had a right to complain, it was Father Joseph.

He covered the hole again. "And which one of you three fine young men is Joe?" he asked. "And would that be short for Joseph?"

I raised my hand. "Actually, it's Joel," I said.

"Ah! Jo-el," he said. "It means witness to God! Well, Jo-el, let me tell you, your father is a fine man—and a good room-mate to have in the hospital. He's kept me in stitches since he woke up."

"Not that you need more of those, Father!" said my dad. Father Joseph laughed. Or, rather, he whistled through his throat, which was creepy, but funny.

"Of course, he didn't say much the first day I was here," said Father Joseph. "In fact, for a while there, we thought he was going back to Jesus."

"We don't believe in Jesus," said Howard. "He would have gone back to Moses."

There was more whistling laughter from Father Joseph. "Well, whomever he'll meet in the hereafter, I'm glad he's here now, because he makes me laugh, and laughter is the best medicine. Bob, tell them what you did this afternoon, when you woke up. Oh dear, that Claudia is not pleased with you, is she?"

My dad's face lit up. "So this morning the nurse came in to get a urine sample. You know, when you're in the hospital they're always doing something to you, taking your blood pressure, or your temperature, or having you pee in a cup. Sometimes they wake you up to give you sleeping pills! Evidently, they hadn't been able to wake me for a couple days, and they're making up for lost time. So this nurse, Claudia, came in and said she needed a sample. She left a cup on the table and went out of the room." He tried to shift to a more comfortable position, then gave up. "Well, I didn't have anything to give—sometimes you gotta go, sometimes you don't. But on the tray I saw a little container of apple juice that came with breakfast, so I just poured some into the sample cup. A couple minutes later Claudia came and got it. Just as she was walking out the door, she said, 'Something about this sample doesn't look right.'

" 'Lemme see,' I said, and she brought it back to me. I held it up to the light and said, 'Well, it looks okay to me! But if you want to be sure, I'll run it through again!' Then I drank it!" My dad started laughing, and so did we.

"The look on her face was priceless!" said Father Joseph.

By then Kenny had set up the candles for Shabbanukkah,

and Howard, who considers himself Mr. Junior Rabbi, took charge.

"We light these candles to commemorate miracles in the days of old," he said, like he was making a speech.

"Oh yes, son," said Father Joseph. "I know all about the Maccabees, Books One *and* Two. You'll find them only in the Christian Bible—in the Apocrypha."

My mom struck a match, and we took turns lighting the candles, singing the blessings quietly. But when we got to "Maoz Tzur," the same thing happened as last night. We sang it out—loud. Maybe because now we actually knew the words. "Rock of ages let our song/praise thy sheltering power . . ." As we sang, a couple nurses came into the room, looking kind of confused, as well as the dancing janitor we had seen polishing the floor downstairs.

"We should say the Shehecheyanu," my mom said, once we'd finished singing. To Father Joseph she added, "That's the blessing to thank God for bringing us to this point in time."

"To be sure," said Father Joseph. "Let's hear it, then."

I guess we were inspired by him, and by the fact that our dad was alive, because we sang louder. As we did, other people who must have been visiting patients started to come in, like it was a party, and soon there were almost a dozen people in the room. Some even knew the words, so they must have been Jewish, and others hummed along.

"Tonight is also the Sabbath," announced Howard. "The Jewish day of rest."

Father Joseph nodded as my mom lit the Shabbat candles. These blessings have a different melody than the ones for Chahanukah, and we always mix them up. But now it didn't seem to matter.

Then Kenny brought out the bottle of Manischewitz, which is this extra-sweet wine that Jews drink for holidays. Some people love it, some hate it—I like it, even though it tastes like cough syrup. He poured some into a kiddush cup, which he brought to my father, who held it up and sang the blessing. Then he drank some, licked his lips, and said, "Man-O-Manischewitz!"

By now there must have been about fifteen people in the room, including a couple of doctors. Kenny held up the challah and started the next blessing. A lot of people joined in, and when we finished, he passed it around, saying, "Everyone take some! Just pull off a hunk!"

That's when Claudia came in. You could tell it was her, because she looked mad, her face all scrunched up.

"What's going on?" she said. Then she spotted the candles. "There are no candles allowed in the rooms. You'll have to blow them out!"

There was a long awkward moment while Kenny, Howard, my mom, and I all looked at one another. That may be the hospital rule, but blowing out these candles is something you just don't do. It's not like birthday candles, where you make a wish and blow them out. The whole point of Ckakanukah candles is that they're *supposed* to stay lit. Same with Shabbat candles. And even if you do blow them out, it's never supposed to be because someone tells you to. Only tyrants make you blow out candles.

"You need to blow them out," she said to Howard.

As we stood there, facing off, I had an idea. I reached into my backpack.

"Well?" she said again. "Someone please blow them out. Or do I have to?"

"Claudia," I said, stepping forward, "these aren't just any candles." She was shocked that I knew her name. "These are Chckahnukkah candles—so they're magic!" With that, I waved my hand, and a ball of flame appeared over the menorah—then disappeared. Everyone gasped and applauded. Flash paper is a wonderful thing.

"You see, Chhhhanukah is a time of miracles!" I said, not at all sure that I believed it. "Like, it's a miracle that our dad woke up." A couple of nurses nodded, and Father Joseph covered the hole in his throat and said, "Saints be praised."

"It's a time when dreams come true," I said, pretty sure this was a complete lie. I had simply learned to swallow chopped liver without gagging. "Take my father! Who knows if, while he was asleep, he dreamed he was a rich man? Like Tevye!"

Jewish or not, everyone knew who Tevye was. *Fiddler on the Roof* is the one thing everyone knows about Jews. "Look!" I said, pointing to a spot just above the menorah, where the flash had been. Suddenly, a coin appeared at my fingertips. More applause, and I was into my routine for the Miser's Dream.

I snapped my fingers and began to hum the melody for "If I Were a Rich Man." A couple people hummed and clapped along with me. "Yidel-deedle-didel-yidel-deedle-didel-deedle-dum!" The only thing missing was the bucket. I stood there with a coin, wondering what to do next. And then I saw something on the counter: a stainless-steel bedpan. Still singing, I walked over and picked it up. It was empty! Saints be praised, I thought. One step ahead! I tossed in the coin—clang! Perfect. Even better than the professional bucket. A moment later, another coin appeared at my fingertips.

I trotted around the room, singing the song and pulling coins from everywhere, tossing them into the bedpan. I pulled coins out of the faucet in the sink, from Kenny's ear, and from under a Shabbat candlestick, tossing each one into the bedpan.

"I wouldn't have to work hard!" I sang. "Yabba-dabbayabba-dabba-dabba-dabba-dabba-dum!" I walked up to one of the doctors who was watching, lifted up his right arm, then pulled it forward, like a slot machine—and three coins came out of his left elbow. Now everyone was singing along and clapping their hands. Father Joseph was the most enthusiastic and—though I can't believe I did this—I pulled a coin out of the hole in his throat. "Praise Jesus!" he said.

"Moses," Howard corrected.

Everyone was loving it but Claudia, who did not look happy. I got to the part in the song about discussing the holy books with the learned men, then marched right up to her and sang, "That would be the sweetest thing of all!" I patted her on the back, and a half-dozen coins fell out of her nose. Everyone cheered, and even Claudia smiled.

Finally, when I came to the end of the song, I stood by my father's bed, shaking the bedpan, which sounded like it had fifty dollars' worth of coins, and belted out, "If I were a wealthy maaaan!" With that, I turned the pan over onto my father's head. Everyone gasped again—and out poured confetti.

There was loud applause—and whistling, from Father Joseph. The loudest applause of all was from my dad. "My son the magician!" he said, and everyone cheered.

When that finally died down, my dad cleared his throat to make a little speech.

"As you may know," he began, "I've been asleep for a

while. I'm told it was almost two days, and they wondered if I would ever wake up. And yet, as my youngest son, Joel, the magician, says, Chhanukkah is a holiday of miracles."

The room got quiet.

"But that's not all!" he said. "On Monday, the last day of Chchchanukkah, Joel will be making a special presentation at his school's holiday assembly! And they've invited our family to light the menorah in front of the whole school!"

People clapped. My mom beamed.

"I was supposed to be there, dancing on my new golden hips. But, as they say, 'People make plans, and God laughs.'" He paused for a moment. "The doctors said I should rest in bed for at least a week."

And thank God for that, I thought.

"But I said, 'Rest? Who needs rest? I've been sleeping for days!'

"'Yes, you have,' they said, 'but you certainly won't be able to walk for some time.'

"When I explained the situation to the folks in physical therapy, including Jose here," he said, motioning to one of the guys in the room, "you won't believe what he did!"

Now Jose stepped forward, smiling.

"Jose, will you do the honors?" my dad asked.

"With pleasure!"

Jose helped my dad to sit on the edge of the bed, then

reached behind the curtain and pulled out a beat-up old aluminum walker.

"Ain't she a beauty!" said my dad, pointing at it like he'd just bought a brand-new Cadillac. "And would you look at the feet!"

There, on the bottom of each front leg, was a tennis ball. But they weren't the normal tennis balls people put on the bottom of walkers to help them slide. These were fluorescent green!

"Jose has connections!" said my dad. "He knows someone who works in a sporting goods store, and they just got these in! You are looking at the only walker in Los Angeles with Day-Glo tennis balls!"

Jose helped my father up from the bed to stand behind the walker. When he turned around, his butt showed for a moment through the hospital gown, but no one said anything. He was as proud as could be. "Just wait until the kids at Bixby School see this!"

"What?" I asked. "Wait—you're coming to the assembly?"

"Like I said, Joel—I wouldn't miss it for the world!"

THE SEVENTH CANDLE:
The Rest of the Matzoh

"So I still don't get it," said Brian. "If they're matzoh balls, why are they red?"

Once again, he had completely missed the point of the trick. I was practicing my sponge ball routine, making them appear and disappear in all kinds of cool ways. I even turned a round red ball into a black square. But from the moment I said, "And now, the Magic Matzoh Balls!" he kept interrupting me.

Explaining things to Brian can be frustrating. He's always interested, which is good, but when his mind gets stuck on something, it won't let go, and he'd been fixated on matzoh since last Passover when I'd brought it in my lunch. He was curious, so I had shown him how it has dotted lines, but never actually *breaks* on those lines, and when you *do* break it, you always end up with a bunch of crumbs. He wanted to try it, so I gave him a piece. He chewed it and said, "It tastes like nothing."

"Yeah," I agreed. "And if you're not careful, you end up eating the cardboard box, because you can't tell the difference."

"You're right," he said, eating some more. "So why do you eat it?"

"It's kind of a long story," I'd said, figuring he'd let it go. But he didn't.

"Yeah? Tell it to me."

I explained how the Jews had been in Egypt, and left in a hurry, so they didn't have time for the bread to rise. He kept on asking me questions until I ended up telling him the whole story, about the plagues and the parting of the Red Sea and everything else. Since then, he keeps asking me if I've got matzoh for lunch. I explained that you only eat matzoh during Passover—why would anyone eat it any other time?

As for Brian's interruptions this morning, I suppose I brought them on myself. I had asked him over to watch me practice for tomorrow's show at my grandmother's nursing home. I wanted to make it a dress rehearsal, so I put on the white tuxedo jacket and black pants I bought last year, and even clipped on my bow tie. I must have grown since then, because now the jacket was really tight and the pants were high-waters. I pulled them down as far as I could and stood on the base of the stairs leading to the living room, while Brian sat on a bridge chair. It was so hot that I was sweating before I began. I'd made us a whole large can of frozen orange juice—one part concentrate to three parts water—and we had nearly finished guzzling it before starting the rehearsal.

My plan was to tailor the patter to my audience, like Mister Mystery says. I figured that everyone at the nursing home was Jewish, and it was supposed to be a Honiqa show, so I had come up with ways to Jewishify my tricks, and even used fluorescent tape on my suitcase to write the words CHAPPY CHANUKAH! The sponge balls had become The Magic Matzoh Balls. Aladdin's Vase—where you pour out water until it's empty and then, a minute later, pour out more, and keep doing it through the show—became The Bottomless Oil Jar, though Brian said it didn't pour like real oil. For the first trick, where Herrmann magically appears in a fancy-looking wooden cage, I realized I had enough room in the secret compartment for a couple of dreidels. I also changed her name from Herrmann to Maccabee, which I figured she wouldn't mind, given that she already had a boy's name and no idea what it was.

"Ladies and gentlemen, meet Maccabee, the dreidel-playing rabbit! Whenever he spins, it lands on Gimel—

because he's so lucky! You can tell he's lucky because he has all four of his feet!"

"Hold on!" said Brian. "Wait a minute. What happened to Herrmann?"

"This is Herrmann," I said.

"But you just said it was Maccabee!"

"Maccabee's a nickname."

"Really? For Herrmann?"

That's how it went with every trick. Brian wasn't heckling me, at least not on purpose—he was just asking a bunch of questions.

"Look, let's just pretend they're matzoh balls, okay?"

I had Brian playing the role of all the volunteers. He had closed his hand around the matzoh ball, and I was about to wave my magic wand over it so it would turn into two balls, but he wouldn't shut up about the color.

"Maybe it's food coloring?" he asked.

"No, Brian, it's just—they're not really matzoh balls. It's . . . a metaphor."

That didn't help. "What's a metaphor again?"

"A metaphor is like a simile," I said, "only different. All right? Look, can I just do the trick?"

"Okay. But just one more thing about matzoh balls," he said. "Tell me again about Marilyn Monroe."

Brian loves my jokes, and when he hears one he likes, he

wants me to tell it again and again. This is his current favorite. He has a poster in his room of Marilyn Monroe standing over an air vent in New York City, with her dress blowing up all around her.

"All right," I said. "I'll tell you about Marilyn Monroe—and then, can we go on with the show?"

"Deal."

"So, Marilyn Monroe got married to Arthur Miller, the super-brilliant playwright, who happens to be Jewish. She went to his family's house for the Passover Seder, where they had—"

"Matzoh ball soup!" he said.

"Right. The next day you know what they had?"

"Leftover matzoh ball soup!" he said.

"Right again. And the next day, the same thing. Finally, after three days of eating matzoh ball soup she said 'Isn't there any other part of the matzoh you can eat?'"

Though Brian had heard me tell that joke a half-dozen times, he laughed like he was hearing it for the first time, and orange juice came out of his nose.

"That's so cool!" he said. "Marilyn Monroe was super-sexy, and could have married anyone, but she liked the smart, funny-looking Jewish guy!"

"Yep!"

"Just like Amy O'Shea likes you!"

"No way," I said. "She doesn't *like* me. She's just my assistant. It's just a job for her. So she can buy food for Daisy."

"Maybe," he said, "but whenever I see her, she's with a group of girls, giggling about something. I think she's telling them how much she likes you. Where is she, anyways?" asked Brian. "Shouldn't *she* be here practicing?"

"She can't come tomorrow—she had to go be with her dad, in San Bernardino. That's why you're here, so I can get used to doing the tricks alone. And I could do that if you would stop interrupting—"

"I wish I was funny-looking. And Jewish."

I stared at him. "I think that's the dumbest thing you've ever said, which is saying something. Now that I've told you about Arthur and Marilyn—again—I want to show you a trick I made up especially for this show."

It was the Menorah Card. First I forced a card on him— the nine of diamonds, though he didn't know it was a force. Then, instead of just telling him what it was, I pulled out this rolled-up banner from my hat, faced backward for the big reveal, then turned around.

"Whoa!" he said, counting. "There are nine diamonds! But that's the card I picked! And it looks like a Jewish watcha-ma-call-it!"

"Menorah."

I was pretty proud of it—I'd worked hard with markers

to make each diamond look like a flame for each of the eight candles and the shammes.

It took some time, but we got through the finale—my biggest illusion, the Square Circle. There's a big box with a hole cut in the front so you can see a tube inside. You show the audience that both the square and tube are empty, and then—Alakazam!—you produce a ton of things: streamers, scarves, feather boas, pretty much whatever you want, ending with Herrmann—or rather, Maccabee. That trick seemed like a good place to Jewish-up the show, so I renamed it the Holy Temple, and figured out a way to produce more dreidels, candles, and even the string of letters, which had lost some, so it now read HAPPY HANUKK. The challenge would be loading all that stuff in—especially Herrmann— without Amy O'Shea. But I managed to do it, and Brian was really impressed.

Afterward we sat on the front porch. Howard had locked himself in his room to study, and Kenny was over at Danny Jarlsberg's house. My mom had gone to the drug store to buy the medicine my dad would need this afternoon when we brought him home from the hospital. On the way we would celebrate by eating at Canter's Deli—my favorite restaurant in Los Angeles—where we would also get my dad some chicken soup so he'd recover faster. Meanwhile, Brian and I sat on the AstroTurf drinking more orange juice—

we'd finished off the first pitcher, so I'd made another—and complaining about how hot it was.

"Winter or not, this is the hottest it's ever been," said Brian.

"Yeah," I said. "It's so hot that when the dogs chase the cats, they both walk."

He made the sound of the rim-shot—"ba-da-bum!"—then added, "It's so hot, you can fry an egg on the sidewalk!"

"Nope," I said. "You can't. Because by the time you crack the egg open, it's already hardboiled."

That was a new one. He laughed, and then, out of nowhere, asked, "So, have you given up yet?"

"What?"

"Your fight."

"What fight?"

"The one you picked with God."

"Oh, that," I said. "You were right."

"Told ya. You got your butt kicked, didn't you?"

"Yeah, kind of. I guess I got off okay. At least my dad's not in a coma. But I'm not even sure if I believe in God."

"Well, that's your problem right there!" said Brian. "No wonder God's on your case. You want to keep God happy, you need to go the other way. Be even more Jewish. Maybe wear one of those beanies."

"They're called yarmulkes."

"Whatever they're called, you need to wear one."

"Yeah, right. I already feel like I walk around with a neon sign saying JEWISH! Wearing a yarmulke would make it flash. No thanks. It's bad enough that my dad's planning on coming to school on Monday..."

The moment the words were out of my mouth, I realized what I'd done. I watched Brian's face slowly rearrange itself into a question mark.

"Hey," I said, trying to distract him, "you just reminded me of a great joke. There's this Jewish guy with a long beard and sideburns named Shloimi. For his whole life he's dressed in a black coat, a hat—the works. Then on his fiftieth birthday, he decides to go for a whole new look. He goes to a barber and says, 'Take it off—the beard, the sideburns, all of it. Gimme a crew cut!'"

Brian wasn't buying it. "Monday? Why would your dad come to school on *Monday*?"

"Then Shloimi goes into a clothing shop. Instead of the usual black suit, he buys a red-and-white checkered jacket, with a pair of purple pants! And white shoes!"

"Monday," Brian said again, scrunching up his face. "This doesn't have anything to do with the assembly, does it?"

"Shloimi is a whole new man! He dances off down the street and suddenly—wham!—he's hit by a bus. As he lies there, dying on the street, he calls out.

" 'God above! For fifty years I've been your faithful servant! And now, you do this to me?'

"Suddenly, the clouds part and a voice says, 'Shloimi? Is that you? Sorry—I didn't recognize you!' "

"Wait a minute," said Brian, not even getting the joke. "The assembly. And your dad is coming . . . Does this have to do with the surprise?"

There was really no point in keeping it a secret anymore.

"Yes," I admitted. "It does. *I'm* the surprise."

Now he looked even more confused.

"You?" He shook his head. "I don't get it. I thought it was Sonny and Cher!"

"Mr. Newton had this dumb idea. That's why Mrs. Gabbler called me into the office on Monday. It wasn't for sneeze-honking. It was for the winter holiday assembly. I'm going to be telling the story of Honnika."

"You mean the one with Judah the Maccabee?"

I nodded.

"In front of the whole school? Whoa. That was one thing when you were a little kid—but now? I mean, you're in seventh grade!"

"Tell me about it," I said.

"All right, that's weird. But what does your dad have to do with it?"

"That was Mr. Newton's other dumb idea. To have my

family with me, lighting the candles and singing the blessings."

"Onstage? In front of everyone?" He shook his head and whispered, "Do you know what will happen when they see your dad walking in? I mean, *I* won't laugh, but everybody else . . ." He whistled. "Man, you're in big trouble. If I were you, I'd put on one of those beanies and start to pray."

There were a million people at Canter's Deli, and the line stretched all the way out the door and into the street. Hot as it was, the ultra-Orthodox Jews hurried by in their black hats and coats, like it was winter in Russia. I never know what to think when I see them. Part of me wants to go up to them and say, "Shalom! I'm Jewish too! Even though I don't wear the costume." The other part of me wants to run and hide. None of them were in line for Canter's. Even though it's a Jewish deli, it's only kosher *style*, which is not kosher enough for them. Besides, they don't spend money on Shabbat, which pretty much rules out lunch at a deli.

But Canter's was still packed, filled with all the other Jews trying to escape Christmas festivities, and everyone was in a bad mood. We'd already waited fifteen minutes outside in the sun, and now that we were inside, it wasn't much cooler. Covering the walls were framed photographs of all the Jewish comedians who had eaten there: Joey Bishop, Woody Allen, Groucho Marx, Milton Berle, Jack Benny, and two of my favorites together, Carl Reiner and Mel Brooks. Beneath the pictures were all kinds of Jewish foods piled on platters in glass cases. On top of the counter were five different kinds of halvah, this sesame candy I love, and baklava, a delicious Middle Eastern pastry with honey and nuts.

"I'm starving!" said Kenny. "How long will it be? I can't wait another minute!"

"Well, you'll have to," said Howard. "Because I've calculated the number of people in line, and it will take at least fifteen minutes until we're seated."

"Well, we're not here for math, we're here for matzoh ball soup, so shut up."

"You just don't want to admit that I'm right," Howard said. "So *you* shut up."

"I don't want to admit that you're an annoying..."

I heard a sigh and turned to see my mom, who looked like she was about to cry. I had to do something, so I nudged Kenny and pointed to a case where there was a pointy slab of bumpy textured meat.

"See that?" I asked.

"Yuck!" said Kenny. "It's a giant cow tongue! That's gross!"

"How do you know?" asked Howard. "Have you ever tasted it?"

"No, of course not. Have you?"

"No, but you should never say anything about anything

until you know," said Howard. "Otherwise you're a preju-
diced ignoramus."

"Oh yeah?" said Kenny. "Well, *your* tongue is a big—"

"Hey, you guys!" I said. "I know *exactly* how tongue tastes."

"You do?" asked Kenny. "How?"

"Easy—I taste mine all the time." They laughed. "But I
would never eat *that* tongue," I said, pointing to the one in
the case. "Because I don't want to taste anything that's tast-
ing me at the same time."

Now the people behind us in line laughed. Just then, a
guy behind the deli counter called out, "Coming through!
Hot matzoh balls!" The servers moved back, and he poured
a whole vat of soup into the pot, with matzoh balls the size
of grapefruit.

"Wow!" said an old man in front of us. "Look at the size
of those matzoh balls!"

"You should see the rest of the matzoh!" I said, borrow-
ing from Marilyn Monroe.

Now everyone was laughing and looking at me to see
what I'd say next. It felt strange—and a little scary—but
kind of fun too. And my mom was smiling again.

"Hey!" said a guy behind me. "The kid's a regular Groucho
Marx!"

That setup was too easy. I held an imaginary cigar to my
mouth and moved my eyebrows up and down, saying, "That's

the most ridiculous thing I've ever heard! By the way, have you met my brothers, Chico and Harpo?" I pointed to Kenny and Howard—there's really no resemblance, but I kept on with the Groucho imitation. "When you're waiting in line," I said, "time flies like an arrow. And fruit flies like a banana."

"The kid's on a roll," said the man standing behind me.

"Yep," I said, "your choice—sourdough, white, or onion. Or you can have me on rye—after all, my mom says I have a *rye* sense of humor. In fact, when I'm complaining, she calls me Kvetcher in the Rye."

That's from this book Kenny's reading in high school, called *The Catcher in the Rye*. If there's one thing Jews agree on—and maybe the only thing—it's that we like to laugh. Now even the waiters were watching.

"But if you don't want rye, how 'bout a bagel?"

This little kid in front of me said, "I do! I want a bagel!"

"Oh yeah?" I said. "Do you know how they make bagels?" He shook his head.

"First they get a hole. Then they wrap the dough around it."

"Really?" he said.

"No," I said. "Just kidding. Actually, a bagel is a doughnut that went to college."

That got a laugh, and right then, someone dropped a glass, which shattered, so I shouted, "Mazel tov! Let's hear it for the shlemiel!"

"What's a sha-meel?" asked the kid.

He was perfect. It was like I'd planted him. "Well," I said, "a shlemiel is someone who falls on his back and breaks his nose. But in a restaurant like this, the shlemiel would be the waiter who spills the soup on the customer! And you know what that makes the customer?"

"Wet?" he asked. The kid was a genius.

"Not just wet, but a shlimazel. You see, the shlemiel spills the soup and it lands on the shlimazel. Then the shlemiel falls on the shlimazel and breaks the shlimazel's glasses! Seated right next to the shlimazel is a guy who says"—and here I used my nerdiest voice—"'I see your glasses are broken. I could fix them if I had one of those little screwdriver kits—but I don't!' That's the nebbish!"

Everyone applauded for that one, so I bowed and motioned to the kid. "And let's hear it for Gimpel!"

They applauded for him too, and when he said, "But my name's not Gimpel, it's David!" they cheered even louder.

Just then a waitress came to my mom and said, "Your table's ready." Then, she whispered, "And because your boy made everyone laugh, lunch is on the house!"

Lunch was great. And because it was free, I ordered halvah *and* baklava for dessert. It's weird how good food and a few laughs can change everything.

We drove to the hospital, and Kenny said, "Look!" Sure enough, there was a parking spot just down the street from Kaiser. When we got to our dad's room, he was sitting on the edge of his bed, trying to button his shirt, joking with Father Joseph.

". . . So, as the plane is going down, the rabbi turns to the priest and says, 'Better than pork, isn't it?'"

Father Joseph laughed, whistled, and coughed all at the same time. It took him a minute to recover.

"It's good to see you again, Father Joseph," said my mom. "How are you today?"

To me, Father Joseph looked even worse than yesterday, and there was some kind of gunk dripping from the hole in his throat, but he said, "Praise the saints, I can't complain! Though I will say your husband and I have been trading priest and rabbi jokes, and I've yet to find one he doesn't know!"

"Telling jokes is hard work!" said my dad. "And I haven't eaten yet, because I thought you might bring me something from Canter's!"

"We did!" said Kenny, holding out a paper bag. "Matzoh ball soup!"

"My favorite!" said my dad. "You want some, Father? It's Jewish penicillin."

"Matzoh ball soup? So I've heard. Never had it, but it

smells wonderful. I'm afraid I can't, though. It would have to go through the blender first, so I could drink it through a straw."

That was not a pretty picture. To change the subject I told them about Canter's, my comedy routine, and the little kid who kept asking questions. As I did, my dad slurped away, although now, no one complained.

When he finished we were ready to go, and Howard brought out the walker from behind the curtain. We all helped my dad stand up and said good-bye to Father Joseph.

"You take care now, Bob!" he said, finger over his throat hole. "I'll be sure to keep you in my prayers."

"That should do the trick!" said my dad. "That and matzoh ball soup! And best of luck to you, Father Joseph!"

As we walked down the hallway toward the elevator, people came out to say good-bye to my father—nurses, orderlies, even a couple doctors. I was amazed at how many people my dad met while he was in the hospital—even while in a coma. It felt like a parade, and my father was grand marshal. Some had been at my Shabbanukkah magic show—even Claudia was there, and smiling. "Rest up," she said. "And no more tricks."

We took the elevator down to the lobby, then opened the door to a blast of heat and light, and began walking down the street to the car. I say "walking," which is what my brothers, my mom, and I were doing. But my dad was doing something else altogether. He took a deep breath, then slid the walker about six inches. Then he pulled his feet forward, shuffling and grimacing when he put his weight on his hip. That was one step. Then he took another. And another. All afternoon we had been spinning like dreidels through the deli and the hospital. Now we were moving in slow motion. My dad, who just a few minutes earlier had been the life of the party, now looked like death warmed over.

I didn't want to look at my dad, but couldn't turn away, so I stared at the fluorescent tennis balls, which were even brighter in the sun. They reminded me of my second-favorite store in the world, which is right down the street from Berg's Studio of Magic, called Aardvark's Odd Ark. They sell things for hippies, like posters in bright colors of rock bands and cartoon characters and anti-war slogans. There's always this spacey music playing and it smells like some kind of perfume, which my dad says is called incense. Once we went into this special room they have, with a huge black light—which isn't really black, but purple. When it shines on the posters, the colors glow like they're from another planet.

I convinced my dad to buy a poster of Donald Duck's uncle Scrooge, which said, in huge red letters, QUACK! We put it up in the hallway between the bedrooms, which is the one place in the house that gets completely dark. My dad got a little black light we could plug in and shine at the poster, which I did every couple of weeks. That's where my dad first got the idea for going into the glow-in-the-dark plastic business.

But it wasn't the poster I was thinking about today. It was a T-shirt I saw on the way out that said I'M NOT WITH THEM—and had an arrow pointing to one side. I didn't buy it, but I sure felt like wearing it now.

We finally got to the car and put the walker in the trunk, then helped my dad into the passenger seat, which took another five minutes. He couldn't lift his legs and moaned in pain when we tried to help. After we finally got him in, my mom said, "Well, that wasn't so bad, was it?"

Nobody said anything, because we all knew it *was* that bad. The freeway was packed, bumper to bumper, as we crawled back toward Temple City.

It was only when we got to our exit that I remembered the Neck-O-Matic. Shoot. We hadn't even thought of it while packing up my dad. It was probably in some closet in the hospital. But I wasn't about to say anything—it would be left behind, like the rest of the matzoh.

This evening I sifted through the boxes of candles, trying to find seven decent ones and a shammes. I mostly managed to do it, except for one that broke when I was putting it in. I considered switching it out, but somehow it fit my family.

My dad was a wreck after the trip home from the hospital. Looking at him in the light of the candles, it seemed clear there was no way he would make it to Monday's assembly. I couldn't help but feel relieved.

He seemed to read my thoughts. "Don't worry," he said. "I'm just tired from the trip home. I'll sleep tonight, rest up tomorrow, and by Monday I'll be as good as new."

That's when my mom spoke up.

"Well, this year, with all that's happened, it's been especially hard to think about presents . . ." I couldn't believe it. Here we were, seven nights into Kchanakah, and she was giving us The Explanation. But then she said, "So, today, when I was at Thrifty's, I saw something and thought . . . well, it's not much, but here you are. There's one for each of you."

She pulled out a shopping bag from behind the chair and handed out three plaid flannel bathrobes—a red one for Howard, a green one for Kenny, and a blue one for me. We put them on over our clothes, then looked at ourselves and one another.

My dad beamed. "My three sons," he said.

It was the first Khchanukkah gift we'd ever been given. Howard and Kenny seemed thrilled with their bathrobes, but I didn't know what to think. Because in my mind I was wearing that T-shirt: I'M NOT WITH THEM.

And tomorrow, I thought, *I won't be. I'll be dressed in my tux, amazing the crowd.*

No more waiting around for miracles—I'll be making magic of my own.

THE EIGHTH CANDLE: An Orange

There are no good sounds that can come from your parents' bedroom. Go through the list if you want—or, as Mr. DeGuerre likes to say, "You do the math." But you may as well take my word for it.

At five o'clock this morning I heard my dad screaming in pain and then, a moment later, shouting, "Where the hell are my pills?" Then there was a lot of shuffling and moaning, which turned into arguing.

I tried to go back to sleep, but kept thinking about my show. I pictured the room full of people clapping, and lines of patter kept running through my head: "I know why you're here! Because you believe in . . . magic!" "These aren't just matzoh balls—they're *magic* matzoh balls!" I was trying to keep track of all the changes I'd made and all the things I would have to do because Amy wasn't there. The hardest part would be dealing with Herrmann—Maccabee—but

I had a little travel cage for her, so I could manage. I had almost asked Brian to be my assistant for the day, but it would have been harder to teach him to do the tricks than to figure out how to do them myself.

I finally did fall back to sleep, and slept a long time. When I woke up and went to the kitchen, my mom looked like she hadn't slept at all. Her hair was a mess—not a hair-in-curlers-and-then-will-be-beautiful mess, but a who-can-think-about-hair-when-your-husband-is-up-all-night-screaming-in-pain mess.

"Hey, good-lookin'," she said, attempting to smile, "what's cookin'?"

"Nothing much," I said. "How's Dad?"

"Well, he had a rough night." That was an understatement. "But I'm sure he'll be better today. He's resting."

"That's good," I said. "So, when do we go?"

"What?"

I thought she hadn't heard me. I said louder, "When do we go? The show's at two, and I should be there by one thirty to set up."

I could tell by the blank look on her face that she had completely forgotten.

"Oh, right. Of course," she said. "Your magic show. Today. Of course." Then she nodded and smiled, like she'd been looking forward to the drive. She took a deep breath, wiped her hands on a towel, and looked at the clock. "Let me just finish cleaning the kitchen, shower, and get dressed," she said. "How about we leave in an hour and a half?"

"Okay," I said, heading off to the den to prepare. But then I turned around and saw her there, looking drained and disheveled. I heard my dad moan in the other room, and realized she had nothing left—nothing at all. And she was willing to give it to me.

But I couldn't take it.

"I don't think so," I said. "You stay here, take care of Dad. I'll take the bus."

"Oh," she said. "Really, it's . . . Are you sure?"

"Of course," I said. "No problem." That was a lie and we both knew it. It was a *big* problem, especially dressed in my tux, carrying my suitcase and Herrmann's cage.

In the kitchen, under the Phone-O-Matic, is a drawer stuffed with maps and phone books and receipts and a bunch of bus schedules. Making sense of which bus goes where and when is a really complicated puzzle. I like puzzles, and this one would have been fun if I didn't actually have to *ride* the buses. I figured out that I needed to take the 259, the 57, and then the 93, which had a stop right across the street from the Jewish Home for the Elderly and Infirm. Looking at the Sunday schedules, I saw it would take three hours and fifteen minutes to get there. Working backward, to get there by 1:30, I would have to be at the bus stop on Baldwin Avenue at 9:57—in thirteen minutes.

No time to shower, no time for food. I downed a glass of orange juice, threw on my jacket and pants, clipped on my tie, put Herrmann in her travel cage, grabbed my suitcase, and dashed out the door. Sure enough, I got to Baldwin just as the bus was pulling up, dropped my quarter into the box, and collapsed into a seat near the front. There were just a few other riders, and with my suitcase and everything else, they must have thought I was running away from home. I suppose, in a sense, they were right.

We stopped to pick up a few people as we rode down Baldwin, but maybe because it was Sunday we were pretty much on time. The air conditioner even worked, which was a first. But the second bus—the longer ride, all the way to the downtown L.A. bus terminal—was crowded and hot as could be. It was stinky too, as if someone had peed in the corner. Wearing my too-small tuxedo, I was already sweating. Evidently neither the windows nor the air conditioner worked on this bus, so the driver kept opening and closing the door every chance he got, trying to use it as a fan. It didn't help.

I scrunched into my corner and ran through my patter.

"Chanuukah is a choliday of miracles!" I said to myself. "Watch this!"

"Hey, man," said a voice behind me. "Nice bunny. What's his name?"

I turned to see the bearded face of a hippie. He had a backpack and bongos.

"*Her* name," I said. "She's a girl. And, well, it's Herrmann."

"Herrmann?" the hippie said. "*Her* name is Herrmann?"

"That's right. But just for today I've changed her name. To Maccabee."

"She's a girl, but her name is Herrmann, and you're calling her Maccabee?" He looked confused, but nodded. "Oh, I see. Maccabee. Like Judah, right?"

"Yeah," I said.

"Far out!" he said. "So, what are you, a magician or something?"

"That's right. I'm going to do a magic show at my grandma's nursing home." I realized this was a great chance to practice the patter that was running through my head. "And this," I said in my deep magician's voice, "is Maccabee, the dreidel-playing rabbit! He's lucky! You know how you can tell? Because he has all four of his feet!"

The guy broke into a laugh, so I kept on going. "And I know why you're here! Because you believe in . . . magic!" I didn't have the feather flowers loaded in my sleeve, but had managed to dig a sponge ball out of my pocket, which I produced from thin air.

"Oh, man!" he said. "How'd you do that?"

"Magic!" I said. "And it's a magic matzoh ball!" I made it appear and disappear a couple times, then produced it from his ear. I was pretty pleased with myself.

"Whoa!" he said. "Trippy! That's totally amazing!"

Suddenly he looked out the window, and called to the driver, "Hey—this is my stop!" Then he said to me, "This lady I met said I could crash here." He grabbed his stuff and ran toward the door. "Hey, you!" he called back. "You're a magic man! Don't you forget it! Happy Haanakah!"

He's right, I told myself as he jumped off the bus. I *am* a magic man.

I was feeling pretty good when we got to the terminal in plenty of time, but the third bus was running late. Really late. I waited ten, fifteen, then twenty minutes before it came rolling up. When it finally did, the driver must have figured it was a good time to tell his life story to all the other drivers, because he stood there talking to them for another fifteen minutes. When we pulled up at the nursing home, it was already five minutes till 2:00, so I ran inside to the front desk, where a woman sat doing a crossword puzzle. I stood there, catching my breath.

"May I help you?" she asked, without looking up.

"Hey there!" I said, still breathing heavily, trying for my deepest voice. "How ya doin'? My name is Joel Edwin—and I'm here to . . . do magic!"

She looked up at me, staring. I felt pretty stupid, but figured I'd try again. "How you doin'?" I said, suave as I could muster. "Is Esther around?"

"Esther? I'm not Esther. Esther's not here."

"That's all right, Not-Esther," I said, reminding myself that I was the magician, and in complete control. "No Esther, no problem." I tried to sound like Mister Mystery. "As I was saying, my name is Joel Edwin, and Esther hired me to perform a magic show for today's Chanuquah celebration. Today. At two o'clock." I looked at the clock. "That's in . . . three minutes."

"Your name is Josh? And you want to do magic tricks?" she said.

"Actually . . ." I cleared my throat. "My name is Joel. And I've been hired to perform for the Hanika party. By Esther."

"Esther doesn't work on Sundays," said Not-Esther. "And she didn't tell me anything about a magic show. Then again, nobody ever tells me anything." She picked up a clipboard, flipping through several pages. "All it says here is, 'Menorah lighting in social room. Two o'clock.' But as long as they're just sitting around, you may as well do some magic tricks. It's not like they have anything else going on."

"Great," I said. "Also, my grandmother, Anna, is a resident here. Would you happen to know where she is? I know she was looking forward to it."

"What's her name?"

"Anna."

"Last name?"

It's the same as mine, and I didn't want to say it out loud. Luckily, I spotted a list of residents' names on the counter and pointed to my grandmother's.

"Oh, her." She frowned. "She doesn't usually come to activities, but I'll ask the orderlies if they can bring her in." She pointed to a doorway. "The social room is at the end of that hall."

I rushed with Herrmann's cage and my suitcase down the hall, opened the doors, and stepped into a room filled with noise and cigar smoke. My dad had said they didn't let people smoke on Saturday, because it's forbidden on Shabbat, but apparently they make up for it on Sunday.

There was a stage at one end of the room, with a big TV on a metal stand, set to a soap opera. On-screen I could see a woman talking to a doctor, but couldn't hear what they were saying, because there were a dozen people in the room talking loudly, some in Yiddish, some in English, all of it kvetching.

"Attendant, it's too hot in here! I'm *shvitzing*!" That means to sweat—a lot. "Why don't they turn on an air conditioner?"

"I'll tell you why—they're too cheap to buy one!"

"Nurse! Nurse! Light my cigar!"

"Yeah!" someone else said. "And then light *my* cigar!"

I figured they didn't let the residents have matches, and that's why, on a table next to the TV, there stood a big electronic menorah with a cord and nine pointy screw-in lightbulbs instead of candles.

I climbed the steps to the stage. There was no backstage, so I went into a corner and knelt down to set up the tricks as quickly as possible. I loaded the feather flowers up my sleeve and prepared the Twentieth-Century Silks—or Escape from Antiochus, as I was calling it—where a multicolored handkerchief vanishes from one place and appears in another. I pocketed the Magic Matzoh Balls, and set up the deck for the Menorah Card, making sure the nine of diamonds was on the bottom, and that the banner was tucked into my hat. I prepped the Miracle Rope, put the linking rings—Eight Rings of Chanukkkkah—in order. I found a drinking fountain and filled the Bottomless Oil Jar. Finally I loaded the coins for Miser's Dream, which I was calling Magic Gelt Trip. I had a coffee can to toss the coins in, though it wouldn't be as cool as the bedpan in the hospital on Friday. They probably had bedpans there, but I didn't want to ask.

Normally I do all my setup in secret, but no one seemed to be watching me, except for an old man who was chewing on something. When I was almost finished, he said, "What are you doing here?"

"Hey there!" I said, turning toward him. "Funny you should ask. I'm doing a magic show for Khanuka!"

"What?"

"A magic show! For Khanukah."

"Why?"

"Because everyone loves magic!" I said, just like Mister Mystery.

He didn't answer, just shrugged and kept staring and chewing. I finished setting up my tricks—except for Herrmann, who needed to go in at the last minute. It was already 2:15 when the attendants, who were big guys dressed in white, began wheeling in the rest of the residents. Soon there was a good-sized audience, but the attendants didn't seem to care which way their chairs faced, and neither did the patients. A few more wandered in, some on walkers, some with canes.

But there was no sign of my grandmother. I waited, running through bits of patter in my mind. "The oil never runs out! It's a miracle!" "Eight rings—for eight nights of Kchaanukkah! Each more magical than the last!"

A white-haired lady near the front said, "Are you going to do a show?"

"Yes, indeed!" I said. "A magic show!"

"Do you sing?"

"No, I don't sing. I'm doing a magic show!"

"Can't you sing instead? I like singing better."

Finally, at 2:30, a couple of orderlies entered the room, escorting my grandmother by her elbows. She was wearing her favorite dress, brown with white polka dots. I waved at her, but she didn't respond. They sat her in a chair in the back. She didn't look like she was having a good day. "Now just sit here and be quiet," they said. "All right?"

Before I could say hello, Not-Esther came to the front of the room with her clipboard. She put on her glasses and said, "All right now, everyone, pay attention. This is the eighth night of Hanuukkaahh so we'll be lighting all eight candles."

That was my cue to load Herrmann—Maccabee—into her hiding place, along with the dreidels, so she would be ready for her first appearance. As I did, Not-Esther twisted the shammes to light it, then each of the eight other bulbs, and read the blessing from her clipboard. *"Baruch atah Adonai elohaynu melech ha-olam . . ."*

"Why aren't you singing?" asked the woman who likes singing. She started clapping her hands and singing the blessing all over again. *"Baruch atah . . ."*

"Doris," said Not-Esther, "we're not singing. And I don't want any trouble from you. Or you're out."

"Yeah, Doris! We don't want to hear you singing," said the man next to her.

"I like singing," someone called from the back.

"Shush!" Not-Esther finally shouted. "Or I'll unscrew the candles!" That quieted them down, though the TV was still really loud. "Today as a special Hanuka treat we have a young man who will do a magic presentation. His name is Josh—"

"Joel," I corrected.

She gave me a look and went on. "His grandmother is a resident here. You know Anna." Not-Esther looked around the room, spotting her. "There she is. In the back. Wave at everyone, Anna."

She raised her arm, looking confused.

"Now, I know you'll all welcome our guest, and behave, not like the last time. So everyone, please, welcome Josh the Magician."

There was some applause and a lot of blank stares, some at me and some in whatever directions people had been pointed. Not-Esther left the room and I leapt up, put on my best Mister Mystery smile, and said, "Hey, everybody— I know why you're here—because you believe in . . ." Then I took the pause, just as I'd planned, pulled out the feather flowers, and said, ". . . magic!"

The woman who liked singing applauded.

"Of course, I can't do magic by myself, even today, the most magical of days—the eighth night of Khanukkah! So I brought a helper along with me—Maccabee the rabbit!" I held up the box. They were supposed to call out "It's empty!" but no one said anything. I pretended to frown. "Of course, being a magic rabbit, Maccabee's invisible. What do you think—would you like to see him?"

Usually, when I do this for kids, they call out "Yes!" But everyone just stared at me. I figured that maybe they hadn't heard, so I said it louder, and slower, enunciating like I do for my mother.

"I said, would you like to meet Maccabee the magical rabbit?"

They still didn't respond and I wasn't going to try a third time. I plowed on. "To make Maccabee appear, we'll need to say the magic words, 'Nes Gadol Haya Sham!' which means, as you all know, 'A Great Miracle Happened There!'" Still silence, except for the TV, where the woman who had been talking to the doctor was now crying about something. "Let's all say it together, shall we? Nes Gadol . . ."

The box was dripping. A puddle was forming on the stage.

"Attendant!" called Doris, in the front row. "Someone had an accident—you'd better clean it up!"

I pulled the lever and Herrmann appeared, sopping wet,

looking none too happy as I lifted her up. "No problem—I've got it," I said, looking for something to wipe my hands on, and ended up using the Twentieth-Century Silks. So much for that trick.

But does a great magician get thrown off when there's a problem? No way. I thought of Mister Mystery—and Houdini. What would they do? Improvise. Like the time Houdini was chained up inside a trunk, then lowered into a hole cut into the ice of a frozen Lake Michigan. He managed to escape from the trunk, no problem, but the current was so strong that he drifted, and couldn't find the opening. Did he panic? No. He floated up to the surface and found a pocket of air between the water and ice, which let him breathe until he finally found the hole.

"Well, that's too bad—but we're not going to let Maccabee's little accident put out the Hanukah lights, are we? Of course not! Especially when we have . . . the Bottomless Oil Jug!"

I had shifted the order around. While nobody was very impressed with the trick, it did let me wash my hands, which had become sticky and stinky. I shook them off and pressed on. "And now, for some Magic Matzoh Balls!" One appeared at my fingertips. "They're made by my grandmother, Anna, so light and fluffy—they disappear!" I said as it vanished.

"If they're matzoh balls," said the chewing guy in the

front row, "why are they red?" He wasn't heckling, just curious—like Brian, but a hundred years older.

"Because they're Hanikah matzoh balls!" I said. That made no sense, but bought me some time. "Sir, may I invite you to come up here, since you're such an expert on matzoh balls? Let's have a round of applause for our volunteer!"

This was good, because I had been looking for a volunteer, and he looked like he could climb the stairs to the stage.

"What's your name, sir?"

"Irving."

"Let's hear it for Irving!" A few people applauded. I made the matzoh ball disappear from my hand and appear in his, then turned it from red to black, saying, "Now it's a burned matzoh ball!" Only a couple people laughed, but I knew I'd get them with the Menorah Card. Pulling the deck of cards from my pocket, I said, "Irving, I'll run my fingers through the cards, and you tell me where to stop." He did, and I showed him his card—which was the nine of diamonds, of course—and told him to remember it. Then, taking my hat from my head, I pulled out the menorah banner I'd made, opening it up high over my head, the menorah facing backward so no one could see it.

"Very well, Irving. If this were a regular magic show, and I were a regular magician, I could simply tell you what your card is. But, this being Hanakka, I've got something special.

You tell me what card you chose, and I'll show you a miracle!"

He stood there for a moment, then said, "Seven of hearts."

"Seven of hearts?"

"Yeah. Seven of hearts. Or maybe five. Of spades. That was it. Five of spades."

"Five? Of spades?"

He nodded. It wasn't his card, of course, but what could I say? I was standing there with the answer over my head. "I believe the card you chose was"—and now I turned the banner around, for all to see—"the nine of diamonds!"

Everyone stared at it, then looked at Irving. He shook his head. "No. I think it was the four. Of clubs."

There was silence now, except for the TV. I was feeling less magical by the minute. I had to take control. "Hey," I said, making my way to the TV set. "I'm thinking this TV makes it hard to concentrate . . . maybe even difficult to remember things, like what card you picked. How about if I turn it off? Just for the rest of the show." I pressed the off button, and the picture disappeared into a spot in the middle. For a moment it was quiet—and then, kvetching.

"Hey, I was watching that!" someone said.

"So was I!"

"So what?" said another voice. "It was a rerun. They're all reruns. She finds out she's pregnant—and the doctor is the father."

"Thanks for ruining it!"

This was my make-or-break moment. With the TV off, I had at least the *possibility* of their attention. Deep down, everyone in this room wants to believe in magic, I told myself. And I am a magic man. The order I had planned no longer mattered; what I needed was the right effect to win them over. Suddenly it came to me—the Linking Rings!

It's a trick that comes in almost every kid's magic set. But those are small and cheap, and you can't really learn how to do it from written instructions—you need someone like Mister Mystery to teach you. I had saved up and bought the deluxe rings, and worked for weeks to perfect my routine.

"Not to worry," I said, holding one ring in each hand. "You'll have another chance to see the reruns, but never again will you see anything—like *this*!" I held up a ring in each hand, bringing them toward each other, and as I did, a hush fell over the crowd. Everything that had come before would be forgotten—it all came down to this moment.

Ever so slowly, the two rings came closer, then actually seemed to *melt* through each other. The crowd actually gasped—then broke into applause.

"Yes," I said as the room quieted down. "A true Khanaka miracle! But what's even more amazing is when they melt apart!"

That was true, and it happens so slowly that it's almost

hypnotic. I took my time. This was what I had been waiting for. They were in the palm of my hand, and I could see the wonder on their faces.

But then . . .

"His mother is a murderer!" my grandmother screamed. "She's poisoning his father!"

The spell was broken. They turned to stare at her, then me.

"That's my grandmother!" I said. "She has some sense of humor, don't you, Grandma?"

"And they throw gas at me!" she said.

"Always making jokes . . ."

"It's true! Every night they come in my room and throw gas!"

That's when I lost it. "Grandma!" I shouted. "I've told you before. You can't throw gas!"

Big mistake. My outburst was the cue for everyone else to start shouting.

"Tell your grandmother to shut up!" someone said. "She's always screaming!"

"*You* shut up!" shouted my grandmother.

"What if it's true? Somebody should call the police!"

"You're more *meshugga* than she is!"

Several patients began calling "Attendant! Attendant!" and others were swearing in Yiddish. A moment later, two attendants barged into the room. "That's it!" shouted a big guy with a crew cut. "Show's over!"

Another attendant came in and began to wheel people out. The one with the crew cut came up onstage, looked at my tricks, and shook his head. "You've upset them," he said. "I think you'd better go." I was shaking as I began packing up. The attendant looked around at the chaos, shook his head again, and unplugged the menorah.

Pretty soon the room was empty except for my grandmother. She wasn't screaming anymore. She just stared as I picked up my suitcase and Herrmann's cage, then walked past her out the door.

When you're a kid who does magic shows, you hear the same thing over and over again from practically every adult you meet. As soon as they learn you're a magician, they say, "Hey, can you make yourself *disappear*?" Then they chuckle, like they're the first person who ever thought to say it.

There are a couple ways to respond—my favorite being: "I've got a better trick—I'll make *you* disappear!" Then I cover up my eyes and say, "Whoa, cool!" Though no one had asked me to make myself disappear at the nursing home, it was all I wanted to do as I sat on the bench waiting for the bus. When I glanced back through the nursing home window, I saw people inside looking at me.

Maccabee—Herrmann—didn't look very happy either, and the little water bottle on her cage was empty. I filled it with water from the bottomless oil vase, and thought about Houdini.

In the end, of course, Houdini did not escape. People who have watched the movie about him—which I have now seen five times—think he died while doing the Water Torture Cell, but that's not true. In fact, it was Houdini's strength that killed him. He had built up his stomach muscles so he could withstand any blow, and would sometimes let a spectator punch him, as hard as possible. Houdini always tensed up his muscles before-hand, so that even if someone hit him really hard, all they hurt was their own hand. One day, while Houdini was reading his mail, a college student asked if he could punch him in the stomach. Houdini wasn't really paying attention, but kind of nodded, and before he could tense up his muscles, the guy hit him as hard as he could—a sucker punch. Houdini got appendicitis. He should have gone to the hospital, but he had a big performance that night, of the Water Torture Cell. It was afterward, as he walked through the parking lot, that he collapsed and died.

I hadn't expected the sucker punch either, especially from my grandmother, but I probably should have.

Someone tapped my shoulder. I looked up—it was Not-Esther.

"I found this in a pile of papers on the desk," she said, holding out an envelope. "Is your name Joel?"

I nodded, taking it, though I didn't want to. Inside were five twenty-dollar bills I did not deserve. My gut hurt.

When the bus finally arrived, it was a crawler, hot and packed, and there was no place to sit, so I stood, right in the center. People gave me dirty looks because I took up so much space with my suitcase and Herrmann's cage. I was getting hungry—I hadn't eaten all day, and all I had with me was rabbit food. The bus stopped at every green light, without fail, sometimes staying two cycles for no apparent reason.

It went like this for about twenty stops until we got to the Fairfax area, where people started to get off. By the time we reached the Farmers Market stop, everyone was gone. Maybe they were going Christmas shopping. Whatever it was, I was glad to have some breathing room. There was a seat open right behind the driver. Though it said RESERVED FOR ELDERLY AND HANDICAPPED, I no longer cared, so I took it—the closer to the door, the better.

The next light was green and so, of course, we stopped. And waited. Finally an old man climbed on, walking with a cane and carrying a shopping bag.

Just my luck—elderly *and* handicapped. He had thick glasses and wore a plaid felt hat. It took him forever just to make his way to the bus driver.

"How much is it?" he finally asked, in a thick Eastern European accent.

"Senior citizen? A quarter," said the bus driver.

"Twenty-five cents?"

"Yeah. A quarter."

Time, which had been crawling along, came to a complete standstill as he reached into his pocket, pulled out a coin, then dropped it with a clink into the box.

"That's five," he said. Then, after more fishing in his pocket, he pulled out another coin. "Ten." A few seconds later, "Eleven . . ."

That was it. I saw my whole life passing before me. I would live and die on that bus, in the shadow of my own failure. I watched the mildew, which seemed to be growing up the window as the light went from green to red, then back to green again. Finally, after the man had put in all his nickels and pennies, the bus driver flipped the lever so the coins dropped, and Mr. Elderly Handicapped began to back up right toward me. He didn't even look—just shuffled backward. Great. A whole bus full of empty seats, and he wanted mine.

I slid toward the window, because if I didn't he might well have sat on my lap. Stuck next to him and feeling awkward, I stared out the window. Porsche, Ferrari, Cadillac—the cars zipped by. But I could feel the old man staring at me. I scooted even closer to the window, but could still feel his eyes on me. Finally, he tapped me on the shoulder, so I *had* to look at him.

He sat there, his head kind of tilted, and said, "Happy Channukah."

How did he know? He must have seen my suitcase. I didn't say anything.

"You don't look very happy, young man," he said. I wanted to get away from him. I'd had enough old people for one day. "So maybe I'll show you something."

He rummaged around in his shopping bag, and pulled something out, holding it up for me to see. It was an orange. I stared at it.

"Vat do you think?" he finally said.

I shrugged. I had a lot of thoughts; mostly, You're a weirdo, like everyone else I've met today, and everyone in the world, and my family, and my grandmother, and my whole pathetic life, and I don't care about you and your stupid orange, so just let me shrivel up and die in peace. But I didn't say any of that. Instead I said, "I think it's an orange." Then I looked out the window.

"Yes." He nodded. "You are right. It is an orange. But vat do you think of it?"

Clearly, he wasn't letting up, so I took the orange, looked it over, and gave it back to him. "What do I think?" Again, I kept my real thoughts to myself. "It says Sunkist, and has a navel, so that means it's seedless. The peel is kind of thick, and a little green in one part, but it's probably orange inside. Basically, though, it's just an orange."

"Just an orange?" he said, nodding, then looked at it for a long time. I turned away from him again, but I could see his reflection in the window. He was rolling the orange between his hands, almost kneading it. Finally, he spoke again.

"You don't understand, do you?"

Here, at least, I had to agree. I had not a clue as to what he was talking about or why he was bugging me about his stupid orange.

"You know," he said, "I'm not from around here."

Duh, I thought.

"I came here after The War." He squinted at me. "Do you know about The War?"

"Yes," I said. "We studied it in school."

"Ah!" he said. "I see. And in this school of yours, did you learn about the place where I spent The War?"

"I don't know." I shrugged. "Where was that?"

"It was called Auschwitz."

"Really? Yeah. I've heard of it. There was a picture of it in our textbook, with a sign that said WORK WILL MAKE YOU FREE."

"Yes." He nodded. "That's right. *Arbeit macht frei.* Tell me—in your book, with the picture, did they say what *color* it was?"

I shrugged again. "Well, the picture was black-and-white. But the place itself was, well, all the colors of a place."

"No," he said, shaking his head. "That is not true. There were no colors. It was black. And white."

"What do you mean? No place is just black and white."

"The guards," he said, "dressed in black, and wore black boots, so shiny, you could see your face in them. And the uniforms they gave us had black and white stripes. Beneath them, our skin was pale white from the lack of light." Here, he rolled up his shirtsleeve and there were numbers on his arm. "You see these numbers? They have turned blue now, but when they brought me into a little room, where a man with glasses burned them into my skin, they were black.

"Everything was black, white, or gray," he said. "The sky was gray. And the snow, when it fell, was white, but only for a day. Then the ashes from the smokestacks would turn it gray too. All around was a tall fence, black against the sky.

"The food—I remember the food—was gray. Every day, after roll call, we would stand in a long line, each holding a black metal bowl, and wait. There, at the front, would be a big barrel, in which they had cooked what they called soup—though you or I would not call it that. It was a few potatoes that had been boiled in a big pot of water until they all but dissolved. It was the color of dirty dishwater, and if you got one small piece of the potato, you were lucky. That was our food for the day.

"But more than hungry, I was cold. Our uniforms were made of paper, and to stay warm, I looked for more paper. That was all we could do. When I found a scrap, I would crumple it into my clothes, or use it to patch the holes in my shoes, so my feet would not freeze."

Hot as it was on the bus, I felt a shiver down my spine.

"One day as I walked near the fence looking for paper, I noticed, in the gray snow, a piece of newspaper. I picked it up and saw that beneath it, the snow was a bright, pure white. But there was something else in the snow, and I stared at it in wonder. An orange! I looked for a long time because, you see, I had forgotten the color. Can you imagine such a thing, to forget a color? When I realized what it was, I grabbed it, and hid it inside my uniform. When I got back to the barracks I slid it into a hole in the wall.

"That night, as everyone slept, I brought it out. You must understand how hungry I was; I had eaten nothing but potato water for six months. I wanted to devour that orange, like you might eat an apple, peel and all. But I knew that if I did, I would have nothing.

"Instead, I rolled it between my palms. I felt the texture against my skin, its gentle roundness." As he spoke, he rolled the orange between his hands. "And then I scraped at the peel with my fingernail, closed my eyes—and inhaled." He held it up to my nose. The scent was sharp and sweet.

"At that moment," he went on, "I was carried away. No longer in Auschwitz, I was in a field outside Haifa, in what was then called Palestine. I had a cousin who had moved there before The War. He had written me a letter saying 'Here, we grow oranges. The smell of their blossoms fills the air, even in winter. It is the smell of freedom.'

"For that moment," he said, "I was free. When I opened my eyes, I was back in Auschwitz.

"I could not eat the orange—it was too beautiful. I tucked it back in the wall. But every night I took it out, rolling it between my hands, smelling its sweet scent. And, for just a moment, it carried me away."

I realized I was now holding the orange.

"I told myself I would not eat it until after a particularly bad day. Well, in Auschwitz, you did not have to wait long for such a day. There came a selection. We stood in a long line, a guard at the front with a bayonet, pointing for us to go to the right or the left. Those who were sent to the right went back to the barracks. Those sent to the left went to the showers, and did not return. When I got to the front of the line, the guard looked at me, then pointed to the right.

"It so happened that it was Hanukkah—I don't know which night. We had no candles, or matches, but that night I gathered those around me, and told them I had something to share. I took the orange from its hiding place, and passed it around. Each one of us rolled it between our hands, scraped its skin, and smelled freedom. When it came back to me, I peeled it—careful not to spill a drop—and handed each person a section. I held mine, closed my eyes, and lifted it to my mouth.

"I will tell you. Nothing before, or since, has tasted so sweet. It was the taste of beauty. Of hope. Of life.

"Afterward, I kept the peel, and smelled it each night as you would Havdalah spices to remember the sweetness of Shabbat.

"Finally, we saw the first signs of spring. The snow began to melt, and there, through the cracks, we saw plants, green with yellow flowers. To the guards they were weeds, but to us, they were a gift of color.

"The war ended. Those of us still alive were liberated. I came here, to America. But that orange—it saved my life."

As he said these words, the bus came to a stop. Using his

cane for balance, the old man stood up with his grocery bag, holding out his hand. I gave him the orange.

He smiled, then smelled it one more time. "That happened many, many years ago," he said, "and from then until now, I have not told anyone about it." Then he handed the orange back to me. "Remember, young man," he said. "Remember the sweet things in life."

With those words, he got off the bus.

I don't remember what happened on the rest of that bus ride, or the two after that. I traveled home in a kind of trance, with pictures whirling in my mind, of the old man, the dirty snow, the gray food—and the orange, which I kept rolling in my hands. The same way he held on to that orange peel, I held on to his story.

When I finally got home, I placed the orange on top of the piano in my room, then looked through the drawers of the living room cupboard, where I found we had another box of candles. I set them up as neatly as I could—with an orange one for the shammes.

I turned out the lights, and we lit the candles and said the blessings. Then we sang "Maoz Tzur," but quietly. There was an open window, and just a hint of a breeze. The flames flickered ever so slightly. I looked at my family. They were all exhausted.

My mom looked at me. "Joel, maybe you'll do a magic trick?" she asked.

I shook my head. "I don't have any magic left in me," I said. "But would you like to hear a story?"

"Yes," said my mother. "That would be wonderful. What would you like to read? Here, I'll turn on a light . . ."

"No," I said. "I don't need a light. Or a book. Just the candles."

With some effort, my dad settled into the couch beside my mom. Kenny and Howard sat on the bridge chairs. I had read the story of "The First Shlemiel" so many times that I knew it by heart. I pictured the drawing of Shlemiel, Baby Shlemiel, and the rooster on the windowsill, and began. "There are many shlemiels in the world, but the very first one came from the village of Chelm . . ."

I told them of the snow, Shlemiel's despair, the sense that all was lost. I found I remembered everything in the book, and a few things besides, and I didn't miss the illustrations, because I had the characters sitting right in front of me. There was Howard, looking like an elder of Chelm, gravely serious, Kenny, another elder, always hopeful. And my mom—the hardworking, long-suffering Mrs. Shlemiel. Then I looked at my father, who is, in his dreams, Shlemiel the King.

I told them of the miraculous recovery. How Shlemiel

didn't die after eating the jam he'd thought was poison, but drifted off to sleep. How he had cried tears of joy when he realized he would go on living. And how, upon hearing the story, the elders of Chelm made a truly wise decision, for once: that everyone should give a little of their own jam to the Shlemiels. Finally, I told them how on the first night of Chanuka, when the family lit the menorah and placed it on the windowsill, there was a flurry in the snow. It was the rooster, who had been lost but, by the light of the candles, had found his way back home. And that year, the Shlemiels had a happy Hanukah after all.

When I finished, there was silence. The stubs of the candles that remained showed just a hint of color, their flames dancing side to side. The one to the far right began to flicker—a moment later it glowed brightly, then faded out, sending up a wisp of smoke. Then another candle—the fifth—flared, then burned out, sending up its wisp of smoke. We watched in silence until there were just two flames left— one on the green candle to the far right of the menorah, and one on the shammes.

The shammes burned lower and lower. After about a min-ute, the flame was so small, I couldn't even be sure it was still lit. The green one was bright—lighting up the room as if all the other candles were burning. Then, all of a sudden, it died down. A wisp—then it was gone.

All that remained was the dim light of the shammes. We stared, barely able to make out its faint orange glow. It suddenly brightened, a tiny flame appeared, and light filled the room. Finally, there was a wisp of smoke—then peaceful darkness.

THE SHAMMES: Just Enough

My first thought this morning—even before I opened my eyes—was of the old man, how he lifted the newspaper and saw that orange against the snow. When I opened my eyes a moment later, I saw the orange on top of the piano. I stood on my bed and picked it up, holding it for a long time, rolling it between my hands, just as he had done. Then I scraped the peel, closed my eyes, and smelled.

Usually, when I hear a story I like, or a joke, I turn around and tell it to someone. Anyone who happens to be around. I'm not sure why. Maybe because part of me just doesn't get it until I tell it to someone else. But not the story of the orange. This one I *got*. And I didn't want to let it go. It was as though a little star had floated down from the sky, right to me, like that old song my mom sometimes sings— "Catch a falling star and put it in your pocket, never let it fade away . . ."

That's what I had: a little bit of light in my pocket. I thought of my grandmother. I wondered if she still had a spark of light somewhere deep inside, or if it's gone forever. That reminded me of something Rabbi Buxelbaum said in a sermon when I was a little kid. When you look up in the sky, on a really clear night, and see millions of stars, some of them actually burned out long ago, thousands or even tens of thousands of years ago. But because they're *so* far away, their light is just reaching us now, and we don't know which are dead and which are alive.

I don't know what to think about my grandmother. But I do know that, from out of nowhere, one little speck of light had come to me.

Nowhere?

Well, not exactly nowhere.

"Hey, God," I said. "It's me. Look, I know I've done a lot of *kvetching* over the past eight days. I guess you really don't like being heckled, do you?"

No response, just the sound of Herrmann spinning on her wheel.

"Then again, I'm not sure you want us humans to just sit here quietly and accept everything. Especially us Jews. If you did, you wouldn't have made us this way."

That seemed to be a really good point. After all, what's more Jewish than arguing with God? Like that story in the

Torah about Abraham debating with God about whether Sodom and Gomorrah should be destroyed. We don't just argue with God; we wrestle. Like Jacob, who wrestled all night with an angel. In the end, the angel dislocated Jacob's hip, which must have hurt. A lot. I'd never thought about it before, but Jacob probably walked like my dad. I wonder— did people laugh at him? Then, before the angel left, Jacob had the nerve to ask for his blessing. He didn't just ask; he demanded it—which is a gutsy thing to do when someone has just busted your hip. But the angel did give him a blessing, saying he would change Jacob's name to Yis-ra-el— Israel—which means "One who has wrestled with God." To me, that proves that wrestling with God is a *good* thing. I was just about to explain all this to God, but stopped myself. Somehow, lecturing God about Bible stories seemed over the line.

"Anyhow, God, I'm sorry about the heckling. I know I don't like it when someone calls out the secrets to my tricks. For what it's worth, your secrets are safe with me. Because I have no idea how your tricks work. All I know is that every once in a while, you come up with a good one. So, I guess what I'm saying is . . . thank you for the orange."

I thought about it for a moment. "Hey, the guy on the bus . . . was he an angel?"

No response. But I didn't need one.

"No, he wasn't. An angel would probably have broken my hip." Then it came to me. "I know what he was—a shammes."

I put the orange back on the piano.

I was still turning the whole business over in my mind as I walked to school, worried about the assembly, with no idea what to say onstage. And here's what I realized: The old man's story would not actually change anything.

Although I had prayed for snow, none had fallen. Nor was it ever going to. Sure, a few flakes of snow might land here someday. They might even come during Kchanuka. But they wouldn't transform Temple City from an endless grid of streets into some kind of winter wonderland, let alone the village of Chelm.

Nor would his story make my dad a healthy man. Dr. Kaplowski had said that he could try the operation again in six months, but my dad would have to stop taking the prednisone, and that might kill him. Even if he does get golden hips someday, he'll never again be truly healthy or able to ride a bike, whistling. He'll never be Normalman's father.

Nor will my family ever be Normalman's family. Howard is, to be honest, strange, and getting stranger. He's not just a grumpy older brother. There's something wrong with him. I don't know what it is. But I do know that it can't be easy being him, even if he is some kind of math genius.

And Kenny. He's really kind, but filled with hopes that keep getting dashed. He's like my mom, who still holds on to the dreams that brought her here from Cleveland, no matter how disappointing life gets. I guess she tries not to see it. Maybe that's the only way she can get by—and take care of us. I was thinking of her this morning as I gathered nine candles, a book of matches, and our menorah. She didn't go into work all last week. Her boss, Mr. Miller, is pretty good about letting her take time off, but when she doesn't work, she doesn't get paid. And my dad sure isn't making any money. Just before I left for school, I dug the envelope out of my tux jacket and looked at the five twenty-dollar bills. I put two of them in my impromptu box. Forty dollars will be just enough to buy that spring-loaded top hat from Berg's Studio of Magic, including bus fare there and back.

Looking at the other three bills, I thought about all the magic tricks I could buy. In the end, I folded them up and dug through the pile of stuff in the kitchen phone drawer to find a rubber band, a piece of paper, and a pencil. I wrapped the bills in the paper and slipped the rubber band around them. Then, while my mom was in the shower, I snuck into her purse, took out her wallet, and stuffed them inside.

On the paper I had written *Happy Hanukkah*.

Because that's how I've decided to spell the word from now on: *Hanukkah.*

H-A-N-U-K-K-A-H. Hanukkah.

I know what you're thinking. With a million different ways to spell it, why would I choose to spell it *that* way?

It's a good question. And I don't have a good answer. All I can do is answer the way Jews always do—with another question.

"Why not?"

Maybe *that's* the real question: *"Why not?"*

Because it turns out that life is hard, and not actually fair. Terrible things happen in this world, like sickness and Nazis and whatever happened to my grandmother before she left Poland. Too often our dreams shrivel up and our hopes turn to disappointment. Then, in the middle of it all, we get a glimpse of something shiny and bright, something that glows in the dark and sets us free, if only for a moment. It's not much, and sometimes we have to squint to see it. In fact, most of the time all we have is the *memory* of the last time we saw it. Or *thought* we saw it, because sometimes we're not even sure it was there in the first place.

"So," you ask, "if it's small, completely unreliable, and usually not even there—why celebrate it?"

Again, a good question. And, again, I can only answer: *"Why not?"*

With the assembly scheduled for second period, Mr. Culpepper decided first period should be a Christmas party,
so he decorated his trailer with tinsel and put a big wreath
on the blackboard. He had pushed the chairs aside, leaving
the room empty except for a table in the middle, covered
with candy canes and a record player, playing a Dean Martin
Christmas album.

"Good morning, students," he said. "You'll notice that
the choir has gone off to prepare for the assembly, which
leaves just you boys. You will also notice that I have placed
candy canes on the table, my sincere hope being that you
will be drawn to them like rats to cheese." He thought for
a moment, scratching his beard. "Or, like bees to honey.
Moths to a flame? How about . . ." Now he smiled. "Like
meatballs to spaghetti?! Whatever your choice of simile, I
hope you will gather around the table, and *not* bounce off
the walls." With this he looked at Eddy, who kind of nodded. "I'll have to leave a little before the end of class—and
all I ask is that you do not destroy anything."

Sure enough, he left about ten minutes before the bell
rang. I slipped out right after him, taking my paper bag to
the auditorium, and climbed up the side stairs to the backstage area. The main curtain was closed, and there was a set
of risers on the stage. I could see Mrs. Gabbler on the other

side of the stage, and all the girls dressed in their blue-and-gold choir robes.

"Hello, Joel," Mr. Newton said, walking up to me. "Are you ready?" I nodded. He pointed to the paper bag in my hand. "Is that the, um . . . menorah?" I nodded again. "Good. You can set it up on this little table, then bring it out when it's time for your part, right after the choir." He looked around. "Where's your family?"

"I'm not sure," I said. "They were supposed to be here already."

"Well, all right," he said, looking at his watch. "I'm sure they'll arrive soon." I could hear the auditorium filling up. "We'll be starting with the choir in a couple minutes." He went across the stage to check in with them. They were warming up, singing scales. I could see Amy O'Shea, though she didn't see me. I peeked out from behind the curtain. The auditorium was packed. Everyone had come.

Except my family.

Mr. Newton walked up to the microphone at the front of the stage.

"Good morning, everyone! Welcome, to Bixby School's special Winter Holiday Celebration!" He said it like everyone should applaud, and they did. "As you've heard, we have a special surprise."

Again, I peeked out. No sign of my family. Where were they?

"But first, we'll be starting off with our own Bixby Girls' Choir!"

The choir took their place on the stage, and Mrs. Balthazar, the choir director, sat at the piano, nodded, then began to play. They started with Israel Isidore Beilin's "I'm Dreaming of a White Christmas," then worked their way from one Jewish Christmas song to the next.

I had heard all the songs before, but something happened as the choir sang, and it caught me completely by surprise. I don't know if you've noticed, but I don't cry very often. When I *do* cry, it's usually at something *schmaltzy* in a TV commercial, or a movie, or a song. And that's what happened when the choir got to "I'll Be Home for Christmas," the only non-Jewish Christmas song they sang. It's about a soldier who's off fighting in The War, but says he'll be home for Christmas. It's really a happy song, about how he's looking forward to snow and mistletoe and everything else—until the last line: "I'll be home for Christmas, if only in my dreams."

I thought about Amy's brother, and all the soldiers in Vietnam who wouldn't be coming home, for either Christmas or Hanukkah, or maybe ever. Suddenly my eyes welled up, and the choir was a blue-and-gold blur.

"Joel?" said Mr. Newton, putting a hand on my shoulder. "Are you all right?"

I nodded.

"Don't worry," he said. "I'm sure they'll be here." He thought I was crying about my family. And maybe I was. He pulled out a packet of tissues and gave me a few, then went off.

Finally the choir came to their last song: "Rudolph the Red-Nosed Reindeer." But when they got to the words "Then one foggy Christmas Eve, Santa came to say . . ." there was a swell of laughter from the audience, and a deep voice sang, "Rudolph with your nose so bright, won't you guide my sleigh tonight?"

Everyone applauded. I looked onstage and there, in front of the choir, was Santa! He had the clothes, the white beard, the huge belly—everything. I'd never seen such a Santa—he looked like he'd come straight from the North Pole! Then he turned to the side, looked right at me—and winked! It was Mr. Culpepper!

Suddenly it hit me—*that* was his secret! The one I stopped him from telling by cutting and restoring his neck-tie. He wasn't going to tell the class about *me*—he was going to tell us that *he* was Santa!

The song ended and everyone cheered.

"They're still not here?" asked Mr. Newton.

I shook my head. I didn't know if I felt sad or relieved. Either way, I was lighting the menorah on my own.

"Well, that's a shame," he said, patting my back. "Something must have come up. But we'll go on without them—and I'll be by your side."

With that he walked onto the stage. "Let's hear it for Mr. Culpepper, our special guest Santa! And for the whole Bixby Girls' Choir!" Everyone cheered as Mr. Culpepper took a bow. "I'm told by Mrs. Balthazar that they'll be back for a special encore at the end of the assembly.

"But first," he said, getting serious, "as you all know, we call this our 'Winter Holiday Assembly.' While many of us celebrate Christmas, it is not the only holiday observed at this time of year.

"There are people of the Jewish faith who celebrate a holiday called Hanukkah, which is also known as the Festival of Lights, and we are fortunate to have a Jewish student here at Bixby School. Many of you know Joel, in seventh grade, who will light the Hanukkah candles and tell us the story of the holiday." He paused for a moment. "We had hoped his family would be joining us but, unfortunately, they were unable to make it. So I'll be his assistant. Joel?"

I carried the little table with the menorah and the candles to the front of the stage, my hands shaking. I pulled a match out of the book and tried to light it, but it didn't catch, so I tried again, and again. I had just managed to light it when Mr. Newton said, "Ah, wonderful!" and pointed to the back of the auditorium. "There they are now!" The door had opened, and there stood Kenny, Howard, and my mom. I blew out the match. Where was my dad?

"We're so glad you're here!" said Mr. Newton. "And just in the nick of time!" He cleared his throat, and I realized with horror that he was going to introduce them—and say my last name. I closed my eyes.

"Boys and girls, please give a warm Bixby School welcome to Joel's older brothers and his mother—and look, Joel! There's your father! Excellent! The whole family is here. So now let's have a big round of applause for—THE ENTIRE BUTTSKY FAMILY!"

I had braced myself for the reaction that always comes when people hear my last name. But there was no laughter. I opened my eyes to see Kenny, Howard, and my mom inside the door, looking back. And there, behind them, standing in the doorway, was my dad, leaning on his aluminum walker with the glowing tennis balls, its bars now spiraled with red fluorescent tape. Everyone was staring at him in complete silence.

From the back of the auditorium to the front isn't very far—maybe one hundred feet—but it may as well have been a mile. My father hunched over his walker, pushed it forward a foot, maybe two—then pulled himself up to it. Then he rested, caught his breath, and did it again. With every step he took, the silence grew louder. Only once was it interrupted, by some sort of scuffle in the crowd, which I couldn't see. But no one paid any attention to whatever it was, they just kept staring at my dad.

When he finally reached the stage, I walked down the steps to help him up, one step at a time, holding him so he wouldn't fall backward. We gathered behind the menorah. My dad leaned on his walker, trying to catch his breath.

I struck the match, this time without a problem, and held it to the shammes. As we sang the blessings I lit two candles, then passed it to Kenny, who lit three more, and to Howard, for the final three. We sang "Maoz Tzur," which we all knew by now. Then I walked up to the microphone.

"I'm supposed to tell you why we light these candles. The story of Hanukkah."

My voice sounded very small. I looked at my family.

"It was long ago, in Jerusalem, when the Jewish people weren't free to be Jews. They were ruled over by the Seleucids, who wouldn't let them do Jewish things, like study the Torah and observe the holidays. They couldn't just be themselves. The leader of the Seleucids was a general named Antiochus. He actually called himself Antiochus Epiphany, which means 'the Brilliant One.' He thought all the light shone on him, and that he knew everything about how people should live, and what everyone should believe. And he told the Jews that they had to worship the Greek gods.

"But you can't do that. Because no one owns the light. And you can't stop people from being who they are, and believing what they believe. Especially Jews. Even if they're different." I looked at my family. "Even if *we're* different.

"But everyone was afraid of the Seleucids, because they had a huge army and rode on elephants. And no one was willing to do anything—except this one family, the Maccabees, who decided to fight for their freedom. They weren't fighting for land or for money—they were just fighting for the right to be who they were. It was the first time in history that ever happened. There weren't many of them, but they fought—and they won.

"And do you know why? Well, in the story, they say it was a miracle. They say we won because God was on *our* side."

I could see Mrs. Gabbler in the wings, looking at me, worried. After the grief my family had given the school about mixing church and state, here I was, in front of the whole school, talking about God.

"So, was it a miracle?" I thought about it. "I really don't know. The Maccabees wrote a whole book about it—two of them, in fact. But, as Mr. Culpepper says, history is the story told by the winners. And throughout most of history, Jews sure haven't been the winners, so I guess when we *do* win, we get to call it what we want.

"But I'm still not sure. The Seleucids probably figured they had all kinds of gods on their side, like Zeus up there throwing lightning bolts, and Poseidon making earthquakes. It's like that Bob Dylan song, 'With God on Our Side.' He's Jewish too, by the way—his real name is Robert Zimmerman, and his family escaped to America from the same part of Lithuania as my mother's parents.

"So I don't know if winning the war was the miracle. But here's what I do know. After the Maccabees won, they needed to make the temple sacred again. That's what *Hanukkah* means—'rededication.' But to do that they needed to light the menorah with special oil, which the Seleucids had destroyed. All they could find was one little jar, enough to burn for a few hours. But they lit it . . ."

I paused, picturing that moment. Everyone was waiting to hear what I would say next. Not a sound came from the audience or the choir behind me. I moved closer to the microphone, like Mister Mystery had taught me, and said, in a low voice: "That tiny flame burned, and kept on burning, all through the night. And the next. And the next. For eight nights and days, growing brighter.

"And that *was* a miracle. Not just the oil—but that we have something inside that keeps us going, no matter how dark it gets. Something to hold on to—something that glows in the dark."

I looked at my dad, who was nodding with a big smile. "Because we're doing the best we can," I said. "All of us. We may *wish* things were different, but ..." *But what?* I thought of all that had happened over the past eight days—and all that had *not* happened, and would never happen, no matter how hard I wished.

". . . but miracles aren't the same as wishes. It's like that old poem my grandmother taught me, which goes 'If wishes were fishes . . .'" *What came next?* I had no idea where I was going with this. I could feel myself turning red. "Hold on. Oh yeah, 'If wishes were fishes, and ifs and ands were pots and pans . . .'" *Then what?* My heart was racing. I tried, once more, for a running start. "'If wishes were fishes and ifs and ands were pots and pans, and if . . . if . . .'"

If what?

I stared in panic. Everyone was staring back at me. It all came crashing down.

Then I heard my dad.

"If!" he said. I looked at him. So did everyone else. He pushed his walker forward, and said, again, slowly and deliberately, "IF!"

He nodded his head and started to hum.

"If?!" I said back to him.

"IF!" he shouted.

I felt my hands tingling, getting light, lifting up, floating in front of my face. When they reached high above my head, I snapped my fingers, stomped my foot, and together, my dad and I shouted, "IF . . . I . . . WERE . . . A . . . RICH . . . MAN!"

There was no turning back. I stomped my foot again, so hard the candles shook, and sang, "If I were a rich man . . . yidel-deedle-didel-yidel-didel-deedle-didel-dum!"

For just an instant, I realized what a ridiculous thing I was doing. But the flame had been lit—and I couldn't have blown it out if I'd wanted to. And I didn't want to. I wanted to sing—and dance.

"All day long I'd biddy-biddy-bum, if I were a wealthy man!" Mrs. Balthazar must have known the song, because she began playing it on the piano, while I sang and danced all over the stage.

My dad had pushed his walker forward and was leaning on it, stamping with his good leg as I sang. Mrs. Gabbler was staring at us, her librarian glasses about to fall off, and Mr. Newton just stood there with his jaw open. Now my mother was clapping along, smiling. It wasn't pretend smiling, but real smiling. And beside her stood Kenny, snapping his fingers and raising his arms above his head. Even Howard looked happy.

Then, from behind the choir, came Mr. Culpepper—dressed as Santa, dancing like Tevye, yabble-deeble-dabbling along with us, but louder, with his baritone voice. That set the whole place off, with everyone in the audience raising their hands, clapping and singing.

The next thing I knew, the whole auditorium was dancing the Tevye. Mr. Newton pulled out his handkerchief and started dancing with Mrs. Gabbler. I couldn't believe it—she had some moves!

Just when I thought it couldn't get any crazier, there was a commotion from the choir, and I heard Amy's voice call out: "Everyone—now! *Encore!*" At her words, the soprano half of the choir called out "Up with Freedom!" and the altos answered "Down with the Dress Code!" That got *everyone's* attention as the choir went back and forth: "Up with Freedom!" "Down with the Dress Code!"

Soon the audience joined in the chant. I heard a fluttering above me, and looked up to see two huge cloth banners unfurling from the rafters on either side of the stage. The one near me read OUR CLOTHING, OUR SELVES! and the other said ABOLISH BIXBY'S DRESS CODE!

Then, all at once, the choir took off their robes!

And, underneath, every one of them was wearing pants!!!

We all stared at them, dumbstruck. And then, the whole choir started dancing the Funky Chicken!

I cheered, and so did everyone else—except Mrs. Gabbler, who looked like she was going to bust a gorgle. For a moment, she just stood there shaking. Then she got a funny look on her face and threw up her hands. And *she* started dancing the Funky Chicken!

Suddenly it was absolute pandemonium, and in the middle of it all I saw Mr. Culpepper, who was doing a combination of the two dances—the Funky Tevye—reach into his Santa costume and pull out a handkerchief, which he waved around, singing even louder. He danced into the middle of the choir, where another hand reached up and grabbed the handkerchief—and out came Amy O'Shea. She wasn't just wearing pants, but jeans that were *covered* with patches. Mr. Culpepper led her over to me, holding the handkerchief, and handed me one corner, with a little bow. The next thing I knew, I was face-to-face with Amy O'Shea.

For a moment we just stood there, staring at each other. Then she smiled, snapped the fingers on her free hand, and stomped her foot. I did the same, and soon we were circling slowly around each other, holding the handkerchief. With my free hand, I was pointing and waving. I may have looked like a complete dork, but I no longer cared.

"You are so weird!" said Amy.

"What?" I said.

"It's your superpower, like King Midas. Except everything he touched turned to gold, and everything you touch turns to *weird*."

I stopped dancing. It felt like I'd been slapped in the face.

"But that's why I like you!"

"Really?"

"Wow," she said. "You really *are* clueless, aren't you?"

"Well, I . . . um," I stammered. "I really like your jeans. They're cool! And the choir—everyone's wearing pants!"

"Yep," she said. "We're finally going to get rid of the dress code. You're not the only one with a revolution. Or secrets."

Then I remembered something. "Wait a minute—on Friday, in class, with Mr. Culpepper's tie. You thought he was going to tell your secret . . . and I thought . . ." I stood there, puzzling it out in my mind.

"You know," she said, "for a magician, you're kind of slow. But," she added with a smile, "you're a good dancer."

I don't know how long the two of us were up there, spinning slowly around. Maybe forever, like dreidels in a dream. Then she leaned in close to me. For a moment I thought she was going to kiss me! Instead, she whispered in my ear: "Happy Hanukkah."

That was my fourth Gimel.

And that's when my dad, who had pushed his walker all the way to the very front of the stage, raised his hands above his head in gnarled fists, shaking them in the air. He was singing so loudly, and with such passion, that everyone else stopped what they were doing and watched him as he sang, "If I were a weaaaaaaaaaal-thy maaaaaaaaan!"

The place went crazy.

We Jews think a lot, about pretty much *everything*. Even so, I'm not sure anyone has given much thought to the last day of Hanukkah.

There's been a lot of discussion—and, of course, argument—about the last *night* of Hanukkah. I read in the *Jewish Encyclopedia* that when the rabbis were figuring out how to celebrate the holiday, Rabbi Shemmai said we should kindle eight lights the first night, seven the second, six the third, and so on until, on the final night, there would be just one left. But another rabbi, Hillel—who always won their arguments—said we should *start* with one light on the first night, add a second the next night, and so on, because it's about the *growing* of the light. So that's what we do, building up to eight candles on the last night.

But what about the last day, which comes *after* the last night? It's usually forgotten. There's no big celebration, just melted wax and pieces of foil from chocolate gelt, the smell of latkes long since fried and eaten, and maybe a few dreidels lying around. You know what happens when that day comes to an end?

Nothing.

You don't gather around to light candles or sing blessings. The moment the sun sets on the last day, it goes from Hanukkah to Not-Hanukkah, which lasts for almost the whole year.

So how do you celebrate the last day?

That's what I'm wondering as I sit here on the AstroTurf on my front porch. It has cooled down now—the heat wave has finally broken. The sky is streaked with colors, and several you might call orange. But there's nothing quite like the color of the one I've been rolling back and forth between my hands as I replay the memories of this Hanukkah in my mind. Right now I'm thinking of Brian's face as he came rushing up to me at the end of the assembly.

"Joel!" he said. "That was wicked cool! Now everyone wants to be Jewish!"

"Yeah, right," I said, remembering something. "Hey Brian—when my family was walking up to the stage, what was that noise in the audience?"

"Oh, that was nothing, really. . . ."

"But I heard something. Did you see it?"

"Well, yeah," he said. "But it's not important."

"What was it?" I wanted to know.

"It was Arnold Pomeroy."

"What did he do?"

"He said, 'Hey, look! Joel's dad's a gimp!'" Then Brian smiled, a little sheepishly. "So I decked him. Like Judah—the Maccabee."

When I told my dad later how glad I was that he had come to the assembly, he looked surprised, then smiled. "I wouldn't have missed it for the world."

That look is something I'll remember, even when I'm grown up. But I'm not going to tell anyone about it. Or anything else about these past eight days. Not now. I'm going to wait.

I don't know how long. That old man on the bus held on to his story for a really long time, since The War ended, over twenty-five years ago! That's twice as long as I've been alive. If I wait that long, it will practically be the year 2000—the next millennium! I wonder what the world will be like. I hope the Vietnam War will be over. Maybe *all* wars will be over. Maybe Los Angeles will figure out some way to get rid of its smog—and its traffic. I'm pretty sure they'll have flying cars by then.

However long it takes, I'll wait until the time is right. And then I'll tell my story to some kid I've never met, sitting on a bus, all confused about life, with dreidels on the brain. Maybe they'll have had a week filled with chopped liver, stuck between two older brothers in the backseat of their parents' flying car—looking through a little hole in the floor at the earth below—wondering whether to believe in magic, or miracles, or anything at all.

I won't be able to answer their questions, of course. So I'll ask another: "Would you like to hear about the Hanukkah of 1971, when I was twelve—and prayed for snow, but was given an orange?"

Acknowledgments

As a child, I learned not to expect presents, for Hanukkah or anything else. Now, as an adult, I am blessed by the gifts I've received, including the many that have come in the course of writing this book. They have taken the form of wisdom, insight, ideas, support, and editing.

My longtime friend and fellow author Jeff Lee, who has helped me in so many ways for so long, came through once again in *Dreidels on the Brain*, working with me to sift through a tangled mass of verbiage so I could figure out what I was doing. Likewise, Pete Neuwirth was the first friend to read a sample chapter. He saw something in it that I did not, and gave me encouragement and support that stuck with me through multiple drafts. Much later, I shared the book with my good buddy Jordan Winer, aka Great Zamboni, who read several drafts, each time offering insights that helped shape conflicts and form characters. Others have also offered suggestions, edits, memories, and support as I have written this book, including Jerry Sontag, Lee Dickholtz, Valerie Lapin Ganley, Rob Saper, Zahava Sherez, Jay Golden, Barry Brinkley, Maggid Jhos Singer, and my in-laws, Hezi and Ruth F. Rutenberg. I thank you all.

I've had some excellent professional help as well. Great thanks to Laurie Fox, who gave sage advice regarding the book contract. And I'm indebted to Rand Pallock, who escorted me as I traveled back to the dark and murky realms of my childhood. It's been said, "The mind is a dangerous place—don't go there alone." I am lucky to have had Rand on this journey.

A book has to be written somewhere, and much of this one was written—and rewritten—in cafés. Two in particular, here in Berkeley, provided writing refuge and multiple macchiati. My thanks to Nefeli Caffé—*Efcharistó!*—and Abe's Café— *¡Gracias!*

This is my second book, and a great deal has changed in my life over the thirteen years since publication of the first one, a memoir—*The Beggar King and the Secret of Happiness.* By far the most amazing transformations I've seen are in our two children, Elijah and Michaela (Izzy), who were five and two years old in the book. Not only have they grown up to be *mensches*, but also insightful literary critics. Each read a draft of *Dreidels on the Brain*, then said, "I really like it, *but . . .*" and went on to point out character problems they were uniquely qualified to notice. Those comments resulted in months of rewriting—and a far better book. I am so proud of them—and grateful for their input.

Penultimately, I am deeply indebted to the folks at Dial. My thanks to Danielle Calotta, who took a bizarre idea and turned it into a cover that captures the spirit of this book, and to Dana Chidiac, assistant editor, who has helped every step of the way, with grace and warmth. Thanks as well to Copy Chief Regina Castillo, who corrected hundreds of my actual mistakes while nimbly sidestepping my many intentional breeches in spelling, and to Nancy Leo-Kelly, who worked typographic magic in the layout of this book. My publicist, Amanda Mustafic, has been wonderful to work with, and I'm glad to have her spinning *Dreidels on the Brain* out into the world.

I am particularly grateful to Lauri Hornik, publisher of Dial and editor of this book. About ten years ago, after reading my first book, she invited me to stop by when I was next in New York. We went for hot chocolate and she asked if I had ever considered writing something for young readers. "Well," I said, "there was this one Hanukkah when I was twelve, and a story about an orange that's been rolling around inside my head. . . ." When I finished telling her the story, she saw the potential for a book, and asked for a sample chapter.

It took me seven years from that meeting to find the right voice and deliver that chapter, then another three years of writing, rewriting, and rerewriting, to come up with the book you've just read. Lauri has been there with boundless patience every step of the way, offering editorial insight, judicious edits, sage advice, writerly perspective, and, most importantly, the belief that this was a story worth telling. One could not ask for a better editor. Thank you, Lauri—it is a pleasure and honor to work with you.

And, finally, I am so, *so* grateful to Taly Rutenberg, whom I must thank twice:

First, to Taly, my wife, without whom this book would never

have been written. She gave me the push I needed, asking, "Are you ever going to write that book about snow and oranges? Or just keep talking about it until you die?" Then, throughout the writing process, she put up with years of my frustration, distraction, procrastination, and other unpleasant traits that can make living with a writer in general—and this one in particular—a total pain in the Buttsky.

Then, to Taly, my writing partner, who, after I had already written numerous drafts, plunged into the manuscript, working alongside me to tweak every sentence, scrutinize every character's psyche, and twist plots as needed. At times, hers were the fingers on the keyboard. Through those multiple final drafts, she became a true collaborator as we spun this story together, resulting in a much, much, *much* better book. And we had great fun.

In light of Taly's tremendous contributions to this book, I am inspired to add something I have never seen, but befits this Hanukkah tale—a *rededication*:

For Taly

I am forever grateful for your gifts.

As the dreidels in my brain spin out into the world,

know that the dreidels in my heart

spin for you alone.

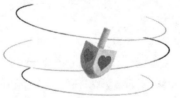

About the Author

In the summer of 1983, after graduating from Stanford, storyteller Joel ben Izzy set off to travel the globe, gathering and telling stories. Since then, he has performed, led storytelling workshops, and served as artist-in-residence in thirty-five countries on five continents.

Over the years he has produced six recorded collections of his stories, all of which have won awards from organizations and publications such as Parents' Choice Foundation, the American Library Association, and *Booklist* magazine.

In addition to Joel's writing, teaching, and performing, he is one of the nation's most sought-after story consultants, working with individuals and organizations striving to make the world a better place. He serves clients in numerous fields, partnering with them to craft their stories, find their voices, and bring their messages to life. Joel also volunteers as a board member of Jewish Family and Community Services of the East Bay, which serves a diverse population including holocaust survivors and refugees from around the world.

Joel's first book was the highly acclaimed memoir *The Beggar King and the Secret of Happiness.* Now in over a dozen foreign languages, it is currently in development as a movie.

Joel lives with his wife, Taly, in Berkeley, California. They have two grown children, Elijah and Izzy, who are off having adventures of their own. They also have a dog named Herschel, the only member of the family who did not help in the writing of this book.